WELCOME TO THE FAE WORLD

ELEMENTAL FAE ACADEMY
Book One
Book Two
Book Three
Elemental Fae Queen

MIDNIGHT FAE ACADEMY
Ella's Masquerade
Book One
Book Two
Book Three
Book Four

FORTUNE FAE ACADEMY
Book One
Book Two
Book Three
Book Four

HELL FAE
Hell Fae Captive
Hell Fae Warden
Hell Fae Commander
Hell Fae Prince
Hell Fae King

FOR FAELICIOUS FUN AND BOOK NEWS, JOIN FOSS & THORN FAENATICS

Hell Fae Prince

USA TODAY BESTSELLING AUTHORS
Lexi C. Foss   J.R. Thorn

Hell Fae Prince

Editing by: Outthink Editing, LLC

Proofreading by: Jean Bachen & Katie Schmahl

Cover Design: Covers by Juan

Cover Photography: Wander Aguiar

Cover Models: Sophie, Alex, Philippe, Forrest, & Camden

Chapter Header Art: Ricky Gunawan

Kingdom Map Art: Tomasz Madej

Melek Illustration: Tyler Finnigan

Published by: Ninja Newt Publishing

Digital Edition

ISBN: 978-1-68530-307-5

Paperback Edition

ISBN: 978-1-68530-309-9

AI Disclaimer: This book does not contain any elements of AI content. All art was designed by real artists, and all of the words were written by the authors.

Careful, little angel. I'm about to tie you up in knots...

About Hell Fae Prince

Ribbons are fascinating.
They curl and twine, yet unravel so beautifully.
Especially when wrapped around a woman's sensual form.

Alas, I've woven so many intricate knots around Camillia De
la Croix that I worry she'll never allow me the privilege of
untying her.

My pretty little captive is stubborn. Powerful. So delectably
perfect.
I've wanted her for many moons now.
To taste her.
Captivate her.
Dress her in ribbons and devour her.

But just as I'm about to make my move, to finally show her
who I really am, she's taken from my grasp to a place I thought
long destroyed.
And I'm the only one who can bring her back.

However, it's going to require a full mate-circle to provide me with the power to do so.

Typhos. Az. Ajax. Me.

Can I convince them all to play nice?
Or are we destined to spend eternity without our beautiful mate?

Don't worry, little angel.
I'll find you. I'll k*ll for you. And then...
All of us will worship you.

Authors' Note: *Hell Fae Prince* is a dark paranormal romance with four tormented mates and no choosing required. If you like your antiheroes dominant and sexy, you've come to the right realm—the Hell Fae Realm, where the romance is hot and no forgiveness is required. This book is part of a five-book series and ends on a cliffhanger.

A NOTE FROM LEXI & JEN

Thank you for picking up *Hell Fae Prince*! We hope you enjoy this dark world as much as we do.

For those new to the series, we strongly recommend reading these books in order, as it is a continued story.

Just a note of caution: This series contains strong sexual undertones, violent scenes, and themes of dubious consent. There are also several strong male-on-male relationships in this world, and these men absolutely love to fuck each other. But they'll be inviting Cami to join them... once she proves her worth. ;)

However, Cami isn't the type of heroine to bend over and take it. She'll fight until the bitter end.

Her mates have a lot of work ahead of them.

As well as some groveling to do along the way.

Their journey won't be easy. But it'll be deliciously sinful.

So continue your adventure through the Hell Fae world. Be careful who you trust. And watch out for the infamous mirages.

Nothing is what it seems.

Just like our Hell Fae mates...

INTRODUCTION

The beauty of rope play is how truly versatile it can be. It's a method of restraint, yet it's also freeing. It takes you to new depths. Introduces you to profound pleasures. All while providing a lifeline you never knew you needed.

Perhaps that's a riddle.
Perhaps it's prophetic.
Or perhaps everything up to this point has been misleading.

Shall we find out?
Turn the page, little angel.
And allow me to be your guide as your *Hell Fae Prince*.

—Melek

HELL FAE REALM

A REVEALED PAGE FROM LUCIFER'S BOOK, VITA

Once upon a time, an angel Fell. His feathers were stripped, his light was extinguished, and he landed in the fires of a broken land.

But this was no ordinary angel.

He knew his world was about to end before the ultimate betrayal arose, and inside him, he hid the source of his light. His true power. His ultimate revenge.

From that fiery ember of energy, he created a new world—the Hell Fae Realm. And within it, he accepted all the creatures every other fae realm rejected.

Nightmare Fae. Abominations. *Monsters*.

As his new court grew, various kingdoms were established. Each one is ruled by a protective Mythos Fae, and beneath them, various Fae Kings.

This entry is considered to be an index of those kingdoms and known species within. It changes and grows daily, but I am Vita, Lucifer's prized book. I know all. I document all. And now, I'll share that knowledge with you, dear reader...

Barren Lands: Desertlike dry areas with rocky landscapes and little to no water sources. Centaurs, Manticores, Minotaurs, Air Dragons, Griffins, and Boggarts make these lands their home. It has also recently been used to house the Hell Fae Bridal Candidates within a unique paradigm.

Hell Fae Kingdom: A centralized kingdom that Typhos Lucifer calls home. All non–Nightmare Fae creatures reside here, as do Lucifer's infamous Hellhounds.

Marsh Lands: Murky waters and swampy plant life make this an ideal home for Nagas and Unseelie.

Morpheus Kingdom: This is the land of dreams, where Nightmare Fae feed on terror and fear. Ghouls and Strigoi call this place home, but one of Lucifer's personal creations lives here, too—the Kuntilanak Fae.

Netherworld Kingdom: Darkness and wisps of dull moonlight haunt the graveyards of this kingdom, making it an optimal home for Corpse Fae and Death Fae.

Underwater Kingdom: Vast oceans and coral-like castles paint this kingdom in a sea of unique colors. Kelpies and Water Dragons call this kingdom home, but some of Lucifer's personal creations, like Sirens, reside here, too.

HELL FAE REALM

MARSH LANDS

MORPHEUS KINGDOM

HELL FAE KINGDOM

UNDERWATER KINGDOM

BARREN LANDS

NETHERWORLD KINGDOM

PROLOGUE: MELEK

"In order for me to offer you solace, a home, your Warden position, access to the Hell Fae Source, and your Hell Fae Bride of choice, you'll need to become my mate, Ajax."

Ty's words played through my head on repeat, causing my lips to curl more with each echo.

Of course, Ajax's reaction hadn't been as exciting as I'd hoped.

"You have one week to decide, Ajax. Choose wisely. It could be the last decision you ever make," Ty had said.

Ajax's eyes had simply narrowed for half a second. Then his features had hardened into a mask of stone, giving nothing away. "You'll have my answer at the Interrealm Fae Ball."

With that anticlimactic statement, he'd vanished. I could have tracked him, but I suspected our Warden needed some space to think.

I'd grant him that.

And entertain my king instead.

Hmm, I hummed, still lounging about on my throne while Ty relaxed nearby. He appeared to be pleased by Ajax's nonchalance. *Potential* and *mate* kept playing over in his mind, followed by a rare hint of admiration.

Admiration he typically reserved for me.

And sometimes for Az.

My eyebrow inched upward as I pushed upright to saunter toward him. "Are you considering what our dear Warden would be like in bed, my king?" I asked him.

Ty's ocean-like eyes met mine. "The only one I want in my bed is you, little prince."

My eyebrow winged a little higher. "Oh?" I paused between his sprawled thighs, his relaxed posture at odds with the turmoil darkening our bond.

The Hell Fae Realm was under attack. Vortex-like portals were threatening our kingdoms. And we were not any closer to discovering the culprit behind the assaults.

There were also several false leads.

Like Maliki in the Netherworld Kingdom.

He'd opened that portal for the Ghouls to escape into an alternate reality to participate in some glorified mating ritual known as *Monsters Night*.

Thus far, it seemed coincidental.

But my king didn't believe in coincidences.

Something larger was at play here, disturbing his bride trials and wounding his previously immaculate reputation.

On top of all that, he had uncertainties within his inner circle.

Uncertainties surrounding Camillia De la Croix.

I might be partially to blame for that.

However, I wouldn't apologize.

She was the key. The *solution*. And the Hell Fae King was slowly learning why. Each layer peeled away revealed more of her potential underneath. Soon, he would desire her as much as I did.

Dropping to my knees before him, I gently palmed his

thighs. "You know what I think?" I asked him casually, my touch gliding upward at a gradual pace.

He canted his head to the side, his long hair falling in dark waves over his muscular shoulders. "That you want to celebrate your victory by sucking my cock?"

My lips curled. "Yes, that," I admitted. "But I also think you're lying to yourself, Ty." My hands reached for his pants, my thumb deftly undoing the button above his fly.

"Regarding?" he rumbled out.

I drew his zipper down, freeing his prominent erection. My gaze lifted to his as the head angled upward toward my mouth. "I'm not the only one you want in your bed, my love." I sealed my lips around him before he could reply, eliciting a low groan from my king. His fingers instantly wove through my hair, holding me to him and forcing me to take more.

"I want Ajax for power," he growled, his grasp turning bruising in an instant. "He's an ideal candidate and a worthy mate. But that doesn't mean I want to fuck him, Melek."

"Mmm," I agreed around his dick. *So what about Cami?* I asked mentally since my mouth was otherwise occupied.

The Hell Fae King's nostrils flared, his gaze darkening. "What about her?"

I merely smiled, my tongue tracing his throbbing shaft and earning another one of those delicious rumbles from his chest.

I bet she would enjoy learning how to please you, my love, I whispered after a beat. *Taking you deep. Choking around your length.*

An act I suspected she was currently engaged in with our Commander.

Because I could feel her arousal searing my bond. Her dark interest a beacon that nearly had me teleporting to the Midnight Fae Realm just so I could watch her and Az play.

He was a beast.

A Shifter Fae with feral needs.

And from what I could tell, she was meeting those needs right now.

Our perfect angel, sinning on her knees.

My king would feel it, too, sense Az's elation through the mate-bond they shared.

Ty might not favor our Commander in a sexual manner, but that didn't mean he was immune to the erotic wave whirring through their connection. He could feel every ounce of pleasure, just like I could, only I was sensing it through Cami, not Az.

The Commander's arousal would be even more intense, his Black Phoenix heritage riddled with primal energy. Ty would have felt Az's pleasure before, particularly when he'd played with our Warden. But this was different. This was about *her*.

I suspected Ty wasn't closing off his connection to our Commander like he normally would.

Because my king wanted our little angel, too.

He just wasn't ready to admit it. Not even to himself.

"Fuck," Ty ground out. "I don't want to think about her, little prince. Not when it's your mouth wrapped around my cock."

Liar, I accused, my teeth dragging along his thick length.

He yanked me off of him so fast I barely had a moment to comprehend his intentions before my back landed harshly against a nearby wall. His gaze burned into mine as he pinned me there, his muscular form taut and intimidating against mine.

"I don't lie," he said through his teeth. "Not to you. Never to you."

I pressed my palm to his heart, my expression softening. "I'm not the one you're lying to, my love."

His gaze narrowed. "Melek—"

"I'll stop pressing," I promised, my lips ghosting across his. "But only if you give me something else to think about."

A tic started in his jaw, one I felt against my mouth as I leaned in to kiss him again. He didn't move. Just held me captive against the wall, his chest slowly rising and falling against mine.

So much pent-up rage.

So much frustration.

So much *excitement*.

He was pleased by his deal with Ajax, eager to hear how the Warden would respond to his offer. And he was darkly intrigued by Az's mounting pleasure. I could feel it radiating through him, deepening his need to fuck.

"I don't want to crave her," Ty admitted in the softest of voices, his vulnerability uncharacteristic and entirely warranted. "She's dangerous, Melek."

My palm slid up from his chest to cup his cheek. "All change is dangerous, my king."

He shook his head. "I don't trust her."

"I know."

"She's a threat to the Source," he went on.

"She's not."

His hands went to my hips, his still-hard cock pressing against mine through my slacks. "You don't know that, Melek."

"I feel it," I countered, my fingers drifting to his nape. "Her intentions are good, my king."

"We'll see," he replied.

"We will," I agreed. "Now, about that distraction..."

"Is it for me or for you?" he asked, crowding me even more against the wall.

"Why can't it be both?" I wondered aloud. "Our mates are playing, Ty. You feel it. I feel it. Let's join them in our own way."

He shook his head, not to deny me, but in a gesture of defeat.

Everyone saw this fae as an intimidating godlike being of immense power. It was true. But he was also my Ty. My king. My love.

"Let me worship you," I whispered, my fingers drifting to the buttons of his dress shirt to begin unfastening the fabric. "And in return, you can take care of me."

"I'll always take care of you, little prince."

"I know," I told him. "You take care of all of us." I leaned down to kiss his throat. "And now I'm going to thank you for it."

"Melek..."

"Shh," I hushed him. "Let me play. I promise you'll enjoy it."

He gripped my nape, forcing my gaze back to his. The world dissolved around us, only for our bedroom to appear, his expression intense.

"It's my turn to play, little prince." He walked me backward into the mattress, a strand of rope magically appearing in his hand.

Mmm, it seemed my king was in the mood to punish. "Tell me what to do, Ty," I dared him, eager to engage in a sensual battle of wills.

"Take off your clothes and get on the fucking bed," he demanded.

I practically purred in response.

Or maybe that was Az's purr I heard through Cami's mind.

Regardless, this was going to be fun.

Just like the weeks to come...

CHAPTER 1

CAMI

I'm on fire.

Not literally.

Or maybe literally.

I... I couldn't say. Everything just *burned*. And it was all because of the powerful male purring beneath me.

Azazel. *Az*. The Hell Fae Commander.

Violet flames danced in his irises, his inner Phoenix peeking out at me while the man evaluated my expression. My mind. *My wants*.

It should be fairly obvious to him what I craved. I'd straddled him on this couch for a reason. Clasped his muscular shoulders beneath my palms. Molded my clothed chest to his bare one. *Kissed* him.

Yet he observed me as though he were debating what to do with me.

"Teach me," I whispered, the plea in my tone impossible to hide.

Fae, I wanted him. *Yearned* for him.

He'd given me something I couldn't define. A truth that

9

knocked down my walls. Penetrated the last of my reserves. Annihilated all my doubts.

A Virtuous Fae—*Vivaxia*—had made him her pet. Fuck, if I ever met that bitch, I'd kill her.

She'd enslaved Az's Phoenix. Forced him to do despicable things.

With a spell.

Similar to the one Ajax cast, I thought, swallowing.

Only, Az had beaten that spell.

Freed himself.

No, not quite. He'd... he'd *mended* his spirit, combined the man and the beast. But he'd left his Phoenix in charge as a way to show respect. To me. To Ajax. To apologize for everything he'd done wrong. To demonstrate his worth as... *as a mate.*

I wanted to demonstrate my worth now, too. To show him that I forgave him. *Accepted* him.

And most of all—that I could handle him.

"Show me how you fuck," I added out loud, the words an echo of the ones I'd just spoken into his mind moments ago. "Please, Az. Please—"

A wave of intense heat stole my voice, leaving me gasping in its wake.

"I don't want to fuck you, little warrior," Az murmured, his lips hot against mine. "I want to *consume* you."

I shivered, his warmth seeping into my skin and strengthening the fire burning through my veins.

"What you're feeling is only a fraction of my need," he continued. "A dose of what I want to do to you."

My throat worked, my body nearly paralyzed by the power sizzling across my being. *You're warning me,* I realized, the words a whisper through our bond.

"I'm preparing you," he corrected aloud, his nose running along my cheek to my ear. "I'm going to fucking devour you,

Camillia." He kissed my thundering pulse. "You need a safe word."

A what? I knew what the term meant, but hearing it from his lips surprised me.

"A word that'll make me pause," he explained, likely having heard my thought. "I don't want to hurt you."

"You could never hurt me," I breathed, my thighs clamping down around his legs.

"I could," he corrected, his grip tightening against my hips as he held me firmly against him. "I'm power incarnate, Cami. When I claim you, I'm going to destroy you. I need to know you can handle it. Now give me a safe word."

"You never gave me a safe word," a deep voice interjected, the owner of it sounding more than a little pissed off.

Ajax, I thought, glancing over my shoulder to see him standing just inside the door with a shoulder propped against the wall.

"All you've ever done is *take*," he went on, his dark eyes on Az. "And lie."

Az bristled beneath me. "I've never lied to you."

"Oh? So you didn't pretend your bird was in control? Thus tricking me into leaving you alone with Cami?" He pushed off the wall, fury making his pupils pulse with power. "And what's the first thing you do—seduce her?" His wand slid into his hand. "I should have known better than to *trust* you."

Az lifted his hands from my hips in a surrendering gesture. "Ajax—"

My Midnight Fae mate was already murmuring magical words, casting a spell of unknown properties.

"*Don't*," I told him. But the magic was already weaving around his wand. A flick of his wrist sent it toward Az.

I did the only thing I could—I dove toward it and absorbed the shock of his enchantment.

"*Cami!*" Ajax shouted at the same time Az hissed.

Electricity zipped up and down my spine, sending me crashing to the floor with a yelp that bordered on a scream.

Or maybe I screamed.

No idea.

Because *fuck,* that hurt. I couldn't move. Breathe. *Focus.*

Static humming sizzled in my ears, irritating my senses.

I couldn't hear or think beyond that noise, nor could I see.

It reminded me of the time Vita had sucked me into her pages and held me captive for a month.

Not again, I thought dizzily. *I am not losing time again.*

I also didn't want to revisit one of Lucifer's infamous memories of his *fall.*

Wincing, I curled into myself—not exactly literally because I couldn't feel my limbs, but figuratively. Or... or I assumed that was what I was doing, anyway.

Shit.

Whenever I came out of this paralyzing state, I was going to give Ajax a piece of my mind. He'd intended to hit Az with this spell, after everything else that had already been done to him.

No.

Not okay.

Ajax was mad. I got that. I'd been pissed at Az, too. At least until Az confided his history to me. Now... now I wasn't as angry.

Well, no. I was angry. At Ajax, though.

Cockblocker, I thought. Az and I had been having a nice moment on the couch, one that had obviously been leading to fun times in the bed or on the floor.

Then Ajax had to storm in here and interrupt the moment.

Although, I was pleased to see him. And hear his voice.

He'd blocked me from his mind before venturing back to the Hell Fae Realm to meet with Melek and Lucifer.

I wonder what they said to him, I marveled numbly, then tried to shake my head. Now wasn't the time or place. I needed to free myself from this sticky web.

Then I would have a word with Ajax about manners.

And spells.

And things.

After that, well, to be determined.

Growling deep inside, I writhed against the mental constraints. They weren't real, but they... they were sort of tangible. Like a spider's silky trap. All glittering ends and thin strands that appeared fragile in nature but were far too strong.

It was actually quite pretty.

I reached for one, surprised when I was able to move toward it. Or, wait, no. It moved toward me. Like I was calling the magic deeper into my mind.

A sigh overwhelmed me as I embraced the enchanted string. It was warm. Right. *Perfect.*

Maybe it wasn't so bad here.

Maybe I could stay.

I blinked. No, that wasn't right. I didn't want to be here. I wanted to be free. To untangle myself. To... *What was I doing, again?*

So much glitter.

All around me.

Wavering. Swimming. *Dancing.*

I nearly giggled at the lightness of it all. So similar to stars. A world unlike any other.

My brow furrowed. *What am I seeing?*

So much white.

Veils.

Feathers.

Wings.

I—

The vision dissolved into a room covered in writhing vines, the ceiling decorated with blossoming flowers. I shook my head, dizzy from the abrupt change in scenery.

Pain shot down my neck in response, the movement entirely unwelcome and causing my stomach to clench with immediate pangs. "*Ugh...*"

"Sounds about right," a cultured voice drawled.

My brow furrowed. *Zakkai?* I hadn't spent much time with the Midnight Fae known as the *Source Architect*, but I'd been around him enough to recognize his amused tones. Or perhaps *intrigued* was the better adjective.

As a current guest of the Midnight Fae Royal Court, I shouldn't be surprised he was here.

Except I was because he hadn't been here moments ago.

Unless I'm missing time again.

"When Melek returns for his next visit, tell him I want to chat," Zakkai said.

"We can relay the message, but I can't promise he'll listen to it," Ajax muttered.

"Oh, he'll listen," Zakkai replied, all confidence.

The sound of a door softly closing followed, then a warm hand drifted down my arm. "Cami?" Az whispered, his concerned features appearing before me. "Are you all right?"

I blinked. "What...?" I cleared my throat, my voice scratchy. "What happened?"

"Ajax cast a paralyzing spell. And you absorbed it."

My brow furrowed. "Absorbed it?" That was a strange phrasing. "What do you mean, I *absorbed* it?"

"The enchantment was just meant to freeze Az for a few seconds so I could pull you away from him," Ajax explained as he moved to stand behind where Az knelt on the floor, placing both men in my line of sight. "You moved and somehow caught the spell."

"Caught?" Another strange phrase, this one from Ajax instead of Az. The latter helped me sit up as I struggled to move, my body oddly weak. "I leapt in front of Az so you couldn't enslave his Phoenix again."

Ajax made a noise in his throat, one that sounded slightly contrite. Or maybe annoyed. "That's not the spell I cast."

Yeah, I understood that now. Sort of. "You can't do that to his Phoenix again," I blurted out, needing Ajax to hear me. I tried to move up to my knees, to stand, but my body refused. Instead, I glared up at him from my seated position. "He's suffered enough."

The look my Midnight Fae mate gave me suggested he felt otherwise.

"I mean it, Ajax," I rushed on before he could say something sarcastic or biting as a retort. "That spell is cruel, especially with his history."

His brow furrowed. "What are you talking about, Cami?" He looked at Az, who was now standing with his arms folded, clearly not liking the direction our conversation had taken. "What history? I've only used that spell once." Fire danced in his gaze. "Had I realized it was from Melek, I wouldn't have issued it. I thought Zenaida gave it to me."

"Melek gave you that spell?" A responding flame flickered to life in Az's gaze. "Fucking meddler."

"I think they both enjoy meddling," Ajax muttered.

"True, but the Virtuous Fae element to the spell should have made it obvious." Az palmed the back of his neck while Ajax blinked at him.

"Virtuous Fae?" he repeated, looking as confused as I'd felt the first time I'd heard that term. "What the fuck is a Virtuous Fae?"

Az winced, his mind instantly radiating annoyance—not at Ajax but at himself. *Shouldn't have said that out loud,* he was muttering to himself loudly enough for me to hear.

"What—"

"Is there somewhere we can go to talk privately?" Az interjected before Ajax could repeat his question.

Ajax glanced around. "You mean, like a bedroom? One where we're the only ones here?"

He doesn't want to risk being overheard by any of the Midnight Fae, I told Ajax via our bond.

Or he just wants to take us somewhere to ensure we're alone when he attacks, Ajax fired back.

I finally managed to stumble to my feet. Ajax grabbed my hips as I nearly fell into him, concern entering his features as he stared down at me.

I need you to trust him, I whispered to Ajax. *Please.*

Not a fucking chance.

Then trust me, I said, my palms going to his chest. *I've heard his story. I understand him better now.*

Ajax snorted. *So he manipulated you?*

No, he confided in me, I corrected. "And before you consider saying something foolish about me being gullible or easy to persuade, think twice," I added out loud, my tone leaving no question as to how I would react to such a statement.

Ajax's jaw ticked, but I didn't back down, my gaze locked on his as he debated his next move.

Eventually, some of the fire left his dark irises, allowing the blue ring to glitter a little more. "All right. A quiet place to talk is probably a good idea," he said slowly, suspicion still evident in his tone and expression but his thoughts focused on trust—not of Az but of me. "I have some things to share with you both as well."

Az arched a brow as he came to stand right beside us, forming a triangle with our bodies. "I assume it's about whatever Typhos and Melek had to say?"

"As if you don't know already," Ajax muttered.

The Commander's eyebrow inched higher. "Actually, I have no idea why he wanted to see you. I just know he vowed not to hurt you." Az looked him up and down. "And you seem unharmed, so he clearly upheld his part of the deal."

Ajax grunted. "And what did he ask you for in that *deal*, hmm?"

Az frowned. "Nothing. I was using it as a figure of speech. He promised not to hurt you, and I believed him because he doesn't lie. But he didn't tell me what he wanted to discuss, which I assume now was a deal of some kind?" An unsettling note entered Az's voice toward the end, indicating he was at least a little disturbed by this development.

I shared that opinion. "What did Lucifer say?"

Ajax's jaw clenched again, his cheekbones sharper as a result of his tense expression. "He proposed an offer that would guarantee Cami's safety, as well as give me a respectable Hell Fae status. But there's a stipulation."

"Which is?" Az pressed, his unease more than palpable now.

Ajax said nothing for a long moment, causing my heart to race. "What's the stipulation, Ajax?" I asked, needing to know. "What does he want in return?" Because whatever it was, it wasn't good. I could see it in Ajax's eyes, feel it through our bond, *hear* it in the way that his mind had gone silent.

"He wants me to mate him," Ajax muttered. "And he wants my response in one week—at the Interrealm Fae Ball."

CHAPTER 2

TYPHOS

Fuck, Melek's mouth was my addiction. My everything. My *life*. The way he played me with his tongue while gripping my base with his hand...

I'd give him anything.

The world.

This entire fucking universe.

Mmm, all I want from you is your cum, my king, Melek purred into my mind as he hollowed his cheeks around my shaft.

I cursed, a growl rumbling in my chest. "Deeper," I demand. "Take me deeper."

Thinking about Cami's sweet cunt? Melek whispered, the taunt in his voice nearly undoing me.

I hadn't been thinking about Camillia at all, but his words created an image I couldn't ignore. A desire I longed to suffocate. An urge that gripped me by the balls and made me that much harder.

Because now all I could think about was how Camillia De la Croix would take my cock. How deep she'd swallow. How hard I would fuck her.

"Melek," I snarled.

Have I mentioned how skilled her tongue is? he asked as he licked some precum from my tip. "If she gives head nearly as well as she kisses, then we'll both be in for a world of pleasure," he added out loud, his lips brushing my damp skin. Then he closed his mouth over my head and sucked me into the back of his throat.

Flames lit up inside me, my desire mounting to a crescendo that tightened my groin and left me breathless. "You'd better fucking swa—"

Blazing agony speared through my mind in the next breath, killing my orgasm and knocking me off-kilter as Az's fury whipped across my senses. *You asked Ajax to mate you?* he demanded, his words underlined with power.

Melek popped up, his expression concerned. "Ty?"

"I'm fine," I ground out, my hand going to my throbbing head as my body caught up with the pain licking a fiery path down my spine. *Az,* I hissed back via my mental connection with my normally levelheaded mate.

What the fuck, Typhos? What the hell are you thinking?

That mating Ajax will allow me to better protect you and Melek, I muttered back to him.

I don't need your fucking protection.

You do, I shot back. *Because without it, I'll kill Camillia De la Croix.*

Silence met my statement.

She's a threat to my kingdom, Azazel. To everything we've built. If you want me to tolerate that threat—to allow her to live—then you'll grant me control where I need it.

Az said nothing for a long moment, but the waves of furious energy swirling between us told me he was still very much present.

I'm doing this for you and Melek.

You're doing this for yourself, Az bit back, his sharp words shocking me to my core.

You know me better than that.

I thought I did, he returned. *But perhaps I don't. We'll have a counteroffer prepared for the ball. See you next week.*

A wall slammed between us, sucking the air out of my lungs.

In all my millennia of knowing Azazel, he'd never locked me out like this. Not so thoroughly. *Angrily.*

I ran a hand over my face. "Shit."

Melek knelt beside me, gloriously naked, but I couldn't even enjoy the view. Not now. Not after...

I swallowed. "Azazel is furious with me."

"He's protective," Melek murmured. "Kind of like someone else in the room."

My gaze narrowed.

"How would you feel if someone propositioned me in the way you propositioned Ajax?" Melek asked softly.

"I would kill the propositioner," I growled without hesitation.

He smiled. "Exactly."

"You supported my offer," I said through my teeth. In fact, I was fairly certain my little prince had orchestrated my every thought, playing me as he always did in his endless games of fucking riddles.

"Because it was the right one to make," Melek murmured, referring to his support. "Our Commander just needs time to come to the same conclusion."

"Why do I get the feeling you're pulling my strings again, little prince?" Although the nickname was typically one I voiced whilst in a sensual mood, there was nothing sensual about my current tone.

"You know me well, my king." Melek reached for my face,

his palm cupping my cheek. "And I know you, too. Just as I know our Commander. We'll be fine, Ty. I promise."

"Nothing about this is fine."

"No, not right now," he replied. "But give it time, Ty." He ran his thumb along my jaw in a warm caress. "We're on the right path."

I leaned into his touch, something I rarely did. However, I felt... oddly vulnerable. Hurt, even. "Az shut me out." It was different from our usual distance, the wall somehow firmer now. Like he'd constructed it with a devastating purpose, one underscored with finality.

The end, I thought, swallowing.

He couldn't dismantle our bond. It was resolute. Infinite. *Eternal*. Azazel might not be my lover, but he was my mate. I loved him in a different way. Like a brother, perhaps. I trusted him.

And he trusted me.

Or he used to, anyway.

"He claimed not to know me," I added out loud, those words having hurt more than I wanted to admit. But to Melek, I'd confide anything and everything. "He accused me of selfishly wanting this bond with Ajax." I met my prince's multicolored gaze. "I'm doing this for you and Azazel. You know that, right?"

Melek considered me for a long moment, his palm going to my neck, then drifting down over my chest to my torso as he straddled my hips.

"I think your desire to mate Ajax is about power." He settled over my thighs, his bare legs warm against mine. "But it's not because you're hungry for power or want to be the strongest fae in the realms. It's because you want to protect everything you've built, and everyone you love. Your Hell Fae. The Nightmare Fae. Your mates."

He leaned in to kiss me, his lips hot against mine.

I indulged in the sensation, let his warmth chase away some of the chill Azazel's rejection had stirred inside me.

"Our Commander knows your soul," Melek added in a breath. "Deep down, he knows you're trying to control the situation in a way that satisfies everyone's interests. That's what makes you a good king, Ty." He kissed me again. "It's what makes you an amazing mate."

His cock touched mine, the intimacy of the embrace making me groan against his mouth.

A groan that turned into a growl as he wrapped his palm around both of our shafts and *squeezed*.

"Fuck, little prince," I breathed, arching into his touch.

"Indeed," he returned. "An inferno of pleasure will tempt our mates into playing, too. It's what we all need."

My eyes had fallen half closed at the onslaught of euphoria, my blood simmering with renewed need. But hearing my prince's words had me evaluating him once more.

"What are you up to now?" I asked, too exhausted to infuse any hint of demand in my tone. I sounded more resigned than anything.

"Just making everyone feel good," he promised, his palm clenching around us below and making my head fall back. "You have your way of protecting us, and I have mine. Now stop thinking and just *feel*."

I wasn't sure I wanted to feel.

Because feeling made me notice the wall Azazel had created.

Feeling inspired a worry deep down that I'd made the wrong decision—something I *never* questioned. I knew my role. My realm. My *mates*.

But Azazel's fury had been very real.

It'd *burned*.

And now I couldn't feel him at all.

"Ty," Melek whispered.

"Can you sense Camillia?" I asked, a new worry touching my chest, one that threatened to blossom into full-blown panic.

"Yes," Melek replied, instantly calming the torrent of emotions blazing inside me.

"Is she all right?" It wasn't the question I meant to ask, but his response would put me at ease.

Because if Camillia was okay, then Azazel would also be okay.

"You're concerned about Cami?" Melek asked, tilting his head.

"I'm concerned about Azazel."

"Hmm," he hummed. "Interesting phrasing, then, my king." He pressed a finger to my lips before I could correct him. "Yes, she's fine. Ajax created a paradigm for them to talk privately within. Unfortunately, I don't think it's as private as they desire."

My brow furrowed. "Elaborate."

"Zakkai," he replied simply. "He's the Source Architect. There are no secrets where he's concerned."

I didn't like the sound of that at all. "What's he learning about?" The words came out with a sigh, mostly because I didn't have the energy to go on the defensive right now.

Zakkai was always going to be a challenge.

I just hoped to turn that challenge into an ally. Eventually.

"About Virtuous Fae and Az's history." Melek's gaze glittered. "He's repeating everything he already told Cami, and she's currently fantasizing about murdering Vivaxia. It's kind of hot, actually. I had no idea Cami could be so... *violent.*"

I grunted. "She's been a threat to my Source for months, and you're just now realizing she has a propensity for violence?"

"She's not a threat to your Source, Ty." Another pump of

his hand accompanied his words. "She's a goddess we are destined to worship."

My nostrils flared. "I will not be worshipping her." Unless he referred to sensual worship, then perhaps I could be persuaded.

He smiled. "Don't worry, my king. I'm sure she'll pray to you in the bedroom." His palm shifted up to our heads, precum dampening his touch. "She'll go onto her knees and suck you off while I take her from behind. Then I'll tie her up for you, spread her thighs, and watch you fuck her bound form."

Hellfire, I thought, the image his words painted a vibrant display inside my mind.

Camillia wrapped up in Melek's ropes. Presented to me like a gift. Her pussy slick with his cum. Her eyes ablaze with lust and fury.

I shook my head, trying to clear the erotic fantasy playing behind my eyes. When that didn't work, I reached for the lube and gave myself a tangible fantasy to play out in real time.

One that involved me taking my prince's ass.

While fighting off images of Camillia's tight cunt.

"You're my lover," I told Melek. "My *only* lover."

"Mmm," he hummed. "For now."

"For eternity," I vowed, rolling us until he was flattened beneath me. "Only you."

He palmed my cheek, his eyes smiling. "I love your loyalty, my king. But she's part of us now. And one day, I will watch you fuck her. Then we'll share her." He nipped my jaw. "And maybe she'll let us stretch her and fuck her pussy *together*."

I bit off a curse, his erotic words stirring a yearning inside me that I couldn't fight. "You're pushing me."

"Yes."

"Stop."

"No." His palm went to my nape, squeezing me. "It's time

to embrace the future, my king. This is happening. Now fuck me while I taunt our intended."

"*Your* intended," I corrected him.

He chuckled. "What's mine is yours, Ty. So stop stalling and prepare me to take you."

"I should fuck you raw for this."

"If that's your wish, I'll happily grant it," he whispered with another bite against my chin. "*Fuck me*, Ty. Fuck me and I'll share every ounce of pleasure with our Cami. Teach her what she's missing. Show her what her life will one day be."

"Fuck, Melek," I breathed, unable to fight him on this anymore. If he wanted to include Camillia De la Croix, so fucking be it. "I'm not going to go easy on you."

"Good."

My mouth slammed down against his as I grabbed his hips to tilt him upward. Then I retrieved the lube I'd released when spinning us on the bed and used it to ready him.

I'd threatened to take him raw.

Alas, that didn't suit my mood.

I wanted to go hard. But I needed him to enjoy it, too.

My fingers speared him, making him groan against my mouth, his dick throbbing against mine. He wanted this. I wanted this.

And one day, Camillia might want this, too, a dark voice whispered in my mind. A voice that sounded suspiciously like my own.

Fuck.

I was losing control of everything.

All because of Camillia De la Croix.

My beautiful little nemesis.

With pert tits.

A perfect ass.

And a rebellious nature that called to my very soul.

I shut my eyes and focused on Melek's mouth. His ass. My fingers. Our cocks.

But a feminine presence lurked between us.

One my prince was no longer trying to hide.

He wanted me to embrace her. To embrace *this*. And as always, I was a slave to my prince's needs and desires.

"I love you," I told him as I lined myself up with his prepped entrance. "Remember that while I destroy you."

"Always, my love," he breathed as he arched his hips to take me. "Now fuck me."

I slammed into him, drawing a groan from us both.

Then I reintroduced my prince to the underworld and reminded him why everyone bowed to me as the *Hell Fae King*.

CHAPTER 3

CAMI

WARMTH FLOODED MY VEINS, causing me to cross my legs in response.

Fae. I was on fire again, just like I'd been while straddling Az what felt like hours ago now. And it was a completely inappropriate response to the hostility unfolding in the small space before me.

Ajax had crafted a living area—not too dissimilar to the one we'd just vacated—in order for us to speak freely. However, he'd created it quickly, as evidenced by the vapid walls and general lack of furnishings.

Not that either male seemed to notice.

They were too busy squaring off on a rug that appeared to be only partially woven.

Az had just finished explaining who Vivaxia was and what she'd done to him, including the part about the taming spell.

All the while, Ajax had simply glared at him. Silently. Broodingly. No questions, just listening while Az had told him about the Virtuous Fae, how Lucifer had basically saved Az from a lifetime of servitude, and was now going into some details about what had led to the creation of the Hell Fae Kingdom.

Lucifer fell.

He took his light with him.

Then created a new source of power in the pit of despair.

The Nightmare Fae, also known as the "abominations" the Virtuous Fae had unceremoniously discarded into said pit, all thrived under Lucifer's freshly created Source.

Kingdoms were born—such as the Netherworld, Barren Lands, and Marsh Lands—where the various Nightmare Fae took refuge. "And the Hell Fae Realm began to thrive," Az went on now.

All while this heat continued to blossom inside me.

Heat that was making me tingle in unspeakable ways.

Why am I so aroused? I wondered, swallowing as I tried to push away the strange hormonal response to Az's words. *This should not be turning me on.*

Mmm, I disagree, a silky voice replied, one that had my breath catching in my throat.

Melek?

Hello, sweet angel. Having fun in Ajax's little paradigm? he murmured into my mind, his mental voice holding a hint of breathlessness that nearly made me frown.

Only, my teeth sank into my lip in the next instant as a fresh wave of fiery need licked down my spine. *Melek!*

Oh, how I can't wait to make you scream my name like that, he returned on a pant I could practically feel against my skin. *Fuck, Ty is going to rip me apart, Cami. And do you want to know why?*

I swallowed, an image slamming into my mind of what Melek's words meant. Because the sensual way he'd voiced them told me he hadn't meant *rip me apart* in a violent way, but in a sensual one.

You... you're having sex right now, I realized. *That's... that's what I'm feeling?*

Yes, he whispered back to me. *Ty is fucking me while thinking about you.*

My lips parted. *What?* He couldn't possibly mean that. *Why...? Why would he be thinking about me?* Did Lucifer know about the dreams?

Melek seemed to.

Had he told the Hell Fae King?

Had he learned about them through Melek?

My heart skipped a beat. I didn't want Lucifer knowing about those forbidden fantasies. Primarily because I couldn't seem to control them. Or deny them.

I *hated* Lucifer.

And he had made it very clear that he hated me, too.

Ajax's furious growl yanked me out of my mind, returning me to the argument unfolding before me. "You should have fucking told me! It was my damn job, Az."

I blinked. *What?*

"Your job as Warden was to guard the prison. My job was to tame the beasts. You were never in any danger."

"Oh, fuck you," Ajax spat back. "This isn't about *danger*. It's about keeping the truth from me. For not *trusting* me." He shoved Az back with both palms on his chest, causing my eyebrows to fly upward.

"It wasn't—"

"I spent ten years guarding Nightmare Fae," Ajax snarled, interrupting Az. "Now you tell me this bullshit about reneged deals and black souls? That those beasts weren't real Nightmare Fae?"

Oh. My brow furrowed. *Ajax never knew about the black souls?*

Ah, is that the direction Az's conversation went with Ajax?

31

Melek asked with a pleased sigh. *I bet Ajax is taking that reveal well.*

He looks ready to kill Az, I whispered back to him as Az and Ajax squared off before me.

"What do you want from me?" Az was demanding after saying something I'd missed while talking to Melek. "You want to tame me again? Hit me? Hurt me?"

Kill or fuck? Melek mused into my mind. *Because I prefer fucking. Which brings me back to why Ty is fucking me now...*

My blood heated again. *Melek—*

I told him that I wanted to tie you up and watch him take you, he went on before I could finish my thought. *Now he's fucking me while thinking about your sweet pussy, angel.*

I gasped, his crass words utterly unexpected. *Melek.*

Gods, it makes me so fucking hard thinking about him being inside you. About me caressing you, praising you for taking our king, and ensuring you feel worshipped while he desecrates your body.

My thighs clenched, my lips parting in shock at the vivid commentary. Melek had flirted with me before, but never like this. Never so bluntly. So *erotically.*

I can't hold back much longer, little angel, he murmured, the sensuality in his mental tones causing my nipples to bead in response. *I need you to know what I intend to do to you. How I plan to please you. The future we're headed toward together as us, and with Ty.*

I shook my head, not caring at all that he couldn't actually see me. *Lucifer hates me.*

Does he? Melek asked, a breathy quality to his voice. *Or is he just scared of what you might mean to him?*

I swallowed, still in denial about everything he was saying. Every hot emotion he awoke inside me. *This is insanity.*

Then it's right, he whispered back to me. *Pleasure isn't meant to be sane. That would be oh so boring, Cami. Pleasure should ignite an inferno inside you. Burn you. Make you question your very existence because all you can feel is euphoria so heavy you can hardly breathe.*

My chest ached in response to his description, my lungs ceasing to function. *Melek...*

That's it, little angel, he praised. *You feel it, don't you? The flames. The intensity. The power brought on by enigmatic sensations.*

His words morphed into a groan I felt through every inch of my being, his mounting rapture rippling through my existence and sucking me in with him.

I gripped the seat beneath me, needing to remind myself that I wasn't there. I wasn't him. But, oh, I felt like I was him. I felt *everything*.

Lucifer's thrusts.

His growls rumbling against Melek's chest.

I could practically see them fucking in the bed, Lucifer deep inside Melek as they faced one another.

He's fisting my cock, Melek moaned into my mind. *Stroking me in time with his punishing pace. Gods, I wish you were here with us, little angel. All wrapped up in my ribbons. Panting. Begging us to take your pussy together.*

I crossed my legs, my core throbbing with renewed need. All I could feel was Melek's pleasure. All I could hear was his pants. All I could think about was what Lucifer was doing to him.

Hot.

Hard.

Masculine.

Energy.

Fuck, Melek groaned. *Ty's using me just like he wants to use you.*

I shivered, my forbidden dreams haunting my thoughts.

Every evening, I woke up aroused. Ready. *Wet*. All because of Lucifer's big, strong body overwhelming mine.

It didn't make any sense.

But I couldn't stop thinking about him.

His heat. His strength. His exotic appeal.

He's thinking about you, Melek went on, causing my nails to bite into my leather chair.

Or was it a bench?

I couldn't remember.

And I wasn't about to open my eyes to find out. I was enjoying the visual playing out behind them far too much to stop now.

He craves your submission, little angel. I can taste it on his tongue, hear it in his mind. He wants to bend you over and make you take all of him. Melek released a sound of elation, one I swore was a breath against my ear. *Oh, fuck, he's picturing his hand in your hair as he forces you to suck my cock.*

I swallowed, Melek's taste suddenly filling my senses. *How are you doing this?*

We're bonded, he panted. *You can feel me. And I can feel you.*

Goose bumps trailed down my exposed arms, his fingers seeming to stroke my skin even from a distance. Because he wasn't here.

Or I... I didn't think he was here.

I opened my eyes, half convinced I would find myself in bed with Melek and Lucifer. And instead found an erotic display featuring two other men.

Az had Ajax pinned against a wall, his chest heaving with the effort. My Midnight Fae mate had blood on his swelling lip, and Az had bruises forming along his jaw.

The marks wouldn't last. But the evidence of a fight certainly existed between them.

Ajax's shirt was torn.

Az's bare shoulders were bulging.

And both men appeared ready to kill one another.

Their chests heaved; their lips parted. A growl emanated from Az, one that made my toes curl in response.

"I'll never forgive you," Ajax snarled. "You made me stand there and watch him punish her."

"I know."

"You never let me in. You never confided in me. You left me in the fucking dark, Az."

"Because you were so forthcoming?" Az demanded, a hiss underlining his words. "You opened up to me about your parents? Emelyn? Everything Constantine did?"

"Fuck you," Ajax spat back at him.

"I'm not wrong," Az pressed. "You never trusted me enough emotionally to open up. That wasn't what we were to each other."

"We just fucked."

Az snorted. "You're my outlet and I'm yours. A healing bond. A friendship founded on mutual need and destructive tendencies. That's more than a *fuck*, Warden."

"*Ex*-Warden, Commander. Unless I accept Lucifer's deal." Some of his ire fled with the comment.

Lucifer offered Ajax his life back in exchange for a mating, I recalled, some of my sanity returning. *You knew he was going to do that, didn't you?*

I hoped he would, yes, Melek replied, his breathless tone reminding me of his current antics. *We're all meant to be together, little angel. And it's time to embrace the future.*

What if I disagree? I asked him, infusing every bit of incredulity that I could muster. Unfortunately, it wasn't much. Because that treacherous inferno was roaring to life inside me all over again, and somehow it was even hotter than before.

Then I'll need to work harder on convincing you, he

whispered. *Consider this my opening argument on why we should mate.*

I frowned. *Wh—*

My thought cut off on a wave of excruciating heat, the sensation rippling over me in a fiery rush of *need* that culminated in an explosion of supreme intensity.

Melek! I vibrated with the passion overwhelming my insides, my core throbbing with a desire to be filled. To be complete. To be *fucked*.

Because I could feel Melek coming. Could feel his immense ecstasy. His violent shaking. His overwhelming, all-consuming *rapture*.

I experienced his climax as though it were my own.

And yet, I wasn't truly falling apart.

It only felt like I was. *In my mind*.

That, coupled with the scene unfolding before me, left me panting. Wet. *Craving*.

"I'll accept whatever deal I want to accept," Ajax was saying, not caring at all that Az had grabbed him by the throat, their faces not even an inch apart.

"I won't share you with him."

"It's not your choice," Ajax retorted. "Your Phoenix might have claimed me, but that doesn't mean I'll acknowledge our bond or you."

Az growled. "Whether you like it or not, we're mates." He pressed his lips against Ajax's before he could reply, causing the Midnight Fae to try to shove him back. "You hate me. I get it. But I'm going to spend eternity earning your forgiveness."

"I—"

Az kissed him again, this time harder, his hand visibly closing around Ajax's throat to cut off his air.

My thighs clenched. My breathing quickened once again. My blood *burned*.

Mmm, that's it, little angel, Melek murmured into my mind. *Feel the bonds. Embrace our future.*

Why are you doing this? I breathed back to him, confused by this new level of seduction. He'd flirted, yes. Kissed me a few times. But this... this was new. It was... a whole new level of intention.

We're moving past our introductory period and into true courtship, Cami. I need you to know me so you can trust me. Otherwise, you'll never let me tie you up. His exhale was a kiss against my senses, as though he stood right beside me with his lips at my ear. *And Cami, I really want to tie you up.*

Power erupted in the room, sending Az back a few steps as Ajax roared in fury. Then he launched himself at the other man, grabbed him by the nape... and kissed him.

My eyes widened at the virile display, the unexpected combustion of male energy coupled with erotic need.

Ajax's violent outburst had culminated in an embrace that was all tongue and teeth as the two males devoured each other.

I practically salivated at the sight.

At the knowledge of Melek and Lucifer having just done something similar.

Of the fact that all these men wanted me, too.

We more than want you, little angel, Melek whispered. *We want to worship you and make you our queen.*

As though Az and Ajax had heard those same words, they stopped to turn toward me, their expressions riddled with savage need.

My heart stopped beating, their feral natures washing over me in a wave of unadulterated *claim*.

"I'm going to need that safe word, Cami," Az said as they both started toward me. "*Now.*"

CHAPTER 4

AJAX

Arousal emanated from Cami, her presence seeming to have taken over the entire damn paradigm. I had no idea what had worked her up to this point, and I didn't fucking care. I just wanted to devour her.

And it seemed Az felt the same way.

Flame me, I thought. Between Az's fiery kiss and Camillia's addictive scent, I was so damn hard.

"This doesn't mean I forgive you," I told Az as I moved beside him. Then I grabbed Cami before she could answer his statement about a safe word and devoured the shit out of her. She was half standing, half in her chair, and shaking.

Az helped her up, his hands going to her hips as he positioned her between us while I claimed her mouth. Thoroughly. Passionately. *Utterly.*

I'd shadowed right to her after Lucifer laid out the terms of his proposed deal. I'd expected to tell her everything. But then I'd found her straddling Az, and all I'd seen was *red*.

Because I'd assumed his Phoenix had seduced her.

After hearing his full explanation, I realized it'd been Az—the man—who had broken through her walls.

She'd forgiven him. I saw that now. Understood it.

But I wasn't ready to do the same.

Not after learning about everything he'd kept from me.

Pushing all that away, I focused on Cami. Her lips. Her pert tits. Her *moans*.

Az was kissing a path up her neck, his existence very much noted. Not just because Cami was arching into his touch, but because I could *feel* his desire. His heat. His *power*.

He was barely holding on to his control, his need for us a sensual presence that threatened to enslave us all.

"Safe word," he repeated against Cami's ear. "Name it."

Cami shivered, her lips trembling against mine.

I released her to hear what she might say, curious as to what word she might pick.

"Camping," she breathed, making me blink.

"Camping?" I repeated, the term one that took immediate effect. All thoughts of kissing her vanished as I asked, "Why?"

"Because I *hate* camping," she muttered, her nostrils flaring with her proclamation. "My parents were fond of it when I was a kid. But every time we went somewhere, it was for some sort of fucked-up lesson. Like setting the Everglades on fire and leaving me with instructions to fix it."

My eyes widened. "Why the hell would they do that?"

"That's how you knew what to do with the vortex in the Marsh Lands, why you blasted it with that maelstrom of warmth and water," Az said, a hint of awe in his tone. "I heard you thinking about the Everglades during our training, but I didn't put it together until now. You learned to do that..."

"During one of our infamous family camping trips," she finished for him. "Yeah."

"Fuck," he growled. "When I find your father—and I will —I'm going to fucking annihilate him."

"No." Cami spun to face him. "That honor is mine." She

poked Az's bare chest. "You can hold him down, or knock him around a bit, but *I* will be doing the killing."

Flames. Her fiery response made my dick that much harder. And it seemed to have the same impact on Az because he actually groaned.

Then he grabbed the back of her neck and pulled her to him in a brutal kiss that had Cami instantly melting into his embrace. I stroked my hand along her spine to the hem of her tank top, my fingertips tracing the material as my lips whispered a spell.

Purple mist-like fire danced along my skin, sending little gold flickers up into the air. It wasn't exactly what I'd had in mind, my magic slightly altered from mating Az, but the spell was what I desired.

With a softly uttered command, the enchantment left my hand to eat through the fabric of her shirt, causing her to still between us.

"Relax." My lips went to her shoulder, my touch gentle. "I'm just removing your clothes so Az can keep fucking you with his tongue."

The Commander growled in approval, his grip on her nape tightening as he re-angled her to receive his sensual assault.

Cami trembled, then sighed as my magic warmed her skin, turning the pale color a pretty pink as the enchantment traveled over her.

Her tank top and pants disappeared, as did the undergarments beneath, leaving her gloriously naked between us.

"*Fires,*" Az rumbled in a purr-like sound before releasing Cami and taking a step back.

My brow furrowed as I stared at him, confused by his sudden move away from the beautiful woman. "Did I burn you?" I asked, wondering if perhaps my spell had tried to attack him as a result of my internal conflict toward him.

He shook his head, his violet eyes meeting mine. "No. But I need you to let me use you, to take the edge off."

My eyebrows lifted. "Are you fucking kidding me? You want me to bend over for you? Take your—"

"I want you to fuck me," he interjected, his unexpected request causing my eyes to widen.

Az *never* let me fuck him.

He was dominant to his very core, always preferring to be in charge while forcing me to his will. That was our dynamic. We'd fight and fuck, almost always with me beneath him.

"Please," he added, the word sounding strange on his lips. "Weeks of being mated without a release... cutting off Typhos... I..."

He closed his eyes, his breath leaving him on a pained exhale, one that didn't sound anything like the man I knew.

"My Phoenixfire is blazing hot, Ajax. A safe word isn't enough. I need you to help me stay in control... by accepting some of my power first." His eyes implored me to help him, yet another abnormality.

Az possessed supreme abilities. He never bowed.

Yet he was practically begging me now, to the point of offering complete submission.

It was a show of trust—he knew he could rely on me to take care of him, to assist him, to *guard* him. Even as he was angry and fighting, his faith in me remained resolute.

Or perhaps it was his knowledge that I would never let him hurt Cami.

That I would do whatever it took to protect her, even from him if needed.

"I can handle your fire," Cami said, reaching for Az.

He let her touch him, but his gaze held mine, his eyes flickering with an erotic mix of black and purple fire.

I could see the power rimming his pupils, his Phoenix dying to explode.

I wasn't sure what he meant about cutting off Lucifer, but I understood the need to *claim*.

His Phoenix had bitten me and Cami, but the man himself hadn't finished the mating. He needed to fuck us to culminate our bonds. And in doing so, he would release an exorbitant amount of power.

Since I'd recently mated Cami, I knew what that pull felt like, how feral the need was to take my bonded female.

Az had that same pressure weighing on him—*times two*. Plus, it'd been weeks since his animal had initiated his claim.

His ability to last this long without begging was just a testament to his steadfast control. Especially since he'd apparently been in charge this entire time, or one with his Phoenix, or however he'd explained it.

He'd followed our lead.

Bowed to us.

All while waiting for a moment to explain himself and ask for forgiveness.

It didn't surprise me that he'd started with Cami. Or maybe their conversation had begun in a different way.

Regardless, it was done. We understood him now. And he needed an outlet.

"Az," Cami pressed, her nails digging into his chest. "I can take this. I can take *you*."

"I have no doubt you can take me, little warrior," he replied, finally looking at her. "And you will. But I need to relieve some pressure first. Otherwise, I'll hold back on instinct, which will ruin the lesson you requested."

He palmed her cheek, his forehead meeting hers before she could reply.

"You want to know how I fuck, and I want to teach you. But I can't do that in my current state." He pressed a kiss to her mouth, the embrace slow and purposeful while he gave me time to formulate an answer.

But I didn't need time.

I'd already decided.

And I told him that by unraveling the paradigm around us, the temporary bubble-like space one I'd created in a hurry to provide us with some privacy while speaking about Virtuous Fae.

However, we didn't need that privacy now.

What we needed was a bed.

One big enough for group play.

The bed in our guest suite would do just fine. It was private enough for what we needed to do. And if anyone overheard us, well, I hoped they enjoyed the show.

Because I was about to rail Az's ass.

Take out every frustration on him with punishing thrusts.

Force him to accept every inch of my wrath.

Then make him come all over Cami's slick cunt.

"Get on the fucking bed," I told him, purposely goading him. He made the demands in our relationship, not me.

But if he wanted to *use* me, then I was going to fucking use him, too.

And I would enjoy every damn minute of it.

A deep rumble came from Az's chest, one that reminded me of the countless hours we'd spent sparring over the last ten years. His eyes opened to reveal black irises, the purple nowhere in sight.

Hello, Phoenix, I thought, staring at power incarnate.

Az tilted his head just slightly, the birdlike move telling me his animal was very much in charge right now. But in a blink, the violet returned, creating an intriguing pattern of obsidian and amethyst swirls.

He'd told me how mating us had joined him with his Phoenix.

Now I could see it.

And had I been paying attention over the last few weeks, I might have noticed it earlier.

Alas, here we were.

I either embraced the future or lived in the past. The story of my life, really. But one look at Cami compelled me to move forward. To step into our destiny. To accept... our existence.

I pulled my torn shirt over my head and tossed it to the floor as I stepped backward toward the bed. Az's heated gaze tracked over my torso, exploring every rigid line before zeroing in on my hand unfastening my belt.

Using his hands on Cami's hips, he turned her to watch, his lips going to her ear. "Isn't he beautiful, little warrior?"

"Yes," she replied without hesitation.

He pressed his lips to her pulse as he hummed in appreciation. "You're gorgeous, too," he told her before tracing the column of her throat. "I fully intend to worship you while Ajax fucks me."

Her nipples beaded in response to his words, her tongue sneaking out to dampen her lips.

"Are you okay with this?" I asked her as I drew my zipper down. "Because I'll refuse him if that's your wish." I meant it. She came first. And I knew he felt the same way. He'd proved that much over the last few weeks.

She swallowed, her beautiful gray eyes flashing up to mine. "I know my safe word, and I have no desire to use it."

My lips curled. "You may need a safe gesture, too. Just in case."

Az grinned, clearly understanding me. "True. Your mouth might not be available." His smile slid a little as I pushed down my pants, his focus shifting to my erection. "Fires, Cami, look at how hard he is. Doesn't it make you want to go to your knees and taste him?"

She took a step forward, something that seemed to be

encouraged by Az's hand on her hip. But her eyes held mine as she knelt before me, her expression hungry.

Cami didn't give me a moment to utter a word, her mouth closing around my pierced tip in a breath before taking me deep into her mouth.

"*Fuck.*" My hand went to her hair as my head tipped back. But Az was there in the next exhale, his palm clasping my nape as he yanked my face back up to meet his kiss.

It was rough. Demanding. *Angry.*

I almost didn't notice Cami pushing my pants off my legs, almost didn't sense my shoes and socks going with it. However, I was suddenly as naked as her with my cock lodged in her throat and Az's tongue fucking my mouth.

This wasn't at all what I'd expected upon returning to them. But I no longer cared about expectations. I just wanted to *feel*.

Az nipped my lip, then fell to his knees behind Cami.

"Such a good girl, deep-throating him like that," he purred against her ear. Then he forced more of me into her and held her in place where she couldn't breathe. "Form a fist with your hand for me," he said as her eyes opened in alarm.

A flurry of words filtered from her mind to mine, none of them coherent.

"No, Cami. I realize we can hear each other's thoughts, but I need you to understand your nonverbal safe word. Now make a fist." Az closed his free hand around hers to force her to comply. "And lift it," he added, guiding it upward into the air. "Like this."

Tears formed in her eyes, but she did what he asked, holding her hand up.

After a beat, he eased her back, causing her to pant against my dick. My head was still in her mouth, allowing me to feel her struggle to catch her breath. Each puff made my balls tighten that much more.

Because flames, that was hot.

"Very good," Az praised, kissing her neck. "This is your nonverbal cue for when we push you too far. And *camping* is your verbal safe word. Anything else you do or say will be ignored. Understood?"

She tilted her head to look him dead in the eye, her mouth leaving my dick. "Choking me with Ajax's cock isn't a limit."

I groaned, the words ones that had me wanting to shove her back down so she could continue her ministrations.

But Az chuckled, clearly amused. "I wasn't trying to push you, little warrior. Not yet. That was just us setting terms."

She arched a brow. "Then you should get naked so we can start this lesson properly."

He arched a brow right back at her. "If you want me naked, then take off my pants."

Cami considered him for a moment, then turned to give my cock a long lick, her eyes holding mine the entire time. I cursed at the sight, my grip tightening in her hair. *Teasing Az, little rebel?* I wondered at her.

A bit, she murmured back via our mental bond. *And you.*

Mmm, I hummed. *I approve.*

She took me deep again, past the point Az had urged her, and paused to stare up at me. *You taste good, Ajax. But Az wants you to fuck him. And I want to watch.*

With those seductive words, she pulled off of me and elegantly went to her feet. Az followed, his focus entirely on her.

Sensuality poured off both of them as she grabbed his pajama bottoms and yanked him toward her. He went, his body all fluid grace. One of those famous purrs emanated from his chest while he watched her untie his pants and push them down.

His feet were already bare, his cock instantly free. Because of course he wore nothing beneath. This was Az. And he was very ready for us both.

He leaned down to kiss her, but she moved before he could reach her, our female falling to her knees to give him the same treatment she'd just bestowed upon me. He instantly stilled, his features contorting in both pleasure and pain as he fought his mounting power.

I observed the fight, witnessing in real time just how close he was to combusting and consuming us with his energy.

Fuck, he'd called me beautiful, but like this... he was the most stunning of us all. Fury personified. Sensual. Powerful.

The way Cami had tamed him was so unlike my attempts of brute force.

Our mate had coaxed him with masterful ease, a sensuous little rebel on her knees.

I moved around them to come up behind him, my hand going to his hip as I pressed my mouth to his ear. "Breathe, Az," I told him. "Let her play while I prepare you. Then you can use me however you like while I fuck you."

He shuddered, his hand covering mine and giving it a squeeze. *I've never willingly done this before,* he whispered to me, his confession making me frown. His words implied he'd been forced to do this before.

By Vivaxia, I realized. When she'd treated him like a pet.

Using a spell.

Like the one I'd cast weeks ago.

Fae, Az, I—

Don't, he said, no doubt following my string of thoughts. Or perhaps sensing my realization in the stiffness of my body behind his. *Just... make it a better memory. One I can use to ignore the others.*

All of my desires to make this hurt fled. Not that they'd been strong, but I had considered this a way to take out my anger on him.

Now... now I wanted to make him feel good.

To do just what he'd asked.

Create a new memory. A better one. A *much* better one.

"Cami," I said, forcing myself to focus. "I need your mouth for a moment."

Peering around Az, I met her curious stare, her lips swollen from sucking our cocks. And maybe from our kisses, too.

I pressed myself against Az's back, my palm still on his hip, but I brought my opposite hand around him toward her. "I'd use your pussy to lubricate my hand, but I want to feel your tongue against my fingers."

Her cheeks pinkened, her pupils wide with lust. A soft pop sounded as she released Az to do what I asked, her focus shifting between us as her cheeks hollowed around my fingers.

My cock pulsed against Az's ass, Cami's clever mouth easily driving me to madness.

But after a few minutes of indulging in her velvety tongue, I pulled away and focused on preparing Az while she returned to her ministrations.

"*Fires*," he cursed, arching back into me as I stretched him with my fingers. "Go deeper."

I did, penetrating him while Cami worked him with her mouth.

"Touch yourself, Cami," Az said, one of his hands still on mine while his opposite one guided her head. "I want to hear how wet you are."

Cami moaned, the sound drawing my attention down over Az's shoulder to where she knelt between his thighs. Lust painted her features, her need a palpable presence that had me yearning to fall to the ground and ask her to straddle my face.

"Fuck, little rebel," I groaned. "I need you to get on the bed and spread your legs. Az is going to eat that delicious pussy while I fuck him."

Our beautiful mate gazed up at us for a beat, then slowly released Az to crawl toward the bed.

Both of us cursed at the sight of her pretty ass swaying in a come-hither motion.

"Crawling looks good on you, Cami," Az said, his voice low and filled with need.

"It does," I agreed as I added a third finger. "I'm going to need more lube."

"Good thing she's wet," Az murmured, watching as our female stood to climb up onto the bed.

She paused on all fours and glanced back at us. "*Very* wet."

"Fuck." Az took a step toward her.

I held him back with my hand on his hip. "Let her get in position, then you can pounce."

"I can't take her like this." He feared his release of power would hurt her, but I knew his limits almost better than he did.

"You can't climax in this state, but you can absolutely get your dick wet," I told him.

Cami continued her sensual show until she was in the center of the bed. Then she slowly leaned down in a catlike stretch, showing off her glistening cunt, her legs purposely parted.

Another languid movement took her to the mattress where she finally lay on her back and spread her creamy thighs.

I released Az. "Go fuck her."

CHAPTER 5

CAMI

Az PROWLED toward me with predatory grace, his eyes a beautiful blend of violet and obsidian flames. "If I fuck her, I won't stop," he said, his words for Ajax.

"Then taste her," Ajax whispered.

"I want you to fuck her first," Az countered, some of his dominance bleeding through as he glanced back at Ajax. "Then I'll lick her clean while you fuck me."

Ajax's eyebrow quirked upward. "Haven't you delayed your gratification for long enough?"

He growled.

Ajax growled back. "I'll use her pussy to lubricate my cock. But then I'm fucking you. There's no going back now." He moved around Az and crawled over me, his dark eyes glittering with wicked intent.

Bracing one hand against the bed, he used his other to stroke his cock before bringing it to my hot center. A hiss escaped him at the contact, his muscles flexing as he drew himself down to my entrance.

Ajax didn't wait.

53

He slammed into me with a force that had my back bowing off the bed, a scream leaving my lips on impulse.

Somewhere behind him, Az chuckled, clearly enjoying the show. "I look forward to you doing that to me," he murmured.

Ajax's eyes widened a fraction, then smoldered as he came crashing over me to claim my mouth. I gasped against his intrusion, shocked and overwhelmed by his tongue claiming me in time with his cock.

The bed dipped as Az joined us, his large form lounging beside us. I couldn't see him, only feel him. Just like I knew he was stroking himself, too.

Being connected to these men allowed me to feel their pleasure. Their yearning. Their *intentions.*

My Hell Fae Warden.

My Hell Fae Commander.

Even... my Hell Fae Prince, a soft voice whispered.

Mmm, thinking about me, little angel? a masculine tone whispered back.

No, I lied, arching up into Ajax.

Thinking about what it'll feel like to take my cock? Wondering how I'll measure up to our dear Warden?

Fae, I breathed. *How do you know what he's doing?*

Because I can feel it, he replied. *How that piercing is hitting you deep inside and setting your body on fire. How Ajax's mouth is claiming yours. How his palm is molded to your breast. I can sense it all, Cami. Every bite of passion. Every pulse of warmth. Every thrust.*

I shuddered, losing myself to his words and Ajax's rhythm.

Only then it all stopped as he pulled out of me, his mouth leaving me as well.

I blinked, confused, then found him kneeling over me while looking at Az. "You need to fuck her."

"I can't."

"You can. I'll be there to ground you. Shove your power at me, but take our mate. She needs this, and so do you."

Fae, he was right. I really did need to feel Az's fierce energy, his strength, his feral claim. "Please," I added, looking at my Phoenix Shifter mate. "I'm done waiting. Take me. Teach me. *Fuck me.*"

"Fires, Cami..." Az rolled toward me, his palm finding my face as he pulled me in for a kiss. "Your penchant for topping from the bottom is going to undo me." He glanced at Ajax. "Both of you..." He trailed off and shook his head, then reclaimed my mouth with a passion I felt to my very soul.

Ajax slid off of me, allowing Az room to claim me with his body. His Phoenixfire blazed across his skin as he settled between my thighs, but he didn't enter me the way I'd anticipated. Instead, he devoured me with his tongue, all while leaving his cock against my heat. I felt branded. Claimed. Yet empty. Needing. *Wanting.*

"Az," I panted.

"Shh," he hushed me. "I've given you enough control, little warrior. Time for you to remember who I am. Time for you to *learn.*" He nipped my lower lip, then kissed a path to my ear and down to my neck.

I arched for him, loving his lips on me. Every part of me was alive beneath him, indulging—

I gasped as he sank his teeth into my skin, biting my pulse with enough force to draw blood.

Ajax hissed.

Az chuckled. "She's mine, too." He laved the wound on my neck and rolled in a way to see Ajax. "Want it? Come get it."

Ajax growled and practically dove over us to claim Az's mouth. Az's chest rumbled against mine as Ajax angled Az's head to the side for a more thorough kiss, all while the two males aligned their bodies over me.

Az's cock pulsed against my heat, his abs flexing as Ajax did something between them. Then they both growled as their bodies *joined*.

I couldn't see it from my angle, but I felt Ajax's intrusion, his rough entry making Az tense. But the pain was quickly chased away by Ajax gentling their kiss, a hint of some unbidden emotion warming our mutual bonds.

They stopped kissing and stared at one another, their faces so close to my own.

More of that warmth passed between them, then Az gave the subtlest of nods, and Ajax began to move.

Electricity shot through our connection, causing me to arch with them, my body alight from within with renewed sensations.

It was like Melek and Lucifer all over again, yet even hotter now because Az and Ajax were fucking on top of me.

Az kissed Ajax once more, their tongues whispering secrets I longed to hear.

I must have whimpered because Az shifted his attention to me, and suddenly their secrets became mine, too. Because he kissed me with the same passion, same *intention*, as he'd just kissed Ajax.

I could taste them both, their masculine flavors an addiction I was growing to love. *More,* I thought. *Give me more.*

Az smiled. "Still trying to top from the bottom, hmm?" He pressed himself against me. "Ajax? A hand?"

I gazed up at them, curious as to what he meant, when Ajax reached between us and guided Az to my entrance. "Fuck her hard, Commander."

"I'm only indulging that demand because I want to," he replied as he thrust into me.

I grabbed his shoulders in response, his intrusion so different from Ajax's, and yet equally as perfect.

My Midnight Fae mate was thick, his piercing placed to create the most exquisite form of pleasure.

But Az was longer, leaner, and pulsating with *power*. I could feel his penetration all the way to my soul, his movements almost otherworldly in nature, like I could sense him claiming every ounce of my being.

I moaned against his mouth, his name a chant in my mind.

He set a harsh pace, causing my head to spin. I was lost to him, his prowess, his *need*.

Ajax's lust blended with Az's to create a euphoric aura, one I dove headfirst into as the three of us moved in unison.

It was erotic.

Intensely beautiful.

Utterly divine.

I'd never experienced anything like it, and from what I could feel from Az and Ajax, they agreed.

Hands roamed.

Az tracing my body. Tweaking my nipples. Rubbing away the pain.

I explored him in kind, my palms moving along his muscular shoulders and arms, then the upper part of his torso, before trekking down his sides to find Ajax below.

He had a tight hold of Az's hips, his body slamming against the other man while Az fucked me.

Fae... I loved this. I wanted to do this again and again, and I told Az that with my mouth.

This is just the beginning, he promised me, his voice a mental caress that shot a fresh wave of heat through my veins.

Because this man—*fae*—was mine. As was Ajax.

And Melek.

I love that you're thinking about me while on the verge of coming, Cami, the male replied.

I ignored him and focused on the men actually in the room with me.

Only, Melek didn't leave. He kept whispering to me, taunting me about his ribbons, telling me how good I was for taking Az so deep, whispering dark thoughts about what it would be like if I were in the middle and being penetrated on both sides.

Add a third to your mouth, and you'll be stuffed full of cock, he went on, causing me to moan against Az's lips.

I clung to him, my insides pulsing with thunderous need. I felt consumed. Alive. Like a queen.

Because even though Ajax was inside Az, his eyes were on me—something I felt more than saw. Az was utterly focused on my mouth. And Melek was still whispering dirty words into my mind.

I was the center of their world.

Their goddess.

Their *mate*.

Az bit my lip, hard enough to make it bleed, causing my eyes to spring open. "I'm inside you right now, Camillia. Focus on my cock. The way I'm fucking you. The way *I* am making you feel."

I gasped as he surged forward, his hands gripping my hips so hard I was certain he would leave bruises behind.

"My Phoenix is possessive, little warrior," he added, thrusting harshly into me again. "We want your undivided attention while we fuck you. So tell Melek to fuck off."

There was a chuckle in my mind belonging to the fae in question. *I'll stop distracting you, little angel,* he whispered. *I don't mind simply listening and feeling through you.*

Az growled, the sound vibrating my chest and teasing my nipples.

Nipples he reached up and grabbed to twist.

I yelped, then moaned as he shifted down to lave the tips with his tongue. Ajax moved with him, pulling out of him as Az started crawling down my body.

My insides wept at the loss of fullness, hands going to Az's hair in an attempt to stop him.

"I'm not fucking you again until I have all of your attention," Az said, a hint of censure in his tone. "Good girls get fucked. Bad girls get edged."

"*Az*."

"Oh, I have your attention now?" he taunted, his mouth near my belly. "Hmm, let's see if I can become your world." He roughly grabbed my thighs, forcing them to widen even more to accommodate his shoulders. Then he pressed his lips to my mound before kissing a path lower.

Only, he didn't touch my clit.

No, he went around it, focusing on every other inch of me instead.

When his tongue speared my opening, I whimpered, needing more. Needing *him*. His cock. His presence. His *heat*.

I cursed his name, my fingers still locked in his hair. He caught my wrist when I tried to yank him upward, his grip forcing me to release him. "Hold her down for me," he said to Ajax.

I glared at the Midnight Fae. "Don't you dare."

He studied me for a moment, like he was debating listening to me. But then he shrugged. "I didn't hear a safe word."

I gasped as he took hold of my wrists and moved them over my head into the pillows.

"Now behave and let Az edge you," he said, his mouth hovering over mine. "He doesn't like being ignored."

"I wasn't—"

Ajax silenced me with his lips, his kiss brutally thorough and making me forget my own name.

Only for Az to remind me of it as he said, "Focus, Cami. I'm the one with my tongue near your clit. It's my hands you feel on your thighs. My teeth aching to *bite*."

My eyes widened at that last part, suddenly terrified that he might actually—

I screamed as his mouth closed around my sensitive bud, the heat of his sensual kiss going straight to my throbbing core.

Please don't bite me, I thought at him.

Mmm, he hummed back. *I might.*

An exotic mix of arousal and terror blended inside me, creating the most intoxicating delirium of pleasure and pain.

I had no idea I could feel both scared and turned on at the same time.

But beneath it all was a layer of trust.

Az wouldn't hurt me without purpose. He'd make it good. Make me enjoy every ounce of whatever he had to give. Oh, and he proved that now by licking me deeply while inserting a finger into me at the same time. It wasn't enough, just a tease of the pressure I missed below, but it held me captive beneath him.

"Play with her tits," he demanded.

Ajax smiled against my mouth. "I knew you couldn't yield for long."

"I'll still let you finish in my ass."

"Good." Ajax pressed a kiss to my cheek, winked at me, and slid down to take hold of one of my nipples. I arched into him, panting as both men played my body to the best of their abilities.

I was so close to falling apart.

So close to *exploding*.

My thighs tensed, my breathing coming fast, their names on the tip of my tongue.

Just for it all to stop.

My eyes flew open as I glared down my body at the two men who had both ceased their movements. One stared at me from a breast, the other from between my thighs. "You don't have permission to come yet," Az told me.

"*What?*"

"I told you, baby. Bad girls get edged." His mouth sealed around my clit as he bit down, doing exactly what I feared and causing my back to bow off the bed. Because *fuck,* that hurt.

Ohhh, but the sensation after... the way his tongue chased away the pain...

I blinked, so confused by the varying sensations. Lost to Az's sensual touch. His mouth. His hands. Already, I was climbing again, nearly reaching the stars.

Only to crash right back down again. "*Az.*"

"Hmm, I almost believe I have your focus now," he taunted, his palms on my thighs. "Does that mean you're ready to behave?"

I growled. "I'm ready to kill you."

He grinned, then slapped me between the legs, drawing a scream from me that sounded suspiciously like his name. A curse was about to follow when his mouth returned to my center and Ajax took hold of my breasts once more.

On and on it went, the two of them torturing me to the brink of insanity, then letting me fall back down only to draw me back up again.

Tears filled my eyes, the pain nearly becoming too much. "Please, Az," I begged him. "Fae, please let me come..."

He didn't.

Because of course he didn't.

I pushed up from the bed, knocking Ajax from my breasts and freeing my wrists, and grabbed Az. "*Fuck me.*"

"No."

I growled.

He returned the sound and flattened me on the bed in the next moment. "You're mine."

"Prove it," I countered.

He smiled. "Finish inside me, Ajax. Make sure Cami feels it."

I gasped. "You're being cruel."

"No, little warrior. I'm *teaching*. You wanted to know how I fuck, and this is how I fuck." His lower half moved against mine as Ajax entered him, the two men joining intimately while Az held my gaze.

"I will consume you inside and out," he said, his voice holding a lethal edge to it. "Every inhale will include my scent. Every thought will end with my name. Every prayer will be whispered to me, *for* me."

"*Fuck*," Ajax breathed, nearly causing me to glance up at him.

But Az filled my view, his gaze blazing with barely restrained violence. "And *you* will consume me in exactly the same way. I expect mutual appreciation. Mutual *obsession*. So if you want me to fuck you, you'd better be ready to *commit*."

I swallowed, utterly lost to this feral fae on top of me.

Ajax was fucking him, which I knew had to feel good for them both, but Az's attention was solely on me despite his throbbing cock between us.

"Are you ready to bow, little warrior?" he asked. "Are you ready to fully submit? Because I'll dominate you in ways you've never experienced before. I'll take you to new heights. But I need your body, heart, and mind to do it."

"You have me," I vowed, unable to think about anything other than what he was promising. "Please accept me."

"Oh, Camillia," he whispered, his gaze falling to my lips. "I more than accept. I fucking love you." His mouth claimed mine before I could even begin to reply to that.

And in the next moment, he was there, filling me, fucking me, and twisting his hips in a way that stroked my abused clit.

I was climbing in seconds, my body so fucking primed, so

fucking *his*, that I could do nothing but hold on to his shoulders and try to match his brutal pace.

His tongue held me captive, his hands on my hips a brand. All I could do was feel, exist, and be with him in this moment.

No thoughts mattered.

Breathing was a former expectation.

My heart beat a rhythm that was all for Az.

And my body bent to his will as he used me, filled me, *fucked* me.

In seconds, I was coming undone, and this time he let me. This time... I *flew*. Right over the cliff. Sailing into a cloud of nonexistence. Panting. Dying. Screaming. Crying. *Shaking*.

It was all so powerfully intense, my orgasm never seeming to end.

All this light.

Exploding.

Filling me with heat.

So much power.

Az existed everywhere. In my blood. My mind. My soul.

He was power personified, his ash-like scent filling me with eternal embers. We were bound. Tied together. Forever mated.

My spirit burned up in excitement, embracing his Phoenix with a fiery kiss that I felt blaze through every inch of my being.

It was... incredible.

Hot.

So undeniably passionate.

He roared in response, his own pleasure seeming to mingle with mine in a searing hot wave of madness. I melted. Reveled in the burn. Indulged in his unique sun-like rays.

So much power, I marveled, feeling it whirling through me, bolstering my soul, and filling some part of me I didn't fully understand.

I was content.

Full.

Drunk on his essence.

By the time I opened my eyes, I was... reborn. A new being. Still me, but utterly complete in the best way.

And staring up into a pair of wondrous purple-black eyes. "You're glittering," Az whispered.

My lips curled. "You mean glowing?" It was a cheesy line, but after that mind-blowing experience, I'd allow it.

"No, I mean *glittering*."

Ajax appeared over Az's shoulder, his brows drawn downward. "You look like a disco ball."

I blinked at my mates. "What?" I lifted my arm to see what they meant and gasped at the sheen of gold glitter decorating my skin. A look downward showed that it was all over my torso, too. And Az. Like we'd just rolled in a fucking pile of...

Melek's sparkly jizz.

A laugh pierced my thoughts in response, one that ended in a soft, *You're welcome, little angel.*

I growled. *Melek.*

Enjoy was his reply. *See you soon...*

CHAPTER 6

MELEK

"You look pleased," Ty murmured as I sauntered out of the bathroom in my favorite robe. He sat against the headboard with just a pair of sweats on, a laptop in his lap. "I assume it has something to do with your Camillia?"

"Mmm, yes." My lips curled even more. "Az just blew *our* Camillia's mind, and she erupted in the way only a Virtuous Fae can."

Ty had returned his gaze to his laptop but stilled his typing fingers upon hearing my words. "Glitter?"

"Yes."

"I see."

I arched a brow. "You're not going to question me? Or comment on Cami's evolution?"

"I'm fully aware you strengthened your bond with the female, Melek," he said softly, his fingers moving across his keyboard. "If you want to shock me, you'll have to try harder."

"I'm not trying to shock you, my love."

"Oh?" He paused to glance up at me. "Just more games, then?"

"Are you upset with me?"

He grinned. "No, little prince." He closed his laptop and set it aside, then slid out of bed to saunter toward me. "I'm simply no longer surprised when it comes to Camillia De la Croix." He wrapped his palm around my nape, his opposite hand going to my hip. "You'll have to try harder."

I matched his amusement. "I mentioned our conversation about me tying her up so you can fuck her. It turned her on."

He froze. "What?"

"Was that hard enough, my love?" I asked innocently, pressing my lips to his in a lighthearted gesture. "Oh, I suppose that's a pun of sorts now, hmm?" I moved against his growing erection. "Well, remind me to tell you about her dreams later."

"What dreams?" he asked right as a buzzing noise sounded.

"You'd better get that, Ty," I murmured, stepping away from him. "We'll discuss your starring performance in Cami's dreams later."

"Melek."

"Ty."

He tightened his hold on my nape, yanking me closer. "I'm never going to fuck her."

I cocked my head. "Who are you trying to convince, my king? Me or you?"

He growled as the buzzing grew louder, the audience demanding his attention. Whoever was behind that alarm clearly possessed a death wish, because no one ordered Ty to do anything.

Releasing me, he walked over to his desk to click a button that brought up a screen. His tension mounted as an unexpected face appeared in the translucent space before him.

Well, that explains the demanding presence, I thought, taking in the dark features of the Mythos Fae staring boldly at Ty.

"Hades," Ty greeted. "What an unexpected call."

"Is it?" the godlike fae drawled, his sinister appearance befitting his role as the deity of the Netherworld Kingdom. "Somehow I doubt that."

Ty slowly moved into his chair, his expression giving nothing away. "Maliki?" was all Ty asked.

"Indeed. I would like him back."

I moved to stand behind Ty as he lounged back into his throne-like seat and brought his hand up to his mouth, his elbow on the arm of the chair. "Hmm. And why would I agree to that?"

"Because he has nothing to do with your Virtuous Fae problem," Hades stated flatly, his English tones giving his voice a haughty lilt.

"And what do you know about my Virtuous Fae problem?" Ty countered, his tone and mind lacking any hint of surprise.

Virtuous Fae were not commonly known, their existence a long-kept secret. Mostly because their destruction had led to the creation of all the faedoms.

Except for one—the Mythos Fae.

They'd been around for as long as the Virtuous Fae had, their kind more godlike than angel-like. Historically, the two kinds tended to avoid one another. But Ty had made it his mission to befriend a few, knowing their presence in the Hell Fae Realm would help keep our fae safe.

Thus far, it had worked with the Mythos Fae enjoying their status as worshipped Gods among the various Hell Fae kingdoms. It resembled the fame they'd experienced eons ago when the Human Realm used to pay tribute to them.

Now humans considered them to be a myth. Just like my kind, or angels, as the mortals often confused us with.

Poor humans. How feeble their minds are. And so easily manipulated, too.

Ty glanced back at me, clearly having heard my thoughts. *Sorry, just musing.*

Hmm was all he said in reply before focusing on Hades. The godlike fae hadn't responded yet, simply stared Ty down with the patience only an old, ancient being could possess.

"I assume the purpose of this call is to let me know you have information I may find valuable, and in exchange for that information, you'd like your pet back," Ty summarized bluntly. "Yes?"

"You've been talking to Morpheus."

Ty huffed a breath. "I would never invite a conversation with him. He has a penchant for fucking with my dreams." Another glance my way. "Have you been talking to Morpheus? Perhaps about Camillia De la Croix?"

I pressed a palm to my heart. "Would I do that?"

"Yes." Not an ounce of hesitation. "Have you?"

I smiled. "No. But I do like that idea, so thank you for sharing." Morpheus, the God of Dreams, could be quite useful to me. "Excuse me, I need to make a call." Ty reached out to grab my wrist, holding me in place.

"Maliki and Azazel are half brothers, and Azazel is mine. Therefore, I have a personally vested interest in Maliki's well-being. Your relationship with him, whatever it may be, has not escaped my notice. Does that response satisfy you?"

"Not really," Hades replied. "I would be more satisfied if you agreed to release Maliki. You've questioned him for long enough. The portal he opened simply offered a few Ghouls and Death Fae the option to claim some potential mates."

"I believe you're forgetting the Strigoi Prince who disappeared, too. As well as his lover, the rival family's heir, yes?" It wasn't common knowledge that the Strigoi Prince and his assassin were lovers, but Ty knew every secret that transpired in his various kingdoms.

Hades steepled his fingers on the desk before him, the shadows of his dark lair reminding me of Ty's favorite den.

The two males were certainly similar.

Yet so vastly different at the same time.

Everything Ty did was for his people. Hades's intentions were... to be determined.

But it was interesting that he'd called Ty for this favor. "What are you offering in exchange for Maliki's release?" I wondered aloud, drawing Hades's midnight gaze up to mine. We rarely spoke, but we'd known each other for a very long time.

"I could simply take him," Hades pointed out.

"You could," Ty agreed. "But you won't."

Hades sighed. "No, I won't. I have no wish to deal with you, Typhos. I mean that in terms of agreements and general conversation."

"Yet you called me."

"Yes, I did. Because you've been questioning Maliki long enough to know he's innocent."

"That would require him to actually speak," Ty replied. "Which he's not doing."

"Because I vowed him to secrecy and his loyalty is with me."

"He's one of my Nightmare Fae."

"In my domain," Hades countered.

"A domain I gave you."

"In exchange for my protection. Don't pretend that you did me any favors here, Hell Fae King. I don't serve you. I choose to reside here because I like it here. But those fae are just as much mine as they are yours, and I would like Maliki back. *Now*."

Ty's eyes narrowed. "I don't serve you, God Hades."

The Mythos Fae snorted. "That's a ridiculous title. The

only one allowed to call me God is—" He cut off abruptly and cleared his throat. "I am not your God, Typhos."

Ty leaned forward, his long hair falling over his broad, bare shoulders. "Stop posturing with me and tell me why I should free Maliki. And don't say it's because you asked nicely."

Hades studied him for a long moment before shaking his head.

"You didn't think you could take all those brides without a price, did you? That all those parents would just accept their fates and move on?" He matched Ty's position by leaning forward. "Come now, Typhos. You, of all fae, are familiar with the concept of revenge."

Ty said nothing, but his mind began dissecting the Mythos Fae's words.

"Virtuous Fae love their deals and their games," he added. "Surely you can see the larger picture here, Hell Fae King."

"Enlighten me."

Hades gave him a look that said he had no interest in providing any sort of enlightenment.

"Maliki doesn't fit the profile you've built for your culprit. His portal was unique, he has full recollection of what he did, and he's not apologetic for it. And most importantly, no one was injured. Some horny fae found mates. That's hardly a crime. Now let him go, or I'll come for him myself."

The call ended with a profound click that left Ty and me staring at a blank screen.

"Looks like I need to have a personal visit with Maliki," Ty said after a beat.

"Likely a good idea," I agreed. "But I'm needed in the Midnight Fae Realm."

Ty looked back at me. "You can't stay away from her for more than a few hours, can you?"

I smiled. "It's not Cami who wants to see me." She was currently in the shower with Az and Ajax, trying to wash off her ethereal energy. I'd stop by to help, chat a bit, and then go meet with the fae awaiting my arrival. "Zakkai has questions."

Ty frowned. "He reached out?"

"Not exactly." I didn't elaborate because I didn't need to.

"Should I be worried?" Ty asked, a hint of concern underlining those words.

"No, love." I leaned down to kiss him, my fingers brushing along his jaw. "I've told you countless times that everything I do is for you. I mean it."

"I know you do," he whispered. "But Zakkai isn't an average player in the game."

"Oh, he's absolutely a threat," I agreed, translating Ty's words for what he actually meant to say. "However, I rather like him. He's quite informative without meaning to be."

Ty studied me for a beat, then shook his head. "Enjoy your playtime, Melek."

"Always," I said, kissing him once more. "Try not to kill Maliki. Hades seems quite fond of him."

My king scowled. "No promises."

I shrugged. "Well, invite me to the eventual battle, then. I'll enjoy watching you and Hades play."

"*Play* is hardly what we would do."

I smiled. "Watching you battle an unkillable godlike fae would absolutely qualify as foreplay, my love." With that, I teleported to the closet to find a better outfit. I couldn't very well show up in the Midnight Fae Realm wearing a robe.

Well, actually, I could.

And if I were going for just Cami, I would.

Alas, there were certain expectations for foreign dignitaries, ones I needed to respect if I wanted Zakkai to adhere to polite customs.

A suit, I decided, pulling an all-black one from the hanger.

As I stepped out into the suite, I found Ty in a similar

outfit, only he'd gone with a midnight-blue dress shirt beneath, the color matching his oceanic eyes.

"I'm surprised you didn't choose red," I told him.

"Red would tempt me to bleed him. Not only would that piss off Azazel—who is already upset with me—but it would also anger Hades." He tugged on the lapels of his jacket. "So I'll do this the old-fashioned way."

"By striking a deal?"

"By charming him," Ty murmured. "I am the devil, after all. If I can't tempt him into sin, who else can?"

"Mmm, I rather like this development," I admitted, sauntering toward him. "I do so wish we could spend more time in bed."

"Later," he promised.

"Later," I agreed, my lips touching his. "Maybe then I'll tell you about Cami's dreams—starring you in her bed."

I disappeared for the Midnight Fae Realm before he could reply, but I heard his growl follow me in my thoughts.

He didn't want to admit his fascination with her, just as she didn't want to indulge in her attraction to him.

But I'd make them both fall.

Preferably with me in the middle.

Oh, the rope play we shall enjoy, I mused, appearing in Cami's suite to find her standing in the middle of the bedroom, fuming. "Oh, yes, let's all stare at the glittering gold orb."

"Happily," I said. Because I couldn't think of anything more alluring than a glittering, naked, wet Camillia De la Croix.

Which was the scene displayed right before me.

Hello, my sweet Hell Fae Queen...

CHAPTER 7

CAMI

GREAT. Just fucking great.

Ajax's "disco ball" comment was way too appropriate. And no amount of water and scrubbing seemed to fix it.

Because I was fucking *glittering*.

I wiped my hand through the fog on the mirror, furious that it still resembled the same golden sheen in the reflection. "*Ugh.*" I wrapped the towel more firmly around myself and stomped out of the bathroom to where Az and Ajax were waiting on the bed. They'd joined me in the shower as well, both of them trying to help me cleanse my skin.

Alas, no.

"You're right. I look like a fucking disco ball," I ground out, causing Ajax's lips to twitch. "This is *not* funny."

"It is kind of funny," he replied, making my eyes narrow at him. He held up his hands, causing all those delicious muscles in his arms to flex. "I can try a few spells if you want."

"She'll just absorb them," Az muttered, causing Ajax to sober. "Just like she took all my energy."

I grimaced. Because yeah, apparently that had also

happened. The power exchange Az had feared—the one he'd wanted Ajax to take the edge off of—had all gone into me.

I hadn't realized it until our shower when Az told me my orgasm had basically yanked both men into oblivion with me, whereby Az had lost all control and unleashed everything he'd been holding back. That was why my climax had been so powerful—I'd literally been riding the high of an energy explosion.

But I was fine.

He was fine.

Ajax was fine.

So... everything was fine.

Except my skin.

Gold. Fucking. Melek. Jizz.

This time, the male in question didn't laugh. Actually, he'd been quiet since telling me to *enjoy it*. Whatever the hell *that* meant.

"I need more coffee," I muttered.

"As you wish," a gravelly voice replied. Sir Silber appeared a moment later with a tray in hand, coffee mugs already steaming. "On the balcony, in the living area, or in bed?"

"The living area would be great," I told the gargoyle. "Thank you, Sir Silber."

The tiny stone creature gave a little bow and went into the living room to set the coffee table. "Do they just lurk in the walls, waiting to be called upon?" Az asked, his attention on Ajax.

Our Midnight Fae mate shrugged. "They're always listening, sort of like figments, only far more useful."

"Better-looking, too," Sir Silber commented as he stomped back into the room. "You know, because you can see us."

Ajax smiled. "Yes, I got the joke."

"You didn't laugh."

"It wasn't very funny."

Sir Silber huffed. "See if I bring you coffee again."

Ajax shrugged. "I'll just ask Sir Fletcher, then."

The gargoyle shuffled, his posturing reminding me of a pissed-off bird, only he had no feathers. "There's no need to be insulting, Master Ajax."

"You're right," my mate agreed softly. "I'm sorry. I will happily accept coffee from you any time, Sir Silber."

The gargoyle nodded, seemingly satisfied. "Good. Call me if you need anything else." He disappeared without a trace, leaving Ajax to shake his head at him.

"He takes away your coffee privileges, you mention another gargoyle, and suddenly you win your privileges back," Az summarized. "Well played."

"The same could be said about your edging game with Cami," Ajax drawled as he rolled off the bed to his bare feet and grabbed his wand. His towel disappeared for a pair of gray sweats in a blink, then he did the same for Az. He raised his wand toward me, frowned, and then dropped his hand. "Actually, you can stay naked."

Az nodded. "Agreed." He reached out to grab my towel, yanking it off me before I could protest.

"Oh, yes, let's all stare at the glittering gold orb."

"Happily," a silky voice drawled, one that had been in my head countless times over the last few hours. Which was why I assumed he was just lurking in my mind, not actually here.

But then Ajax cast a spell to give me yoga pants and a tank top as he demanded, "Do you not know how to fucking knock?"

"Of course I do," Melek replied. "I just chose not to."

Ajax grunted.

Meanwhile, Az folded his arms. "What do you want, Melek?"

"To talk about Ty's offer," Melek replied. "I've been helping Cami learn more about deals over the last few weeks, and in my experience, reviewing real-time examples often provides the best teaching moments."

I shook my head. "We're not talking about any of this until I have coffee." I started around him, then paused. "No, actually, we're not talking about it until you get your sparkly jizz off my skin. *And* after coffee."

Yes. That was the deal I was willing to offer him—*get your glitter shit off of me, give me a few minutes to drink coffee, and then I'll talk to you.*

It's not my glitter shit, darling. It's yours, he murmured into my mind. *It's Virtuous Fae energy, something I believe our strengthening bond has brought out of you.*

How do I get rid of it?

He caught my wrist and whirled me toward him, causing both Ajax and Az to step forward. But a pair of wings suddenly blocked them from my view, my eyes widening as Melek showed me his Virtuous Fae form.

My lips parted, my gaze on his white plumes tinged in gold dust.

Gold dust like what's covering my body right now, I realized as his wings came around me in a hug, hiding me from view.

I stared up at him, starstruck by his beauty. Mystified by his nearness. Lost to the multicolor swirl of his irises.

Melek was stunning without wings. But with wings... with wings, he redefined the meaning of *impossible*. Because he was the most glorious sight I'd ever witnessed.

All sharp angles.

Chiseled features.

Alluring eyes.

Thick hair.

Muscular stature.

Glorious feathers.

I wasn't even sure how his wings existed while he wore this suit, but I didn't care enough to ask. It was Melek. Everything about him was enigmatic and defied reason.

He pulled me into him, his hand leaving my wrist for my nape, his lips ghosting over mine. I sighed in his embrace, a sense of protection warming my skin. Or maybe that was just his soft plumes settling around me.

I wasn't sure.

But I felt at peace.

Safe.

Pleased.

"I can't wait to fly with you, sweet Cami," he said against my mouth. "But until that day comes, I'll help you." A flurry of movement whispered all around us, then his wings suddenly disappeared.

As did the gold covering my skin.

Frowning, I glanced at my arms—which I'd apparently woven around his neck—and blinked. "How...?"

He shrugged. "I absorbed some of your energy. Much like you did to Az." He glanced over his shoulder. "That was one hell of an explosion, Commander. A whole new level for you, if I'm not mistaken."

Az grunted and moved around him. "Cami's right. We need coffee."

"I think I liked it more when you looked like a disco ball," Ajax muttered, following Az but pausing to glance my way. "Now you just smell like Melek."

My eyebrows came down.

"You two are going to have to learn to share," Melek said before I could comment. "She's my mate, too. And while I may have chosen a slower seduction method, I still fully intend to fuck her. So you'd better stop trying to piss all over her."

"Says the guy who dusted her in gold jizz," Ajax clapped back.

"She did that to herself," Melek replied. "And it's not *jizz*, which is a very crude word, by the way. It's ethereal magic. Very potent and powerful." He looked down at me. "I can teach you how to use it."

"Why am I suddenly sprouting *ethereal magic*?" I asked with a sigh, honestly not all that surprised to learn that I'd inherited what seemed like yet another ability.

"I assume it has something to do with our mating." He leaned down to press his lips to mine once more, reminding me that we were still locked in a somewhat intimate embrace. When I attempted to release him, he held me tighter. "I mean it. I can teach you."

"Like you're teaching me about deals?" I asked.

He smiled and pulled me around in his arms, bringing my back to his chest. "It helped you forgive Az, didn't it?" he whispered against my ear. "Brought Ajax and Az back together, too."

I frowned. "How did your deal lessons help with this?" But even as I asked, I realized the answer. It was obvious. "Vivaxia's deal."

"Vivaxia's deal," he echoed. "Everything I've done has been in your favor."

"Why?" I asked, turning to face him again. "Why me?" It was something I'd never understood.

"Because you're the key to our salvation, little angel," he replied, his lips brushing mine. "You were meant to be ours. And soon, you'll understand why."

"Or you could tell me," I offered.

His lips curled slightly. "No, love, I don't think I could."

I shivered, his endearment reminding me of what Az had said before claiming me with his cock.

All these men.

All their words.

So much chaos.

I shook my head. "Coffee." That would fix everything.

Except, no, not really.

Because Lucifer wanted Ajax to mate him.

How the hell were we going to counter that?

CHAPTER 8

AZ

I HANDED Cami a cup as soon as she reached the living area, the coffee fixed to her preferences already by the helpful gargoyle.

She took a sip and moaned, the sound going straight to my dick.

We'd only fucked once. I needed more. *So much more.*

Ajax did, too.

He'd enjoyed taking my ass, his desire to do it again humming between us. *You can take Cami's ass next,* I told him. *While I fuck her pussy.*

He nearly choked on his coffee, his dark eyes finding mine. *I'm never going to get used to you being in my head.*

I shrugged. *I've been there for weeks, Ajax.*

Yes. While I thought you were imprisoned and your bird was in charge.

Why is now different?

Because I know the truth, he replied, still looking at me. *Or at least what truths you've told me.*

I've confided everything, I told him. *If there's something I'm missing, I'll share it. You can ask me anything.*

85

He swallowed, then set his cup down. *It's going to take time to trust you, Az.*

I know, I admitted.

But I'm sorry for... using that spell.

I grabbed him and pulled him to me, not caring at all that Melek and Cami were in the middle of saying something about food.

"You didn't know," I told Ajax out loud. "But I did know what happened to you with Constantine, and I still held you captive. Forced you to watch. What I did was worse. Much worse. So don't apologize to me. I'm the one who owes you the apology."

Ajax gaped at me. "Okay."

"Okay?" I repeated.

"Okay," he echoed.

"I'm sorry."

"Okay," he said again.

"I know you don't forgive me, and you don't trust me, but I promise never to do anything like that to you ever again. I might be tied to Typhos, but you... you are *my* mate. You and Cami come first." I meant it. I might owe Typhos an eternity of gratitude and loyalty for what he'd done, but Ajax was mine now. Cami, too. I'd always put them first.

It was why I'd closed off Typhos.

He wanted my mate.

My Ajax.

And he hadn't even told me about his offer or his plan.

It was unacceptable.

"You're not mating him," I said out loud, causing Ajax to frown. "We'll devise a counter. Together."

"It's my choice," Ajax argued. "And his offer—"

"Is too good to be true," I interjected. "We're going to dissect every word. Develop a counter. And if you choose to mate him, then fine. But I won't let you feel coerced into it because of a shiny deal."

"I was there for the offer. I can help," Melek murmured from beside us.

Releasing Ajax, I focused on Melek. "And run back to Typhos with our counter language? No."

Melek's eyebrows rose. "You think I would do that?"

"Yes," I replied instantly. "He's your priority. Your king."

"And your mate, too," Melek shot back, a hint of uncharacteristic annoyance in his tone. "I realize you're upset that he propositioned Ajax without talking to you first, but you know Typhos would never hurt you, Azazel. Both Ajax and Camillia are extensions of you now, which means he would never hurt them either."

Cami coughed.

Melek looked at her. "Oh, little angel, he wants to punish you. And yes, that'll hurt. But he always makes it better. I promise."

Her eyes widened at the sensual undertones of his words. "He hates me."

Melek smiled. "He fears you and wants to tame you. Trust me, there's a difference."

I frowned, Melek's commentary betraying Typhos's true intentions. "That's why he wants to mate Ajax—to have control over Cami."

"Obviously," Melek drawled, surprising me with his candor. He never showed his cards, especially when his hand involved Typhos.

I narrowed my gaze, waiting for him to say more. Because I didn't trust a candid Melek. He loved his games. I just had to figure out which one he wanted to play now.

"It's Ty's way of taking charge of the situation while protecting his circle." Melek shrugged. "It's a rather straightforward deal, but I love a good counter. So shall we discuss options?"

"Why? So you can share our plans with him?" I tossed back, reiterating my original concern regarding Melek basically spying for Typhos.

"I have no intention of sharing anything, Azazel." The serious quality of Melek's tone was very unlike him. "You don't realize the importance of what we're creating here because you're allowing possessive anger to cloud your vision. But Ty's offer is good for all of us."

"How?" Cami asked, her coffee mostly gone already. "Tell me how."

Melek gave her his attention. "Ty's deal unites us as a circle. It gives you freedom to reside safely in the Hell Fae Realm, grants Ajax status and power, and allows us to better protect the Hell Fae Source."

"By allowing Typhos to control Cami through her mates," I reiterated. "That's what he wants."

"No, it's what he *needs*," Melek countered. "Trust takes time, Azazel. Especially when one possesses a history of betrayal."

My jaw clenched. I didn't need a lecture on Typhos's past; I'd lived it. While I understood what was required to gain trust, I didn't agree with Typhos's methods. "I won't let him use Ajax."

"It's not about using Ajax. It's about protecting Ajax," Melek replied.

"Ajax is also standing right here and more than capable of making decisions for himself," the male in question deadpanned. "Stop talking for me, Az."

"I'm not. I'm—"

Ajax's mouth silenced me, his kiss so unexpected that I froze, then immediately leaned into him only for him to pull away. "Thank you for trying to protect me. But I can handle this."

"What do you want to do?" Cami asked, her hand going to Ajax's shoulder.

"I don't know yet," he admitted. "I want to talk through all of it." His gaze went to Melek. "But not with you."

Melek stared at him for a beat and nodded. "All right. I have a meeting, anyway. However, if you do decide you would like my help, Cami knows how to find me." The prince blinked out of the room before any of us could comment, leaving a single feather behind that landed on Cami's shoulder.

She picked it up and stared at the glittery ends, then yelped when it exploded into a puff of sparkly dust. Her eyes closed, her body vibrating with fury. "If I'm a disco ball again, I will scream."

"You're not a disco ball," I said, fighting a smile. "But Melek just coated you in his scent."

Cami pinched her nose, her head falling forward as she audibly sighed. "All this possessive energy is going to kill me."

"Good thing you're a fae and can't die that easily," Ajax drawled. Then he pulled her in for a kiss, his mouth laying claim to her in a way I desired to do as well.

By the time he finished, she was panting. But I didn't care. I kissed her, too. Branding her with my tongue. Telling her without words that she was mine.

Her eyes took on a lustful gleam when I stepped away, her expression clouded over with need. "We have to talk about Lucifer's deal."

"We do," I agreed, taking the coffee cup from her trembling hands. "But we can do that after I fuck you again."

"*We*," Ajax corrected. "After *we* fuck you. Together. At the same time."

Cami's eyes widened. "We should probably prioritize food and conversation."

"Why?" I asked. "We don't need to eat, and the conversation isn't going to change."

"We need to plan."

"And we will," I promised. "After we fuck you again."

She shook her head. "You men only think with your cocks."

"Oh, this is about more than our cocks, little warrior," I told her as I crowded her against Ajax. He caught her hips, his chest meeting her back, as I grabbed her throat. "This is about us getting rid of Melek's imprint and laying our own claim."

"You're ours," Ajax echoed. "And sharing is overrated."

"Sharing is overrated," I agreed. "Melek might have a claim on you, but it's our cocks you'll be feeling all day. Our cum that'll saturate you all night. Our taste that'll linger on your tongue and in your cunt."

"Our marks you'll wear on your skin," Ajax added, his lips against her neck.

Cami gasped as he bit down and took a deep pull from her veins.

I smiled. "We're going to possess every inch of you. And when we're satisfied that Melek is a distant dream, we'll talk about how to handle Typhos."

"Your priorities are... interesting," she breathed.

"I've lived a long time, Cami. But for the first time, I feel truly alive." I stepped into her space, firmly holding her between me and Ajax. "I'm going to indulge in this sensation for a little longer. Then we'll return to reality and figure out how to counter Typhos."

Her lips parted like she wanted to argue, but all that escaped her was a moan as Ajax worked her with his mouth, his throat moving as he swallowed more of her blood.

"The best part of a deal is that you can refuse it. So worst case, we decline and offer him something else." I spoke the words against her mouth. "Regardless, we'll be ready. And most importantly, we'll face him as a team."

I reached around to thread my fingers through Ajax's hair, holding him to her throat and encouraging him to take more of her blood.

"We're a mate-circle now. Together for always. Unbreakable and powerful." I squeezed her throat with one palm and tightened my grip on Ajax with the other hand. "And very fucking aroused. So lose the clothes and let us claim you. *Again.*"

CHAPTER 9

MELEK

My lips curled as Cami moaned, her clothes seeming to disappear in a wink.

I shouldn't have stayed to watch, but I couldn't quite pull myself away.

Az and Ajax were ravenous, their need to overpower my scent turning them borderline feral. Too bad for them, I was under Cami's skin now. She was mine just as much as she was theirs.

Soon, it would be me she moaned for. Me she begged to feel inside her. Me she wanted to touch and stroke and lick.

Alas, that time was not today.

Little prince? Ty murmured into my mind. *You feel... sad.* The way he said it suggested it was a strange emotion to sense from me. Hearing the label on his tongue was also a bit strange, as I... I hadn't even realized that was how I felt until he'd voiced it in my head.

I suppose I am, I admitted. *Ajax and Az won't let me help them craft a counteroffer for you.*

Ty remained silent for a long moment. *You want to help them.* Not a question, but a statement.

I want to join them, I replied. *But they're not ready to trust me yet.*

And a part of me—a very small, rather unique part of me —worried that they may never be ready.

They've determined that I'm the enemy, Ty said, and a flicker of sadness seemed to underline those words. It was barely there, but a fleeting realization that had my king feeling a bit perplexed. *Azazel...*

Is currently consumed by his Phoenix's instincts, I finished for him. *He knows you're not the enemy, my love. But he's also not pleased with you propositioning Ajax in an attempt to control Cami.*

Ty sighed, long and heavy, into my mind. *Camillia De la Croix is slowly dismantling everything I've built.*

No, my love. She's simply challenging you in a way you've never experienced before. It's both refreshing and terrifying, and you're attempting to face her in your own way. Unfortunately, it may not work. It was probably the most straightforward response I'd ever given him, similar to the ones I'd awarded Azazel with a few moments ago as well.

Perhaps Ty wasn't the only one feeling out of sorts over Cami. She wanted me. I could sense it every time I stared into her eyes. Yet she seemed just as determined to push me away. I typically enjoyed a good game of cat and mouse, but lately, all I'd wanted to do was beg her to let me worship her.

It was as though a part of me had become lonely without her. Which was strange, as I had Ty. I was complete.

Or I should be, anyway.

Perhaps it was initiating the bond without finalizing it.

I didn't want to force her—I *wouldn't* force her.

However, I would seduce her.

I nearly connected to her mind now to do just that, but a presence lingering nearby captured my focus. *My meeting is about to start,* I told Ty. *Are you with Maliki?*

Yes. He's just sitting across from me and not saying a word.

I arched a brow. Most fae bowed to Ty's every demand, his intimidating presence a force of nature they could feel lingering all over the Hell Fae Realm. He wasn't an unkind ruler, just a powerful one. And most fae yielded to such power. Yet Maliki didn't seem to fear Ty at all.

That's impressive, I admitted.

It's infuriating.

I smiled, but it didn't quite feel as natural as it should. *Sounds like you have many challenges to keep you occupied, my love. At least you're not bored.*

He snorted back at me. *With you in my life, I'm never bored, little prince.*

With the compliment fresh in my mind, I materialized in the Midnight Fae Palace corridor just as Zakkai rounded the corner. "So you're a Virtuous Fae," he said in greeting.

I could deny it.

But why bother?

"I am." I leaned against the vine-covered wall, ignoring the hissing sounds telling me I wasn't welcome to be there. If one of the snakelike creatures bit me, they'd be in for a hell of a shock. Literally.

Zakkai paused a foot away from me, his magic prodding mine as it always did when I visited. Only this time, he didn't even try to hide his intrigue, instead weaving his power through mine in an attempt to learn it for himself.

"It won't work," I told him, my voice betraying my exhaustion. "For as powerful as you are, my essence is supremely other. Your Source came from mine. To try to understand it—to *rewrite* it—is impossible."

He pulled his power back a fraction, but not completely. "You're a threat."

"Of course I am. But so are you." I cocked my head. "Do you want to measure wands, Zakkai?"

"I want to protect my mates."

"As do I."

His jaw ticked, his silver-blue eyes tracking over me as his long white hair billowed in an invisible breeze. "Walk with me."

"I'm not one who typically follows demands well," I warned him. "Just ask Ty." But I pushed away from the wall anyway and waved a hand, signaling for Zakkai to lead. "So just be aware that I'm following out of curiosity. Nothing more."

He shrugged. "I just thought you might want to leave before your mate starts screaming the names of other men."

With that, he turned.

She might scream their names, but it's my essence permeating her skin when she comes, I thought, my focus shifting to the female in the room beside me. Her mind was utterly consumed by Ajax and Az as they worshipped her with their mouths, her beautiful form writhing between them like the goddess she was.

They'd decided to take turns with her pussy rather than introducing her to anal play. A shame. I suspected my angel would enjoy being filled on both sides.

Maybe Ty and I would have the opportunity to introduce her to it soon.

If she ever accepts me, a dark voice whispered. My lips curled down at the unwanted thought. It was unbidden and entirely unwelcome.

Camillia De la Croix was mine. She'd been mine from the moment I'd found her reading Vita in the library.

Your agitation is making it difficult to focus, little prince, Ty murmured into my mind. *Is your meeting not going well?*

I blinked, realizing Zakkai was waiting with an expectant expression at the end of the corridor. *No, it's just beginning.*

Is Zakkai threatening you? Ty asked, suddenly even more alert. *Shall I join you?*

Zakkai is fine. I'm... My brow furrowed. *Az and Ajax are playing with Cami, and I wish I could join them. But they don't want me there. And it's...* I trailed off, irritated. *It's nothing. I'll be fine.*

My king obviously understood what I was feeling because he softly replied, *They're fools not to want you, Melek. You'll have your revenge one day... with your ribbons.*

I smiled at the notion his words provoked in my mind—an image of Cami tied up and begging me to let her come, all while I teased her like she was doing to me now. *Hmm.* That was a nice distraction. *Go back to Maliki,* I told Ty as I started after Zakkai, my mood instantly improved.

I've already released him, Ty informed me.

I stopped walking. *That quickly?*

Hades appeared.

My eyebrows rose. *And?*

And he's still here.

Oh. I canted my head. *That's interesting.*

Indeed.

I resumed walking. *Well, let me know if he says anything intriguing.*

Hmm, Ty hummed back, his way of agreeing.

Two discussions with a Mythos Fae in a decade was rare. Two discussions in a day was practically unheard of. They typically kept to themselves, choosing to reign in silence and only occasionally appear in public spaces.

And Hades was the most reclusive of them all. He usually sent his cousin Orcus out to do his bidding. Whatever he needed from Ty must go beyond Maliki.

I'd follow up on that later.

For now, I had an even more intriguing conversation to be had with the Midnight Fae Source Architect. He'd resumed walking again, not saying a word to me about my strange delay. I suspected he knew I'd been talking to Ty, or perhaps was used to those around him holding mental conversations.

When we reached the palace exit, I glanced at him but followed him down a grand set of stairs to a waiting cloud below. "I typically prefer my feathers," I told him.

"If I had wings, I would, too," Zakkai replied, stepping up to the mist. "After you."

I smiled. "I would rather eat a burning thwomp branch."

He chuckled. "I can arrange that." But rather than insisting I walk into the mystic fog, he went first.

And completely disappeared.

I waited a beat, then sighed and followed him into the unknown.

Midnight Fae portals were strange, their magic tacky and unwelcome against my skin. Fortunately, they were also short.

Three steps and I was suddenly at a closed door, the knob nowhere to be seen. "You don't belong here," a voice informed me.

I found the source of it hanging on a door knocker. "I'm aware, thank you. But your Source Architect asked me on a date, so here I am."

"I wouldn't call it a date," Zakkai replied from the other side of the door. "More like a necessary shopping trip."

My brow furrowed, not understanding until the gargoyle-like knocker huffed and removed the wooden panel barring my exit.

A shop appeared on the other side, just beyond a cobblestone street. Glancing left and right, I realized we'd entered a village of sorts. "Cute," I said, liking the gothic spires and midnight skies. "Very appropriate."

Zakkai shrugged. "Aflora likes a tavern nearby; they have spritemead and other Elemental Fae cuisine."

"Do they have lava drinks?" I wondered aloud.

"Probably," Zakkai replied, heading for the shop entrance. "They offer food and beverages from all the realms." He glanced at me. "Even the inhospitable ones."

I snorted. "We both know that's not true; you visit Zenaida all the time."

"Do I?" he asked, feigning innocence. "Hmm."

I didn't bother replying to that; the truth was already clear.

What wasn't clear, however, was our purpose for being here.

My brow furrowed as we entered a shop filled with formal gowns. "Need an outfit for the Interrealm Fae Ball?" I asked him.

"In fact, I do," he replied. "Aflora requires a dress. I assume Cami does, too?"

I studied his profile, noted the way he took in every corner of the store, searching for threats. But all I felt around us were some figments waiting to play. Otherwise, the shop was very empty.

"You didn't have to take me dress shopping to garner my RSVP, Architect," I told him. "We'll all be at your little soirée."

"Your king, too?"

"Of course. Typhos is in the middle of negotiating terms with the rest of our mate-circle. He's hoping to hear their counteroffer at the ball."

Zakkai smiled. "You mean Ajax's counter?"

"No, I mean *their* counter," I murmured as I ran my fingers along a particularly beautiful dress.

Cami would look stunning in this gold sheen.

And not just because it reminded me of her ethereal magic.

"Ty might not be ready to embrace our growing circle, but it's already done," I added softly, somewhat enchanted by the silky fabric. "Az, Ajax, and Cami are all thoroughly mated. Anything Ty offers to Ajax is offered to all of them."

"So you're expecting Cami to offer herself up in Ajax's place," he replied bluntly.

I paused my admiration of the gold dress to look at him. "Zenaida recently asked me to indulge her in a game of chess. I believe you should join us."

"I'll take that as a yes."

"You can take it however you like," I said, fully facing him. "Why am I here, Zakkai?"

"Multitasking," he replied. "I really do need to pick up Aflora's dress, and I decided you would be entertaining company for the journey."

I huffed a laugh. "Testing out our new friendship?"

"Considering possible alliances, yes."

"Hmm. And what is your evaluation thus far?"

"Cocky, arrogant, powerful, and playful," he replied without hesitation. "Zephyrus is going to hate you."

I arched a brow. "And you?"

"Will very likely favor you in every argument against Zephyrus," he admitted, his lips twitching just slightly before he sighed in frustration. "Please stop fondling my ass and bring me Queen Aflora's gown."

A tinkling giggle responded to his statement. "As the king wishes."

Zakkai rolled his eyes. "I'm not the king."

"Four kings, one queen. Oh, but my... she is a very lucky queen indeed." The feminine voice floated all over the room, followed by a chorus of agreement.

There were figments in the library near the Hell Fae Bride dormitories, making me quite familiar with the ghostlike creatures. They possessed penchants for trouble and flirting.

My kind of fun.

"I'd like to procure a gown, too," I told them. "But I'll need some jewelry and shoes to match."

"Ohhh, the Hell Fae Prince wishes to speak to us, he does," a figment breathed. "So handsome, he is."

"Very handsome," another cooed, rubbing up against me and pinching my ass.

I merely smiled. "Thank you, lovelies." Then I provided Cami's measurements—numbers I'd committed to memory long ago—and focused on Zakkai. "Would you mind delivering the garment to her guest suite? Or, better yet, pretending it's a gift from the Midnight Fae Royal Family?"

"Worried she might reject it if she knows it's from you?" he asked, sounding amused.

"I know she will," I told him, not sharing his amusement. "Az and Ajax have rightfully claimed her. I... I have not."

He sobered a bit, his silver-blue eyes flashing. "I may know a little about being on the outside of a mate-circle." He glanced at the gold dress now hovering over our heads thanks to the helpful figments. "Consider the task handled."

"Thank you," I replied. "And consider me available to you, should you think of anything you'd like to ask."

If Zakkai desired an ally, I'd accept. Besides, he might be useful to me. He was a Source Architect, used to unraveling complicated strands and realigning them in ways that benefited him and his mate-circle. Perhaps he could help me untangle the snare I'd created with Cami.

I'd wanted Ajax and Az to mate her, but it seemed my plan had worked a little too well.

Because now they didn't want to share.

Zakkai nodded, responding to my offer to answer questions. "I gathered the gist of the history lesson from Az, but I am sure there will be follow-up queries."

"From your mates?"

"From my mates," he echoed, confirming that he fully

intended to inform them of his recent *history lesson*, as he'd called it.

"Anything else for now?" I asked him.

"A drink?" he offered.

I considered it and nodded. "A drink might be nice."

"Charge our guest's items to the royal account," he told the figments. "I'll be back to pick everything up."

"Royal account, he says," one of the voices tittered. "Jewelry, the other requests."

"Ohhh, expensive, yes?"

"Expensive."

"Just make sure it glitters, please," I interjected. "My intended is quite fond of..." What was the term? Ah, yes... "*Disco balls.*"

CHAPTER 10

CAMI

SEVERAL DAYS LATER

"Wow," I breathed, staring at my reflection. The gold silk clung to my hips and breasts, accentuating every curve.

This wasn't a color I would have picked for myself, but it actually brought out the golden highlights of my dirty-blonde hair. And it complemented my skin tone.

Maybe because gold is my new color, I thought sourly.

Every time I'd come over the last week, I'd ended up covered in glitter.

Fortunately—or maybe *unfortunately*—Melek had left a special cleanser in the shower for me.

Consider this a token of good intentions, little angel, his note had read. I'd almost thrown out the bottle it'd been attached to, but morbid curiosity had gotten the better of me. And, well, I no longer resembled a disco ball post-shower. Pre-shower was a completely different story.

I loathed it.

Ajax and Az, however, were starting to love it.

Because apparently it tasted like ambrosia to them.

"Your pussy was delicious before," Az had said the other

day. "But now, it's fucking divine. Come again, little warrior. I need *more*."

It was... an interesting development. One that made my thighs clench as the male in question stepped into the bedroom. "Holy fires, Cami, you look..."

"Amazing," Ajax finished for him.

"You both look pretty amazing, too," I admitted, admiring the snug fit of their matching suits. All black, of course. Only, Ajax had an interesting addition adorning his shoulder. "Nice owl."

Az grunted. "He's an asshole."

The owl bristled like he understood that and snapped his beak in Az's direction.

My eyebrows lifted.

"Kuro is slowly warming up to Az's Phoenix," Ajax said with a slight smirk.

"You're enjoying this," the Commander muttered.

"A little," Ajax admitted as Kuro's wings flexed and unflexed.

"He doesn't seem as mad at you now," I noted, recalling the only other time I'd seen Kuro—he'd been on Shade's shoulder, not Ajax's, and he'd snubbed Ajax by refusing to look at him. "Did you, um, make up?"

I wasn't quite sure what term applied here. Kuro was Ajax's familiar, but when Ajax had become the Hell Fae Warden, he'd left his owl behind in the Midnight Fae Realm. And from what little Ajax had said, his animal hadn't been pleased. But he looked content now.

Or rather, he looked a little miffed.

Only at Az, not Ajax.

"I'm not sure," Ajax said, replying to my question about *making up*. "He showed up to help me get ready. Pretty sure this is for you." He held out a bag I hadn't realized he'd been holding, mainly because I'd been too busy ogling the tight fit of the suit and not his hands.

I accepted the small bag, my brow furrowing. "What's this?"

He shrugged. "I think it's a gift from Aflora and her mates. Shade probably sent Kuro to give it to me."

"Which means his job is done and he can go," Az said, his attention on the owl.

Kuro hissed in response.

Az growled.

And the two locked eyes.

My lips twitched. "I think I rather like your familiar, Ajax."

He returned my smile with one of his own. "Me, too."

Az's irises turned black, his head cocking in a birdlike way. Kuro responded with another ruffling of his feathers, his posture stiff.

I fought a laugh and focused on the bag, pulling out a small box. My brow furrowed as my curiosity piqued. "The royals sent me jewelry?"

Ajax's expression matched my own. "I guess." He grazed his finger over the box. "Open it."

I didn't. Instead, I asked, "Did you just test it for a spell?"

"Not exactly." He paused. "I was feeling for magic."

"Did you sense anything?"

"I wouldn't let you open it if I did," he replied.

Fair enough, I thought, lifting the lid. A pair of earrings and a matching necklace glittered back at me, the pendants on both circular in nature.

"An interesting choice," I mused out loud, wondering if the orb-like symbol meant something. "Is it supposed to resemble the Source?" Because it kind of reminded me of the Hell Fae Source, only the gems were more golden than blinding white.

"I have no idea," Ajax said, sounding somewhat perplexed. "But it's pretty."

"Yeah," I agreed, taking the necklace out first. "Can you help put this around my neck?"

"An excuse to touch you while you're in this dress?" he countered, taking the glittering item from my fingertips. "Yes, please." That last part was a low murmur as he swept my long hair over my shoulder to better access my neck.

His warmth bled into my skin as he slowly clasped the strand against my nape, his gaze on my throat and the gem hanging just above my breasts.

"Seriously, Cami, you're gorgeous." His voice had deepened, his gaze tracking over the deep V neckline. Then he took the box from my hand to grab the earrings and helped affix them.

Az said nothing the entire time, his Phoenix still in some sort of standoff with the owl.

But as Ajax stepped back to view the finishing touches on my outfit, Az groaned. "I'm going to be hard all fucking night, Cami."

"Same," Ajax muttered. "If we didn't have to attend this ball, I'd have already ripped that dress off."

"We still could rip it off," Az said conversationally. "Fuck. A few times. Then head down to the party?"

I gave him a look. "I doubt Aflora and her mates would appreciate you ruining the gift they gave me." I gestured to the gown. "You can't rip this off of me. Not yet."

"Fine. I'll just take it off of you," Az murmured, moving forward to play with the strap against my shoulder. "Slowly..." He started tugging on the silky strand, bringing it down toward my arm. "Gent—"

Magic hummed across my skin as the fabric snapped free of Az's fingers and righted itself once more.

I frowned. "That was weird."

Az grabbed the strand again, tugging it off my shoulder with more force.

Only for it to jerk right back into place.

My eyes widened. "What the hell?" It reminded me of that chain dress Lucifer had made me wear to his nightclub. Goose bumps pebbled along my neck, trickling to my shoulders and arms.

I grabbed the zipper at my side and yanked it down, then yelped as it flew upward in response.

"*Noooo*," I growled, refusing to be trapped in another garment. This one might be silky and cover me in all the right places, but it still functioned as a prison.

At least it's not rubbing my clit, I thought.

Yet, another part of me whispered.

My eyes widened. *No. No. No.* I bent to lift the dress and tried to take off my underwear beneath. The lacy panties—the same color as the dress—reached my knees before magically gliding back into place with a resounding snap.

"What the hell is this?" I demanded, only belatedly realizing both Az and Ajax were already deep in conversation on the topic.

Kuro was nowhere to be seen, the owl having disappeared while I'd been freaking out.

"Typhos wouldn't do this," Az was saying. "He manufactured the chain dress as a sensual punishment. It was his way of making a statement. I'm not saying I agree with his methods, nor am I trying to explain them away. I'm simply stating that this doesn't match Typhos's usual methods."

"Then who?" Ajax demanded. "Because I highly doubt Aflora did this."

"Did what?" a deep voice asked as Shade materialized in the room with Kuro perched on his shoulder. "I assume whatever we're discussing is why you sent Kuro to peck at me?"

"I didn't send him; he left," Ajax replied without looking at his best friend. His blue-rimmed black eyes were on me. "Is the jewelry spelled, too?"

I reached for the necklace and unclasped it. The pendant slid down as I pulled the chain away from my nape. "No, seems to—" The charm slid back into place, the necklace clasp re-clicking. "Never mind. It's the jewelry, too."

Shade frowned. "That's an interesting trick."

"What do you mean by 'interesting'?" Ajax demanded. "Aren't the dress and the jewelry from your mate-circle?"

I didn't like the way Shade's frown deepened. Because it told me without words that this wasn't from him or any of his mates.

Which didn't make sense.

Before Shade could confirm what I really read from his features, I said, "Zakkai brought the dress to me last week and said it was a gift for tonight's ball."

Shade glanced over the gown in question, his gaze lighting up. But it wasn't in an appreciative way so much as an amused way. "Ah, right. His shopping date with the Virtuous Fae."

I blinked.

"How do you know that term?" Ajax demanded, stepping between me and his best friend to capture all of Shade's attention.

"Zakkai," he replied with a shrug. "Your paradigm-crafting abilities could use some work, by the way. Perhaps you should go back to Headmaster Granton's class and take it again?"

Ajax visibly bristled. "You heard our conversation last week."

Shade arched a brow. "Believe it or not, I value your privacy. Zakkai, however..."

"Fuck," Az muttered. "He heard everything, didn't he?"

"He did," Shade confirmed. "And he shared it with Aflora, whose privacy I also value, but I'm connected to her mind, so…" He shrugged again. "It's fine. Your Virtuous Fae mate offered to answer any questions Zakkai might have, and that's that."

"My Virtuous Fae mate?" Ajax repeated. "I don't have a Virtuous Fae mate."

"He means Melek," Az ground out. "It seems he and Zakkai have become friends."

"Zakkai doesn't have friends," Shade replied at the same time Ajax said, "Melek is *not* my mate."

Shade chuckled. "You're in a mate-circle now, old friend," the Midnight Fae drawled. "What's Cami's is yours and what's yours is hers, and all that jazz." He waved a hand. "You'll learn. Anyway, I need to get back to Aflora. Kuro?"

The owl hopped from Shade's shoulder to Ajax's, then Shade vanished in a cloud of purple smoke.

"Melek," Ajax growled, ignoring what Shade had just said. "He must have spelled the dress."

"Why?" Az asked.

"Because he knew I would tear it off the moment I realized it was from him," I seethed, grabbing at the gown in an attempt to do just that.

The silky fabric gave a satisfying rip.

Then mended right back together.

"No. No, I fucking refuse to wear this." I spun around, determined to shred the damn material. "Give me a blade, Az."

He didn't argue, just handed one over out of thin air.

I sliced through the straps.

They reconnected in a blink.

I yanked on the slit in the skirt, trying to extend the split up through the bodice. But the fabric bled back together in a swirl of magic.

Ajax whispered some spells. They basically bounced off the offending outfit, creating sparks of purple and gold in the room.

I snarled, determined not to lose this battle.

But the damn dress wouldn't budge!

Maybe this was Melek's way of staking his claim or providing me with one of his trademark protection spells.

I didn't care about the reason. Because I would not be caged, not anymore.

A scream built inside me in frustration, the memory of those chains weighing heavily on my thoughts.

The masculine jeers.

The metal against my clit.

Trying not to outwardly react. To be strong. To endure it all without blinking.

I didn't want to go through that again. I couldn't. It was horrible.

And it had ended with that portal explosion.

Absorbing Lucifer's power.

Helping him only to end up in hiding here in the Midnight Fae Realm.

Now I had to face him. To follow through with our counteroffer. To... to play out our plan.

In this prison-esque dress that glittered like the fucking Source.

"*Cami.*" Az's voice echoed through my mind, his domineering presence pausing my frantic movements.

I hadn't realized I'd still been spinning, trying to tear off the magic gown.

One look at his concerned face suggested I'd been doing it for a while because he almost appeared to be afraid. Or maybe remorseful.

"I shouldn't have let him put you on that stage," he whispered, confusing me. "I should have stopped him. I'm sorry."

I blinked. "What?"

"Typhos," he ground out. "I shouldn't have let him punish you like that."

Ajax stood beside him with an equally worried expression. "You don't have to go tonight," he told me. "He wants a response from me. I can give it to him."

I blinked again. "I'm not afraid of him," I said. Which wasn't exactly true—Typhos Lucifer was a frightening beacon of power—but I didn't want to hide from him anymore.

He wasn't the one who'd gifted me this dress.

Melek had.

That was what Shade had implied when talking about Zakkai's new whatever-it-was-called with Melek. Friends. Allies. Secret exchangers. Who the fuck knew how to define it? Nor did it matter.

Because Zakkai had brought me this gown. And it had clearly been on Melek's behalf.

I'd curse him in my mind, but that would require dismantling the barricade I'd built between us—a barricade that Az had helped me craft and perfect a few days ago.

I was still learning how to compartmentalize my mate-bonds. Thus, I didn't trust myself to break the wall now to reach Melek. With my luck, it would permanently dismantle the barrier, and I'd have to start all over again.

Which meant I had to go to the ball.

Dressed like this.

For one single purpose—to find Melek.

And when I did, I'd fucking kill him.

CHAPTER 11

TYPHOS

Don't frown so much, my love. You're going to make Queen Aflora think you don't want to be here, Melek interjected into my mind.

I don't want to be here, I informed him.

Really? Or are your feathers ruffled because a certain trio has not yet appeared? His multicolored eyes glittered with mischief, lifting my mood despite my irritation. *It's a party, my king. Have a little fun.*

Yes, I was supposed to be having *my* version of fun.

I should be deep in the verbal sparring of making a deal, but that required a certain little Hellion Bride, my Warden, and my Commander to play.

Alas, they were nowhere to be seen.

Instead, I was subjected to the display of overdressed fae of all heritages dancing on a glassy floor, its otherworldly sheen surface one that reflected the moon. The succulent scents of nightshade and charred burning thwomps in the distance were distinctly different from the aroma of home, but not entirely unpleasant.

Any other night, I would have appreciated Queen Aflora's

invitation and what she had accomplished with the Elemental Fae Queen. The Interrealm Fae Ball was one of the few events I had already planned on attending, given its purpose.

To celebrate those who were otherwise suppressed and ostracized.

Abominations, as the purists among the fae called them, were frolicking about and enjoying themselves. "Abominations" were ironically closer to the original fae kind than any Elemental Fae or Midnight Fae could possibly realize. Still, to see so many out in the open was refreshing indeed.

This level of freedom and acceptance reminded me of my own realm and all that I'd worked to achieve.

This was an echo, though, a blip of peace that wouldn't last.

Such achievements had been made before, and they always ended the same way—in failure.

Of course, there were little records or history of those uprisings because whenever fae of mixed heritages gained a foothold, some overseeing entity unraveled it and then destroyed all evidence of its existence.

I was surprised that this effort had come as far as it had.

And I feared for its inevitable collapse.

This peace, though, was nice to witness. The ambience around it was suitable as well.

Half-built walls stretched over the room in massive arches, as if the palace itself was about to cradle us all in its dark grip. The main stairway, one I kept checking while waiting for a certain female to appear, remained empty at the top of the walls, with the steps delving deep through cut stone.

Craggy spears formed of woven trees and vines—courtesy of the Midnight Fae Queen with an Earth Fae heritage—sent shadows stretching over the venue with an ominous prophecy only I seemed to be able to see. The structures created a sensation of being both trapped and freed.

Appropriate for tonight's festivities, and its inevitable failure.

I hoped I was wrong. Only time would tell.

And if I'm right, then these very fae might require the safety of my realm.

Meaning I needed to get a handle on Camillia De la Croix and the threat she served to my Source.

My chest tightened. Camillia was the first entity in several millennia to challenge me and make me question the future.

And now she's making me fucking wait for my *Warden,* my *Commander.*

With the way that Melek had pined over her, I felt like I was losing him, too.

I was losing everything.

But not for long.

Tonight, the unraveling of everything I held dear ended.

I would do that by doing what I did best.

Bringing chaos under control.

They'd better not be trying to run, I growled inside Melek's head. *Because I have no qualms about leaving this soirée right now and hunting them down myself.* I didn't say the words aloud because they would likely thunder through the ballroom and cause a stir.

I was already tired of the attention. We'd been here much longer than I had intended, which had invited more than a few unwelcome greetings.

They're not running, at least not away *from you, my king,* Melek assured me as he grabbed a fizzy drink from one of the wandering gargoyles. He took a delicate sip.

Ask her where they are, I demanded. I would have asked Az, but he hadn't let me back in yet, his barrier a solid fixture in my mind that I didn't want to touch.

I can't, Melek muttered. *Az taught her how to block me at some point over the last week, and, well, it's impressive... and frustrating.*

She blocked you? I asked, surprised that this was the first he'd mentioned it.

Melek's expression fell just for a moment, the blink of time too quick for anyone else to notice. But I'd seen it clearly, and I'd felt how much the knowledge had pained him, too.

I frowned. *You're hurt.*

She doesn't trust me yet, he replied. *I need to give her time.*

I snorted. *You've given her everything. She's a fool if she doesn't see how lucky she is to have earned your affections.*

Melek had chosen Camillia as his mate months ago, blessed her with his gifts and his guidance, his *protection*, but she continued to reject him in favor of the two other fae.

And now she was putting up walls?

Melek didn't deserve rejection, but to mend this situation required me to mate Ajax so I could bring all of the danger that was wrapped up in a pretty little package named Camillia De la Croix under control.

This will be settled soon, I promised him.

"Hmm," Melek replied aloud as he sipped his bubbly beverage again, now winking at a certain Selkie Shifter who was clearly checking him out.

I rolled my eyes. *Norden.* A fucking Winter Fae Prince, thanks to his recent mating with Lark, the Winter Fae King.

The Selkie was sinful, sensuous, and downright flirtatious. Just like Melek.

Which made it no mystery as to why the two had crafted a friendship.

Norden plucked a blue stick of crystal-like candy from a container and gave it a generous lick, keeping eye contact with my prince the whole time.

Bristling, I clasped Melek's nape in a clear demonstration of my claim.

Jealous, my love? Melek chimed in my head, clearly delighted to be the center of attention.

Why doesn't he flirt with his own mate-circle? I ground out.

Because he knows I like your possessive side, Melek purred back. *He's goading you as a favor to me. And he's taunting me with his candy. I want the recipe, yet he refuses to share it.*

I didn't ask him why he wanted the recipe because I already knew. Selkie candy caused orgasmic dreams, and I could only imagine who Melek wanted to give a piece to.

He asked me recently if I would give him a rope demonstration, Melek went on. *Apparently, he wants to tie Artica up as a Christmas present for Lark and Kalt. I told him I'd do it in exchange for the recipe. He refused.* He paused as Norden popped the candy into his mouth and closed his eyes. *Maybe he's reconsidering.*

I was about to issue a retort—something along the lines of *Maybe the Selkie has a death wish*—when the hairs along the back of my neck stood on end.

My attention snapped in the direction of the electric wave, my lips parting at finding the source of static.

Camillia De la Croix.

She stood at the top of the winding staircase, her golden appearance reminiscent of an angel.

Fuck. She was absolutely stunning.

The anger that had been simmering inside my chest twisted into a sensation I dared not name. Perhaps it was the way her dirty-blonde hair curled over her pert breasts or the way the slit in her glittering dress ran all the way up her thigh.

She was the embodiment of desire—of a *queen*—and her smoldering anger as she flexed her fists at her sides made my mouth water.

I had expected her fury, craved it even. *Mmm, let the game begin,* I thought as my Warden and my Commander stepped up behind her, their symbolism not lost on me.

A united trio.

Soon to become a circle, I mused.

The golden goddess glided down the stairs with lethal thunderstorms brewing in her gray eyes. But it wasn't me she was glaring at.

That look was for Melek.

What did you do, little prince? I asked him, not able to hide my amusement. Because the furious female practically oozed sex appeal, her heels clicking with tumultuous resolve with each step she took.

I have no idea, Melek said, a hint of unease in his tone. Yet he appeared to be just as enamored with the sight of her. *I'm not sure if I should be frightened or turned on. The latter seems to be winning.*

Hmm, I hummed, forbidden images playing through my mind.

Images Melek had implanted, thanks to his sinful thoughts over the last week.

Every time we'd fucked, he'd whispered words and scenarios about Camillia.

Typically involving her being helpless and at our mercy. Begging to be fucked. Whimpering with *need.*

All I could see was Melek tying her wrists with matching golden ribbons that glittered over her skin, her bent over as I slid the dress aside to indulge in what waited underneath.

"*Melek,*" Camillia hissed as she approached. Fiery energy practically licked off of her skin, and I couldn't help but entertain the fantasy of taming it.

Of taming *her.*

Just like Melek wanted me to do.

But that will never happen, because the last thing I need is for this vixen to unravel me like she's unraveled the others. If I couldn't keep a level head around this tempting female, then we were all doomed.

"Hello, little angel," Melek murmured, ignoring the venomous way she'd uttered his name. "You are positively radiant, love."

"Oh, you mean this?" Camillia asked as she plucked at the strap of her dress. It snapped back into place as if it had a mind of its own, causing me to raise a brow. "What did you do to it, Melek? Why can't I take it off?" An adorable growl accompanied her questions, making me wonder what that sound would feel like against my cock.

She crossed her arms, which only pushed her cleavage upward and drew my gaze down to the glittering golden necklace hanging from her neck.

The orb at the bottom settled nicely like a puddle between her breasts, the waterfall effect rather enticing. It made me picture Melek's cum dripping down those mounds in a similar fashion. I didn't try to dispel the pleasant imagery. My prince would have his fun with her, when she came to her senses.

And I would watch. I would allow that small indulgence, at least.

"Let me guess," she fumed, not giving Melek a chance to respond. "I'm going to spontaneously orgasm in the middle of the dance floor and shoot glitter jizz over everyone?"

Melek's multicolored eyes brightened with delight. "Well, that would be a sight to behold."

"I'm serious, Melek," she snapped, leaning in as she practically shoved me out of the way.

Did she not notice that I was right here?

"What did you do to it?" she demanded, her cheeks turning a crimson shade that complemented her pink lips. "The last time you gave me jewelry, it earned me the wrath of the fucking Hell Fae King."

A chuckle practically purred out of me. "*Wrath* is a rather strong term, isn't it?"

Her sea-gray eyes finally shifted to me, and she went completely rigid, her violent summer storm turning to ice in an instant.

"I-I... I didn't see you there," she admitted.

I had not been overlooked by anyone in, well, ever. And the sensation that gave me made my entire mood shift to something lighter, something ready to play with this enticing female who clearly didn't fear me like she should.

Melek summoned over one of the gargoyles and took another one of the drinks, then glanced at the Selkie candy on the tray and snatched it up, too. "You're looking parched, little angel. May I suggest a fizzy drink and a little sugar to dip in it?"

I could practically feel Norden's approval from across the ballroom.

Camillia waved the beverage and treat away. "N-no, thank you. I just want to know what you did to this dress and why I can't take it off." She swallowed, her focus returning to me again. "Or is this... another punishment?"

I stared at her, a myriad of *punishments* spilling through my mind.

But then I caught the edge of Az's ire, the wall between us beating with a hint of barely restrained fury.

I glanced at him. *What is it?* I asked him, aware that he could hear me now since I could feel him.

The chain dress. The anger underscoring his tone caught me by surprise.

What about it?

It left an impression, he told me. *Look at her, Typhos. She's angry, but she's also terrified. You obviously traumatized her with that damn spectacle, and now she's anticipating another one.*

I frowned. "I've never seen this dress before in my life," I informed him—and Cami—out loud. "Melek?"

"I selected it, but I didn't bespell it." His brow furrowed as he reached for the fabric, but Cami took a quick step back like she was terrified of his touch. His arm fell to his side, his hurt at her rejection whipping through my mind and heart.

I barely suppressed a growl in response.

This female was a menace.

Melek hid his pain behind an apologetic look. "I went shopping with Zakkai for your dress, but I promise, I didn't enchant it."

"Then who did?" Cami demanded.

Melek and I shared a look.

Is Melek telling the truth? Az asked me, his tone a little less irritated.

Yes. I didn't elaborate because it wasn't needed. Az knew Melek and I didn't *lie*. Melek liked to play, yes, but he wouldn't outright deny something in this manner. He would be coy and maybe counter with a *Would I do that?*

"Maybe the figments did?" Melek suggested. "I asked Zakkai to give you the dress, as I knew you wouldn't wear it if it was from me. The figments heard me. Perhaps they did something to prevent you from removing it before the ball ends?"

Cami gaped at him. "That's your story? That a figment did it?"

Melek's lips curled downward into an uncharacteristic frown. "If I bespelled it, I would tell you."

"As would I," I added. "It seems plausible that the figments enchanted the dress. They're meddling little creatures. Which explains their love for my prince."

That comment chased away Melek's frown, causing him to glance at me. "Thank you, my love."

"I'm not sure that *meddling* is a compliment," I replied dryly, fully aware that he could hear the teasing in my mind.

Because while Melek's meddling created certain annoyances, his devious nature was what had initially drawn me to him.

Cami plucked at her dress, that hint of fear still lurking in her eyes.

Fear of what? I wondered.

Or maybe *fear* wasn't the right term.

Haunted seemed more accurate, like she was reliving some memory that deeply upset her.

The chains, I thought, recalling what Az had said about me traumatizing her with that punishment. *Hmm.*

That knowledge twisted something in my heart, making me feel a bit ill at ease. Most of my sensual games were appreciated in the end.

But Cami's punishment hadn't reached that sort of climax.

Because the portal had opened in the Marsh Lands, dragging my focus away.

Then she'd come along and touched my Source.

To close the vortex-like portal, I thought, my gaze running up and down her goddess-esque form.

"I think you and I need to have a conversation, little temptress," I informed her softly.

Her eyes widened as she looked up at me, then she quickly schooled her expression into one that reminded me of a queen. Calm, cool, collected, and confident.

Very alluring.

"Ajax has a counter—"

I tsked and shook my head. "Not yet," I murmured, extending my hand. "Let's dance first."

The deal could be discussed in a bit. First, I wanted to...

talk to Camillia. I wasn't quite sure what I wanted to say, but it was a need I couldn't deny.

An invitation to dance was not what Melek's betrothed had expected. Her gaze lingered on my hand, then slowly returned to my face.

It should have bothered me how I could see the power of my own Source burning within her, see how she had tampered with my very soul already, but there was an innocence there, one that Melek had been trying to help me to recognize.

Perhaps she didn't mean any harm.

That still didn't mean she wasn't a threat, though.

"Dance?" she parroted back at me.

Melek seemed to make the decision for her as he took her hand and placed it in mine. Heat stirred in my lower belly at the simple action, one that was a precursor of all the fantasies Melek wished to make reality.

I wouldn't give in to his desires on this one, but it would be one of my greatest challenges of control yet.

"Yes," I told her. "A dance."

She swallowed, and I prepared for her to reject me.

However, some part of her bowed.

Not her soul, exactly, but perhaps the female inside her.

I witnessed it in the glazing of her eyes, a subtle hint of submission. The type I would enjoy coaxing out of her in bed.

"Okay," she agreed quietly, the single word stirring elation deep inside me.

Elation that quickly died as Az whispered, *She thinks she has no choice.*

She has a choice, I informed him. *But I'll make that clearer while we talk.*

No deals, he told me, causing me to meet his burning gaze. *She's mine, Typhos. And my Phoenix is fucking possessive. Don't make me choose between the two of you.*

I arched a brow. *I believe that choice has already been made, hasn't it?*

With that, I tugged her away from the bristling males at her back.

"Wait—"

"I won't hurt her," I told Ajax before he could finish his protest. "And I'll hear your counter when I'm done speaking with Camillia."

"Let them talk," Az said, his hand on Ajax's shoulder. "There's nothing he can do here. Besides, you're the one who said we have to let Cami do what she wants."

Ajax shot him a look. "That was in the Marsh Lands when she was trying to fix that portal. This is different and you know it."

"I'll be fine," Camillia promised him, her confidence returning. "The Hell Fae King and I are just going to *talk*."

My formal title on her lips reminded me of how I'd once commented on her use of informalities with my prince.

"Lucifer," I told her, as I pulled her away from the others and toward the dance floor.

"What?"

"Or Typhos, if you prefer," I added.

She gaped at me. "I don't understand."

"I think the time for titles between us is over, Camillia." I leaned down to press my lips to her ear. "The only situation where that may change is in the bedroom. But here, you can call me Typhos or Lucifer. Your choice."

The word was intentional, a play on what Az had said about Camillia not having a choice but to dance with me.

Perhaps we could use it as a launching point for conversation.

Because where Camillia De la Croix was concerned, I no longer wished to remove her options.

I simply wanted to strike a deal in the end that protected us all.

And gave me back control of my Source.

CHAPTER 12

CAMI

This was a very bad idea. But what choice did I have?

Typhos Lucifer was the Hell Fae King.

Probably one of the most powerful beings in existence.

And he'd asked me to dance.

Fuck.

I'd said yes because, well, I'd been a little tongue-tied. I'd dreaded this meeting for weeks, knowing that my life might very well end upon seeing Lucifer again.

Yet I'd entered the ballroom in a whirlwind of rage, searching for a Hell Fae Prince, and not even thinking twice about the Hell Fae King.

Until he spoke up to comment on my word choice. *Wrath*. He'd called it a *strong term*. I called it an accurate one.

Though, he didn't seem all that wrath-like right now.

Actually, he seemed almost pleased.

But that didn't stop the crowds from parting as he guided us onto the glass dance floor.

Everyone turned to stare, curious as to who had inspired the infamous Hell Fae King to join them.

He ignored all their interest, his focus entirely on me.

Which was unnerving, to say the least. And not just because of how sinfully beautiful he looked in his tux.

Because yeah, he wore it well.

But of course he did. He *always* fit his suits perfectly. A feat, considering his height and muscular width.

"You appear to be perplexed," he said as he pulled me into his arms. "Struggling to decide on what to call me, Camillia?"

I swallowed, recalling the words he'd said just moments ago. The ones he'd breathed against my ear.

"The only situation where that may change is in the bedroom. But here, you can call me Typhos or Lucifer. Your choice."

How would that change in the bedroom? I wondered.

But that was a dangerous line of thought, especially as it reminded me of my dreams.

Which I very much needed to ignore.

Particularly as he resembled sin incarnate in his fitted suit. His sapphire shirt highlighted his oceanic eyes, his dark hair was neatly arranged around his shoulders, and he wore a smile that served as both a warning and an invitation.

Clearing my throat, I went with "Lucifer" because it made the most sense to me.

He was the literal devil. And he possessed the same kind of sensuality that my mother's books had once warned me about.

Or... or were those my father's books? He'd always been the one giving me things to read.

Except I distinctly remembered my mother being obsessed with demonic symbolism—probably because of my father being a Hell Fae.

Did she know about my father's deal the whole time? I wondered. *The one that committed me to life as a Hell Fae Bride?*

Well, sorry to disappoint you, Mom, but I'm no longer a Hell Fae Bride.

Instead, I was a perceived threat to the man currently holding me on the dance floor.

I had no doubt this dance was some kind of sordid punishment, just like the chain dress.

And the one I'm wearing now, I thought, glancing down at the offending fabric.

Melek had suggested that figments had bespelled the material.

I doubted it.

This was all a game, one where the Hell Fae King would probably end up killing me for fun in the middle of this dance floor.

"Typically one moves while dancing," Lucifer murmured, his palm a brand against my lower back, his opposite hand holding mine.

"What?" I asked dumbly.

"You're as still as a statue," he said, guiding me closer to him. "I invited you to dance, not to stand awkwardly in a partial hug, Miss De la Croix."

I frowned. "You're the Hell Fae King. Aren't you supposed to lead?" The quip fell from my tongue before I could think better of it, my entire body freezing as I repeated the words in my head.

To my surprise, Lucifer laughed. *Laughed*. And wow, what a beautiful sight that was. His eyes even crinkled at the sides, his lips curling into a true smile, not one of his deviously charming expressions. But an actual grin.

"Touché, Camillia." His fingers tensed against my back, his arms flexing as he guided our movements.

My heart stuck in my throat, my stomach churning with discomfort while I waited for his mood to shift. For him to reveal the true nature of this punishment. For his amusement to turn deadly. For my entire world to go up in flames.

But all he did was sway our bodies in a sensuous rhythm, one that reminded me of my dreams all over again.

Lucifer on top of me.

Kissing me.

Branding me with his hands.

I shivered, my body and mind fighting a battle I couldn't quite define. I should hate this male, not crave him. He'd put me through literal Hell, bargained my life away in a deal with my father, and then tossed me aside the moment he considered me to be a threat.

I'd helped him with that portal.

He'd chosen fury over gratitude.

And he put me in that damn dress, I thought, trembling again.

Was it really that bad? another part of me questioned.

Yes! It was terrible. He's a horrible fae. He should die for his sins.

My brow furrowed, that angry voice coming from a part of me that I didn't quite recognize. Was I angry with him? Yes. Afraid of him? Also yes. But to want him to die...?

"You're frowning," Lucifer noted, his voice dropping a little. "Everyone is going to think I'm a bad leader now, hmm?"

I blinked. "Oh, I..." I had no idea what to say to that. I felt awkward. Oddly out of sorts. Conflicted about issuing retorts or... or... apologizing?

"It was a joke, Camillia." His serious tone had me glancing up at him. I wasn't sure when I'd even dropped my gaze, but I obviously had because I hadn't been looking at him until now.

He studied me with his ocean-blue eyes, his expression giving nothing away.

All I could see was his chiseled cheekbones and square jaw, his impossibly handsome features making it difficult to focus on the details.

Hell Fae Rule #66: The Devil Is in the Details.

The random rule rolled through my thoughts, reminding me once more of my parents. They were the reason most of these rules existed.

Well, my dad specifically.

Yet that rule in particular was one my mom used to whisper to me.

Shaking my head, I cleared the unwanted memories away and focused on the Hell Fae King. "I didn't realize you had a sense of humor." Again, the quip tumbled out of me unbidden.

And again... the Hell Fae King chuckled. "There's a lot you don't know about me, little temptress."

I shivered again, the endearment rolling over me in a subtle caress, one I really didn't want to experience. But those dreams were messing with my head.

As were Melek's sensual words. Thank the fae that I'd been able to block him.

Of course, the damage was already done, the images of him tying me up for Lucifer a fantasy that haunted my dreams.

"What would you like to know?" Lucifer went on, drawing me back to our dance—one that was really more of a subtle sway of hips than anything else.

A sway that changed as the music evolved around us into something a little faster in pace.

My nipples beaded as our chests met, Lucifer's proximity short-circuiting some part of my brain. But a chill from my necklace grounded me, awakening me to my current situation.

Because the sensation was one I'd experienced before— from Melek's magic.

So he did bespell my outfit, I decided. *Because of course he did.*

"Camillia?" Lucifer prompted.

"Why are we doing this?" I asked him. "Why are we dancing?" It had to have something to do with the enchanted gown; I just couldn't see the purpose.

"Because it's a ball," he murmured, his mouth curving into an alluring smile. "One typically dances at a ball, yes?"

"I wouldn't know," I replied flatly. "This is my first one."

"Ah." He nodded. "I suppose you did miss the Hell Fae Bride event."

My jaw clenched. Because yeah, I had missed that gathering... *as punishment for wearing an enchanted necklace.*

Recalling that event had my veins running hot, just for the charm to cool against my skin once more.

I wanted to rip it off. Burn it. Destroy every piece of magic.

Alas, I had no idea how to do that. Because it was like that chained dress all over again.

Although... with the chained dress, I'd... I'd *absorbed* the magic.

Maybe I could do that again?

No, better yet, maybe I *should* do that again...

I focused on the energy around me, my soul seeking a connection, anything that I could latch onto in an effort to break the spell. I should have thought of this before entering the ball, but better late than never. *Ah, there—*

Lucifer whirled me into a dip, one that distracted me from the strand I'd nearly caught. When he righted me, I grabbed his shoulder with my free hand, my heart skipping a beat.

His blue eyes were so intense. Like whirlpools of madness and chaos and *power*.

"I've been hard on you," he said, his gaze holding mine. "Perhaps unfairly. Perhaps not. That remains to be seen, but I can acknowledge that I've not made things easy for you, Camillia."

I huffed a humorless laugh. "I think that's a bit of an understatement, Your Majesty."

"Lucifer," he corrected. Another dip and twirl, one that ended with my back to his chest and his lips at my ear. "No more formalities, Camillia."

"Why?" I asked on a pant as he whirled me again. "You've more than insinuated that you have no interest in getting to know me." At least, not in real life.

In my dreams, well, that was a very different story.

I ignored that and added, "You've also said that I'm too familiar with your prince. Why the sudden change of heart?"

He whirled me again, catching me deftly by the hips and holding me flush against him. "Because my heart belongs to that prince, and he's made his feelings for you quite clear."

The seriousness of his tone matched the gleam in his gaze, causing me to swallow. "He's playing with me." I'd been a shiny toy from the beginning that Melek had plucked out of the Hell Fae Bride pool. His reasoning remained to be seen. But his intentions weren't long-term. "I'm a temporary fixation."

Lucifer stopped moving, the full force of the ocean swirling in his irises. "There's nothing temporary about what he's doing. He's tied his soul to yours for eternity, and while it may feel like a game—because my prince is playful in nature—it's forever for him."

He twirled me before I could respond, dipping me so far down that my hair skimmed the floor before he pulled me back up in a deft move that left me breathless and speechless against him.

Or maybe the vehemence in his words had done that.

But he wasn't done speaking.

"Melek has made his desires clear with every gift, every thought, every *trick*. You mean so much more to him than you realize, than I even realized. But I see it now. And I'm...

attempting to respect it." He reached up to brush my hair away from my face, our twirling having tangled my long strands.

I held his gaze, my heart seeming to stop beating.

We were so close, our lips only a few breaths away from one another.

If this were one of my dreams, he would kiss me. Then tie me up in Melek's ribbons and torture me with his mouth and hands.

I swallowed, unsure if I hated or loved that idea. If I hated or craved him.

"He didn't enchant your dress, Camillia," he said softly. "Had you not blocked him out, you would have heard the hurt that notion caused him when you accused him of it."

I stared at the Hell Fae King, some of my earlier frustration returning at the mention of my gown. "He's enchanted things before."

"Yes, to protect you," he replied. "I punished you as a way of punishing him; he knew the Hell Fae Bride rules and chose to cheat. I couldn't let that go unanswered."

The song changed again, the tempo slowing once more.

Lucifer followed it, holding me in his arms and guiding us to the new rhythm.

For all his faults—which I supposed he didn't have many other than being a bit of a control freak with a punishment fetish—he could dance.

"More so," he went on, "I was jealous of his affection. Melek's soul is faithful to mine. He sometimes plays with others, but he doesn't fuck them. He simply uses them to satisfy a need I can't fulfill. However, with you, it's spiritual. And it shocked the life out of me."

CHAPTER 13

CAMI

"Oh."

It was a poor response.

But I had no idea how to react to Lucifer admitting he was *jealous*.

This was also the longest Lucifer and I had ever spoken to one another, and he was being... candid. I wasn't sure how to interpret any of this. "Are you... still jealous?" I hedged.

"Extremely," he murmured. "But the reasons for that jealousy are shifting."

My brow furrowed. "What do you mean?"

He shrugged. "It's not relevant to my apology. I'm simply trying to say that I acknowledge I haven't gone easy on you. You've not just threatened my Source, but my heart, too. Fae have died for much less, Camillia."

My chest tightened at his mention of an apology, then my heart sped up at what I perceived as a threat. "I'm not trying to be a threat, Lucifer."

I meant that.

But the chilling magic against my breastbone appeared to

139

contradict me, because the necklace was humming with cool energy.

It seemed to grow colder with each passing minute, Lucifer's closeness intensifying the chill. I wasn't sure what it meant. Was it a warning of some kind? Or a way to help chase away his heat?

"That remains to be seen," he murmured, twirling me again. His response had me wondering if he'd heard the questions running rampant in my mind, but then I realized he was replying to my statement about not being a threat.

"I don't want your Source," I promised him. "And I don't want..." I trailed off. I'd almost said *your prince*, but I caught Melek standing nearby with Az and Ajax, his focus entirely on me.

Actually, all three of them were studying me, likely searching for signs of discomfort. Or perhaps just wondering what their Hell Fae King had wanted to say to me.

"My prince is very alluring," Lucifer said as he spun me in his arms, placing my back to his chest and his lips to my ear once more. "Were you about to deny craving his touch?"

I held Melek's sparkly gaze, noting the concern flickering deep within. It was an uncharacteristic gleam, one that I wasn't sure I'd seen on him before. "Is he worried about what you're going to do to me?" I asked, ignoring Lucifer's question.

"No, he knows I won't harm you."

I nearly glanced over my shoulder to check his expression, but I already knew it wouldn't give anything away. "I wish I could be that confident," I muttered, more to myself than to him.

"You have every right to not be confident in my intentions," Lucifer replied, his words shocking me into silence. "I've threatened you more than once, punished you in foreign ways, and more or less expressed my deep disdain at mating my prince."

He spun me around, my legs clumsy due to my shocked state.

"I don't trust you, Camillia," he told me, his statement far less surprising than everything else he'd said. "So you shouldn't trust me either. But I think it's time for us to determine a way forward, to perhaps learn to trust one another... for our mates."

That last part was uttered as he moved me toward the floor again, his lips near my throat.

I could hardly breathe by the time he righted me, my body on fire yet cold at the same time.

It was such a juxtaposition of climate, my skin burning while my necklace resembled ice against my chest. *Is the spell meant to make me feel submissive? To willingly agree with whatever deal he's about to propose?*

"What are you offering?" I hedged, trying to discern his true intentions, as well as test my theory.

"We're not making a deal, Camillia," he replied. "Not here. Not yet. I promised Az I only wanted to talk to you, and I'm not one to break promises."

I stared at him. "But your entire world revolves around deals."

"Not to sound repetitive, but you don't know me very well. While, yes, deals are of significant value to me, there are some things in life that can't be dictated by formal agreements. Sometimes, we have to put faith in others to test their true intentions."

"Is that what this is?" I asked. "You putting faith in me to see if I'll betray you?"

He considered me for a moment, our hips subtly swaying to the slow beat. "Honestly, Camillia, I suppose I'm trying to encourage you to have a little more faith in me and my intentions. And in return, I'm going to try to do the same with you."

"Does that mean you don't want to kill me?"

His lips twitched. "Oh, I still want to kill you, Camillia. Whether intentional or not, you're a threat." His palm moved against my lower back, his arm enveloping me. "But just because I want to do something doesn't mean I will." Those words were uttered against my ear, his tone shifting downward an octave.

"That doesn't make me feel safe around you," I admitted in a whisper.

"Then we're even, Camillia De la Croix. Because I don't feel safe around you either." His lips ghosted across my pulse, causing my earrings to flare in time with my necklace.

It sent an ice cube down my spine, one that had my eyes going wide in response. It was so unexpected and bizarre, and contrasted deeply with the heat pouring off Lucifer's muscular form.

Again I tried to decipher the magic imprisoning me in this dress.

Something was happening.

Something strange.

"I could never hurt you, Camillia," Lucifer said, his voice whisper-soft. "You're tied to my heart now, to my very soul. Which is why I'm going to confide in you."

I gripped his shoulders, his nearness making me dizzy. Or maybe that was the bizarre temperature battle occurring over my skin.

Whatever he was about to *confide* was likely related and would hopefully explain these conflicting sensations.

"Melek loves his games," he started, confirming what I suspected.

Melek enchanted this dress.

He lied about the figments.

The true punishment is about to begin.

I squeezed my thighs, hoping against all hope that the sensual torment wouldn't begin between my legs. I couldn't handle that embarrassment again, the chain having been too much.

But was it, though? I thought, recalling the Hell Fae nightclub experience. I'd been overwhelmed and humiliated, yes. However, I'd also been furious. I'd held my head up high. I'd battled that room with my confidence.

It was horrible of him to do that to me, another part of me thought, the voice coming from that strange, unrecognizable place again. A place of insecurity, one I hadn't even realized I possessed.

"But something you need to understand is that my prince plays games with those he fancies," Lucifer went on, drawing me back to his comments on Melek. "It's his way of courting you."

I frowned. *What?*

"Everything he's done has been for your protection, from the necklace he once gifted you to his mating vows to his visits here in the Midnight Fae Realm. He's not trying to hurt you, Camillia. He's trying to win your affection and to prove his own worth." Lucifer finally pulled away from my neck, his eyes blazing with passion as he stared down at me.

I gazed back, confused and a little lost.

I'd expected him to *confide* his intentions. To finally reveal his punishment.

Not talk about Melek and his affections for me.

"He's sad, Camillia," Lucifer whispered. "I can't tell you how rare an emotion that is for Melek."

I blinked at him. "He's sad?" I didn't doubt that it was *rare*. I hadn't known Melek for nearly as long as Lucifer had, but I knew enough to understand how abnormal that had to be for the playful Hell Fae Prince.

"For lack of a better explanation, I think he's feeling rejected." Lucifer canted his head, our bodies still swaying to the beat, which hadn't changed much over the last two songs. "Is it your intention to reject him as a mate?"

My eyes widened. "I..."

"You'd been about to tell me that you didn't want my prince, yes?" he prompted, referring to our conversation from minutes ago. "You said you didn't want my Source, then started to say you didn't want something else. I assume you were going to name Melek. Am I wrong?"

I wasn't sure how our conversation had evolved into my feelings for Melek, or how we'd even ended up on the dance floor.

Typhos Lucifer wanted to kill me. He hated me. He thought I was a threat.

Yet he was holding me with care and trying to have an intimate conversation with me.

All while my mates watched.

I glanced their way but found the three of them conversing amongst themselves. It seemed they were no longer concerned about me being in the arms of the Hell Fae King.

Maybe now that nothing terrible had happened, they didn't see Lucifer as an immediate threat.

Do I see him as a threat? I wondered, thinking back to what he'd said about never being able to hurt me, how I was tied to his heart and soul.

Yet he'd also expressed his desire to end me.

An honest depiction of our relationship, I supposed. Perhaps the most honest he'd been with me to date.

Oh, he'd admitted to wanting to kill me before, but tonight he'd said desiring something and doing something were two very different actions.

"Camillia?" he prompted, trying to draw my focus back to him.

My gaze slid his way, only to pause as a head of blonde hair caught my eye, the glimmer shining beneath the moonlight. I swung my attention back to it, the color reminding me of my mother.

But the woman was nowhere to be seen.

A trick of the light? I wondered, frowning.

Lucifer's lips grazed my cheek. "I want an answer, Camillia. If you're going to break my prince's heart, I need to know so I can pick up the pieces and heal him."

"You're not going to threaten me into being with him instead?" I asked, somewhat surprised by my own response, as well as the tone I'd used to issue it. There was a lot of deep-seated anger inside me, perhaps being bolstered by that foreign voice I'd heard twice now in my thoughts.

"If you don't see how worthy my prince is, then your punishment will simply be to never experience him in all his beauty," Lucifer said, a hint of anger underlining his tone. However, it wasn't the kind of anger that frightened me. It was a different kind. The kind spoken by a man possessive of his mate.

He twirled me as a new song started, his movements a little harsher than before. Not violent, but dominant. Like he was trying to bring me to heel.

"Melek is a gift from the heavens," he told me. "A beautiful soul. I may not always agree with his actions, but everything he does is for a reason. He's not malicious. He's pure. And the games he's played with you have all been in your favor."

"They've all pissed you off," I countered.

"Indeed they have," he agreed. "But that's because Melek is pushing me on purpose. He believes you're tied to our future. Sometimes, I understand why. Right now, I do not."

I bristled. "You say that like it's an insult."

"Because it is one," he returned before dipping me to the

floor once more, his nose touching mine. "You're rejecting my heart. And I think you're a fool for doing so."

"I haven't rejected him."

"You haven't claimed him yet, either."

I grabbed Lucifer's lapels, holding our bodies together as he righted us once more. "It's hard to claim someone who is always playing games."

"Then open your eyes and realize that he hasn't been playing a game since you arrived here. He's been trying to help, to ensure your safety while I calmed down enough to see reason." He whirled me around, pressing his chest to my back yet again. "He's your guardian angel, Camillia. Accept that. Or be kind and reject him."

He released me to step around me, ending our dance.

I grabbed his hand on instinct, not willing to let him have the final word, and a thunderous energy rippled up my arm. Both of us glanced down at where we were joined, his brow furrowing.

I went to release him but couldn't, my palm seemingly glued to his.

"What is this?" he demanded.

"I... I don't know." I tried to take a step back, but my legs refused to move.

No. Not my legs... my *shoes*.

"It's this... this *dress*," I hissed, my free hand going to the fabric to pull it away from me.

Lucifer frowned at the offending material, then reached out to touch it himself. A snarl left him as he yanked his palm away, only the gown went with him as ice-cold power rippled through every inch of my being.

I shuddered in response, the sensation overwhelming and crawling over every inch of my skin.

Az, Ajax, I thought, trying to find them in the crowd.

Instead, I locked gazes with a ghost.

One I hadn't seen in... in ages.

But those ice-blue eyes belonged to Mystika De la Croix. *My mother.*

"*Camillia*," Lucifer growled, snapping my attention back to him.

I gasped at the sight before me, his pained expression and gritted teeth utterly at odds with the man I'd just been dancing with.

But it was the strange lock of white hair that really captured my focus.

It reminded me of the Source.

And it was a glaring difference from his otherwise dark hair.

"What...?" I... I didn't...

His hand was still stuck to mine, his opposite palm holding my dress.

My now-*glowing* dress.

Gold flickers. White sparks. *Freezing cold energy*.

I inhaled, the power seeming to seep into my veins, reminding me of the time I'd borrowed his Source to fix the portal. Only this was different. It wasn't intentional at all. It was... it was *forced*.

The magic in the dress, I thought again, immediately trying to latch onto the strand I'd noticed earlier. The cool power reminded me of Melek again, except this couldn't be him. He would never do this to Lucifer.

"*Fuck*," the Hell Fae King gritted out, still trying to free himself from whatever was happening between us.

It had all gone down so fast, the crowd just now seeming to notice something was wrong. *Very, very wrong*, I thought, searching again for my mates.

The three of them were coming toward us now.

But I couldn't let them reach me and Lucifer.

If they touched us, they might get sucked into whatever the hell this was.

"Take us to the Hell Fae Realm," I told Lucifer.

He glared at me. "No. No fucking way am I letting you near my Source."

"I don't know what's happening!" I snapped at him. "And I don't want to risk Az, Ajax, and Melek being stuck in whatever the fuck this is!"

His attention went to the three fae trying to get through the crowd to reach us. Meanwhile, mine went to the ghost lurking nearby.

She was still here.

Her blonde hair waving in an invisible wind.

Her lips pressed into a disapproving line.

Her gaze piercing.

Only for her visage to be obscured as someone moved right through her ethereal form.

A fucking ghost, I thought, trying to shake the image from my head. *I'm losing my mind.*

The strands of power were growing rapidly around me, the icy kiss tracing goose bumps over my arms and legs.

I tracked the energy, searching for the source of the spell again, wanting to unravel it.

Zakkai, I realized, trying to find him in the crowd.

But there were too many fae.

And this was all happening in the blink of an eye.

"Lucifer!" I shouted as he tried to again yank himself away, only for more of his power to surge into me. *Through* me.

I felt it pouring into my being and going somewhere deep, to a cavern I didn't quite understand.

But that cavern was linked to the magical energy swirling around my dress. I could see it now, the energy strands almost tangible.

I tugged on one as Lucifer wrapped his arms around me. "Hold on," he demanded.

Then the world disappeared.

As did Lucifer's touch.

But the energy remained, capturing me in a cloud of chilling fog.

The frosty tendrils writhed, pulsed, and beat at my spirit. Angry and cold. Fierce and terrifying.

I yanked on the mist-like strands anyway, determined to free myself from their frigid grip.

Searing warmth sliced through me, drawing a scream from my throat as fiery fingers dug into my very soul. I shoved it away, not wanting any of it.

Only the ice.

The spell.

The fucking dress.

I clawed at the fabric, my mind unraveling as the tendrils of energy fractured around me. I could feel it failing. Feel the invisible bars around me shaking beneath the force of my fight.

Just a little more, I thought, pummeling at the now-visible energy with my own force of will while I ripped off the necklace.

It didn't fly back up to my throat.

The earrings were next.

They didn't return to my ears.

Then I focused on the remains of the golden material, shredding the threads with my fingertips and mind. It was all connected—the entangling spell, the cold energy, the *siphon.*

I dug deep into the well inside me, found Lucifer's energy, and shoved it out of me with as much force as I could muster, shattering the final bars on my energy-like prison.

Hot white light responded in kind, causing me to blink into oblivion.

I was nowhere and somewhere at the same time.

Floating. Lost. No longer corporeal.

My eyes opened and shut, but all I saw was white. Pure, blinding *white*.

It was silent.

Still.

And cold.

Oh, so very...cold.

Until someone stepped into view. Someone framed by gorgeous white wings.

I blinked at the angel, startled to see her before me.

She was no longer in an ethereal state like she'd been in at the Interrealm Fae Ball, her ghostlike appearance more solid now, too.

"M-Mom?" I said, my voice raspy with disuse. Or perhaps from screaming for an undetermined amount of time. I really didn't know. I couldn't even remember why I'd been screaming or how I'd ended up here.

Maybe I'm dead?

"Hello, Camillia," my mother greeted, ensnaring my attention. "Welcome to utopia."

"Utopia?" I echoed.

She smiled. "Yes, my dear. *Utopia.*"

CHAPTER 14

TYPHOS

MY HAIR WHIPPED around my face, my stomach churning as the distinct sensation of falling made me feel weightless and helpless at the same time.

It was not a sensation I was used to, but one that I remembered all too well.

My nightmares occasionally brought back the old memory now and then, reminding me of the day when everything had ended.

And my new life had begun.

Flames encased me, transforming me into a ball of fire as my Source reveled in my power. I had created it like this, once, long ago.

Now, it had somehow returned to its full glory, but it wasn't pleased.

It was angry.

Camillia, I thought wistfully as I pieced together what she had actually done.

I hadn't reclaimed my Source.

She'd *returned* it.

Little temptress, I was so wrong about you.

She hadn't even realized how powerful her release had been when she'd dismantled the icy energy of her dress. It'd been cementing us together, forcing her to siphon my power into a void inside her soul.

I'd felt it happening, *knew* she wasn't in control.

"Hold on," I'd told her as I'd opened the pathway back home.

Then I'd tried to bring her with me.

But she'd severed that connection and thrown all of my power back at me, sending a blast radiating through my domain.

I had not been prepared to receive the return of my power, and as a result, it had ricocheted.

And now I'm falling all over again.

Bracing myself, I closed my eyes and accepted what would happen next.

After the fall would be the landing.

And it was going to hurt.

My ears popped as I broke through the barrier of the Hell Fae Realm, and the inferno of my Source roared to life.

The sound that echoed across my territory would be heard for thousands of miles—a roar of the Hell Fae King's fall.

And then all I knew was pain.

Stone and rock burst around me as my body slammed against the unforgiving ground.

Or was it a building?

Oh, my palace, I realized, catching a glimpse of the skyline as the walls crumbled around me.

So, I'd be landing in the same place as my very first fall.

That was somehow fitting.

I smashed through walls and stone as my Source sought the familiar hollow. I'd constructed my palace here on purpose, the location serving as a memorial to remember how far I'd once fallen.

My capital was built on top of this sacred crater, all height and grandeur. But in reality, my original fall had carved out an entire cavern beneath the fiery ambience of the Hell Fae Kingdom.

Fortunately, I didn't appear to be revisiting that secret cavern today, my fall impactful, but not *that* impactful.

Blood filled my mouth as every bone in my body shattered. I would heal in a matter of moments, but first my physical body would be destroyed by the collision.

I accepted it with ire.

To be made whole again, I first had to submit to the pain.

A hiss left my deflated lungs as the stone exploded around me into walls of Hellfire, then settled into dust that filtered through the air. My palace would only be partially decimated by my fall.

The Hellfire was from the power of my Source. It would remain eternal.

Just like me.

My bones re-formed in seconds that felt like hours, working to pull all of my organs back into shape as my body knit itself together again.

How the fuck did this happen? I wondered as I stared up at a statue that was miraculously unharmed. The stone displayed my prone form on the ground, lifelike with gold threads through red marble. Its depiction was one of agony, of my fall and the horror I had endured.

The pain had not been purely physical, despite the evidence of bloody slashes down the statue's back.

It had been an emotional wound, one that had never healed.

Now, I'd landed at the entrance to my personal wing, specifically where the impact of my original fall kept the stone warm.

The molten material had been the foundation of this

entire realm. I'd built it up from dirt and dust, forging a new world where others rejected by those they trusted could seek refuge.

Molten hatred and *resolve*—that was what my realm had been based on.

No one will reject you here.

It was what the statue was made of. The ground underneath me went on for miles, and I'd built my palace around it. The broken balcony overlooked a city that I had grown from nothing but desperation and pain.

But now I felt like I was being reborn all over again. That day I had fallen, I had lost everything.

This time, I wasn't the one who had made the sacrifice.

Camillia had.

Where is she? As I curled my fingers into the molten rock solidifying around my form, I crawled to my hands and knees.

Everywhere.

My nostrils flared as I drew in her scent of decadent roses, this time with a tinge of ambrosia and fire.

A mixture of Melek and me.

It was an intoxicating combination, one that settled a craving deep within my soul that felt strangely whole.

I hadn't felt like this since... before.

Before Camillia De la Croix.

Because she gave it back.

All this time she had been stealing my Source, but now I was certain it hadn't been on purpose.

Someone had been using her ability to siphon my power, but she'd figured it out the same moment I had.

And she had fought back.

Just like I would expect of a future queen.

The thought came to me like a reflex, taking me by surprise. She wasn't meant to be mine. She belonged to Melek. To Ajax. To Az. Not me. I didn't want her.

At least... I *shouldn't* want her.

But her loyalty rang true, her honor a beacon my soul desired to repay.

She'd saved my Source. Forced it back inside me. Proved through her actions that she'd meant what she'd said about not wanting my power.

It could all still be a trick. A dangerous game to lure me into her inner circle. However, I'd seen her expression, her fear when she'd realized what was happening.

And even more than that, her *anger*.

She hadn't wanted to be used in that manner, and she'd shoved back against the magic in response.

Since the moment we'd met, she'd vowed she was innocent. I'd just refused to see it because of her ability to reach right into my soul and take my power for herself.

Except, she had never used that power for her own gain, not really.

Camillia had only tried to survive.

She'd closed the portal that would have killed my people.

She'd never outright defied me, and instead she had followed my demands, if only to protect those she loved.

Ajax and Azazel were part of my inner circle. Seducing them hadn't been a tactic to control me; it'd been a natural course of action for the female my own prince had chosen as his eternal mate. The very fact that she hadn't fully mated him yet, that she even seemed reluctant to do so, proved that she had no desire to steal from me.

Because if she genuinely wanted to hurt me, Melek was how she would do it. She would have eagerly taken him up on his offer and claimed him long ago, then destroyed me from the inside.

Her very hesitation proved she wished to take her decisions seriously. She didn't see what Melek was offering her, not yet.

The irony of it all was that she didn't see her own value, or who she really was.

A future Hell Fae Queen, if Melek had his way.

And she fought like one.

Camillia De la Croix had dismantled that damnable dress —*absorbed* it—and found a way to return the power of my Source to me. Then she'd literally imploded in a grand display of power.

Melek had chosen his mate well, and now I finally understood everything he'd been trying to make me see.

Camillia wasn't my enemy.

She was the most powerful ally I could possibly ever have.

So, where is the little temptress now?

When I searched my palace for any sign of her, I only spotted my personal guard. My Hellhounds waited like nightmares on the edges of the foggy destruction, their gazes more curious than concerned.

They didn't approach me but waited for my command, their pointed ears angled in my direction. Those fiery tips were the only parts of them that moved while they watched me expectantly with their glowing red eyes.

Everything felt strangely quiet after the impact of my second fall.

The rest of my realm would be listening for my order, for my instructions, and for my reassurance.

They would want to know what had just happened.

Melek appeared in a glittering golden flurry of feathers, right on cue. "Typhos," he breathed. "Take my hand."

He held out his palm without hesitation as he stepped over the cooling rock.

I stared at his fingers, unable to shake that this was exactly how it had happened the first time.

Except now, I knew that Melek had not betrayed me.

When he had offered me his hand so long ago, I had pushed it away.

This time, I took it.

My prince gave me a smile that broke my heart, because this little reenactment healed something inside of him. We rarely spoke about the tricks he had played back then. Those tricks had saved my life, but they had still hurt.

His perceived betrayal had broken me.

However, my rejection had broken him, too.

That deep scar was something I had never been able to fully heal, and yet, here we were, mending it.

Thanks to Camillia De la Croix.

Melek and I held hands long after I had managed to stand. My suit had burned off my body, but I wasn't broken any longer. I wasn't suffering the loss of my wings like my first fall. Instead, a rush of fire echoed in their place like a haunting memory.

My Source blazed across my skin, healing me with fiery waves that I could see reflected in the golden threads of energy pumping through my veins.

Just like the statue, I marveled.

As though to finish my return to power, heat blazed at my back and my inferno-like appendages stretched to their full grace.

I sighed, renewed. Replete. Fulfilled.

And my Source finally began to calm, its core throbbing like a gentle heartbeat, pleased with its restored balance.

"Where's Camillia?" I asked, because even though her essence was everywhere, she was clearly not physically here.

And I had questions—as well as concerns. She had expelled an incredible amount of energy all at once.

Melek had come alone, which only made that concern grow.

What if...

Shadows twirled in the air as Ajax appeared, followed by the fiery ash of my Commander on his heels.

They both stared at me for a moment, and I realized this was the first time either of them had ever seen me like this.

Reborn.

New.

In my raw form as the Hell Fae King.

My hair waved around my face from an invisible wind as power crackled through my veins. Melek released my hand and reached for me, paying the snapping energy no mind as he took a lock of my hair between his fingers.

My hair was dark, but the piece he held now was white.

Is that from whatever Camillia had done to me?

Not when she'd returned the Source, but before. When she had been *taking* instead.

And now that all of my inner circle was here, it was apparent that Camillia was... not.

All of my men seemed to come to that realization at the same time. Ajax's eyes widened, and Azazel's head tilted to the side as his irises took on a deep shade of black.

Melek's jaw clenched before he spoke. "She's not with you?"

"She's in the Barren Lands," Ajax announced, surprising me with that vague declaration before disappearing in another flurry of shadows.

My Commander's brow furrowed. "He's wrong. She's still in the Midnight Fae Realm," he muttered before puffing into a pile of ash, no doubt heading back to the realm we had just been in before.

Melek's chin dipped as his attention swept away from my palace. "I sense her somewhere else, too. I feel her..." He frowned before he glanced up at me. "Why would she be on the Hell Fae Bride campus? That's where I sense her, but I still can't reach her with my mind. I can only feel her."

Something was wrong—because I felt Camillia, too.

Except, it was here.

Everywhere.

"Go," I told him, because if my men were drawn to those locations, perhaps there was an answer to the riddle they posed. "And tell me what you find, my prince." I gripped his nape and pressed my forehead to his. "But please, beloved, be careful."

I didn't have to say it aloud. He knew.

He had already known, likely long before I had.

We have an unseen enemy who has been pulling the strings all along.

And it terrified me how close they had come to winning.

He smirked. "When have you ever known me to get into trouble, my king?"

With that playful retort, he vanished.

And a sinking feeling of dread settled into my soul.

For the first time since I'd met Camillia De la Croix, I wished that I could feel those delicate little fingers tugging at my energy again, because at least it would tell me that she was still here.

That she was alive.

That she was *safe*.

But that last part wasn't true. I felt it deep within my soul —Camillia De la Croix was in trouble.

And it was my job to find her.

Wherever you are, little temptress, you won't be lost for long. I vow it.

CHAPTER 15

CAMI

WHITE.

Porcelain siding.

Bright blue skies.

Pristine glass.

Vibrant green courtyards with lively flowers and buzzing bees.

Utopia.

That was what my mother had called it during my tour—one I couldn't remember agreeing to, but I must have since she'd just taken me all around to show me her home.

Or was it *our* home?

I still wasn't sure how I'd arrived here. But that was rather normal when it came to my parents—they often took me places without any explanation at all. I'd fall asleep in my bed, just to wake up in the middle of a burning field.

As far as random field trips went, this one seemed okay thus far.

Everyone we passed nodded a hello, the glittering wings at their backs confirming their inhuman status. I studied some of the feathers, a memory nagging at the edge of my mind. One of white plumes tinged with gold.

But before I could grasp it, we turned a corner to admire a large fountain surrounding a feminine statue. She stood in the middle with her arms high, praising the skies.

I... I'd seen something like this before. A statue of intensity, only masculine in nature with scars instead of wings.

I frowned. *Why—*

"I'm so sorry about your father, dear," my mother said, causing me to blink.

"My father?" I repeated as a gray shadow fell across the fountain, making it appear sooty and burned for a fragment of a second.

But when I blinked again, the vision returned to all white. *Strange.*

My mother cleared her throat. "Well, yes. His death. But you have to understand that it was needed."

"Dad's dead?" I asked, confused as to how we'd reached this topic.

Did I already know about his death?

Had we been speaking about it earlier?

I... I wasn't sure. I couldn't remember most things right now. *Like how I got here,* I thought for the millionth time. *Where am I? What's utopia? Why do I feel so lost?*

"Have you not heard a word I've said?" my mother demanded, her tone one I knew all too well.

"I'm sorry," I immediately replied, lowering my gaze. "I... I'm not feeling like myself."

None of this made any sense. I wasn't even sure how I'd arrived here. *Or why...?*

My brow furrowed, my gaze scanning my mother's white dress and... "Why do you have wings?" I blurted out.

She pursed her lips, her expression the epitome of

disappointment. "I'm a Virtuous Fae, Camillia. Honestly, how you've survived this long with your naïveté is beyond me."

I frowned. *Virtuous Fae.* That was familiar. Angelic beings. Original fae. Something about a light and the shattering of a Source...

And a Virtuous Fae falling...

I looked at the statue in the fountain again. The feminine lines were all wrong. They should be masculine. Agonized. Bent over, muscles taut, and showcasing bloody tears where the wings used to be.

It again bled to shades of gray, the visage darkening before brightening once more.

What is that? I wondered, glancing up again. The clear sky couldn't be casting any shadows. And yet—

My mother snapped her fingers in front of me. "If I'm going to explain this, then you're going to listen."

An apology lingered on my lips. But I didn't voice it because my jaw was clenched too tight. It was like my body refused to issue the words while my mind screamed them.

However, a small voice whispered, *Something isn't right.*

I clung to that small voice, curious as to what it meant.

"As I already said, your father was a means to an end. I seduced him to create you. He made the deal at my request. Then he helped me train you. After that, well, there was no need to keep him anymore." She shrugged like everything she'd said made perfect sense, whereas I didn't understand a word of it. "It wasn't like he would be allowed here."

She waved a hand around us, showcasing her utopia once again.

So perfect. Clean. Quiet.

What happened to all the other fae? I wondered, glancing up at the crystal-blue sky. *Are they flying?*

And when did my mother grow wings? She's human...

I nearly asked aloud, but she was already speaking again, something about my purpose.

"You should have finished the job by now," she told me.

What job? The question lingered on my tongue, only to be swallowed as the sky shifted and turned a murky brown color. I gaped at it, then startled when it returned to its blue shade. *How...?*

"You were born for this, Camillia. I'm not sure why it's taking you so long to complete the task." She shook her head. "Well, your grandmother will be here soon for an assessment. Perhaps you just need a little nudge in the right direction."

She started walking again, guiding me toward an arch that bridged two of the pristine buildings. Flowers and vines decorated the white stone, the greenery spelling out a word I couldn't quite read. It was right there, lurking on the edge of my mind, but the more I concentrated on it, the more illegible it became.

Weird, I thought, frowning at it.

"*Camillia*," my mother hissed.

I blinked.

Oh.

I'd stopped walking.

I hurried to catch up to her, a sick feeling curling in my gut. She was no doubt taking me to another infamous training exercise. Perhaps that was the cause of the flickering shadows.

Would a storm approach overhead? A tornado? Something destructive that I would have to use magic to fight?

At least we seem to be the only ones still here, I decided. Everyone else had disappeared.

Although, it was quite strange to be wandering these too-clean streets alone with my winged mother.

Am I dreaming? I wondered.

That... that actually might make sense.

Mainly because my mother was dead.

I halted again. *My mother's dead.* That realization struck me in the heart, making my breathing quicken.

"I'm not dead, Camillia," she said, facing me once more with a look of utter exasperation.

Did I say that out loud? I wondered, startled by her response.

"I'm a Virtuous Fae, not a human," she went on. "And you're a mixed breed, but your Virtuous Fae heritage is stronger than your Hell Fae genetics. Once you finish your task, your grandmother will ensure you're a pureblood by burning that wretched side of you to ash."

"What task?" I blurted out, completely lost. Her words were registering, but the meaning behind them was too unbelievable to make sense.

"Taking back the Virtuous Fae Source," she replied, like it was the most obvious answer in the world. "You're a siphon, darling. Created with my blood and that of one of his Hell Fae creations. You were designed to absorb the light and restore Virtuous Fae kind."

She stepped forward and pressed a palm to my cheek, her affection all wrong.

My mother had never liked touching me.

And I didn't like being touched by her either.

"It's quite a gift, really," she murmured. "But you need to use it properly."

That last part was stated with her trademark annoyance, her hand falling away.

"Honestly, Camillia, I have no idea what you were thinking on that dance floor. All you had to do was hold on to him for a few more minutes, and the charms would have done their part in weakening him."

Charms?

And who was this *him* she mentioned?

"Instead, you shoved the light back into him, returning

him to his throne." She shook her head. "Your grandmother is going to be very disappointed in you."

"Grandmother," a feminine voice echoed with a snort. "Fae, I hate that term."

My mother winced, her attention turning upward as a black-haired woman with glorious golden-tipped wings floated toward us.

She resembled the woman from the statue in the fountain, but that wasn't what caught my eye the most. It was the flickering sky behind her that held me captive.

Smoky and black, not blue.

But with a blink, it showcased a beautiful day.

How bizarre...

"Apologies," my mother said, her focus on the angel touching the ground.

I stared at her, a unique form of familiarity striking me in the gut. *I know her*, I realized. Yet I had no idea how, as I was certain I'd never seen her before.

But there was something about her eyes...

Piercing gray in color.

And cruel.

So, so cruel.

I... I wasn't sure how I knew that. She didn't look particularly evil. But there was just something exceedingly wicked about her, an instinctual response that I couldn't explain. All I wanted to do was *run*.

No.

Not run.

Fight.

My brow furrowed at the conflicting urges. Part of me wanted to flee, and the other part wanted to hurt this woman.

Where is this coming from? I wondered, dizzy from the insane instincts rioting inside me. *How do I know this woman?*

Grandmother, a voice instantly replied. Because my

mother had just used that term and the woman had scoffed at it. *This is my grandmother.*

Only, I'd never met her before.

Yet I knew her. Deep down, my soul recognized hers. And I did not like her.

"Well, let me look at you, Camillia," the female said, standing a few feet away, her wings disappearing in a wink. "You did a number on that dress."

Frowning, I glanced down at the gold fabric hanging in tatters around me. *Uh, that's... hmm.* I was covered in the appropriate areas, but practically naked otherwise.

"She fought the charms," my mother explained.

"Yes, I know. I watched." My grandmother—an odd noun to use in reference to this stranger who wasn't a stranger— sighed. "I know we decided to keep her innocent in order to help her better assimilate and go undetected, but she was clearly a little too innocent."

"Pierre and I went through all the exercises you recommended," my mother responded, her voice holding an edge to it. "I'm not sure what we could have done to better prepare her."

The cruel-eyed woman waved away the commentary. "I don't want to hear excuses, Mystika. What I want to hear are solutions."

"We tell her everything and explain what's at stake," my mother instantly replied. "He already knows she's a threat. But he can't kill her."

"But he can imprison her," the female replied. "And we know how much he enjoys his prisons."

Who are we talking about? I wondered, staring between them.

I was missing details.

Hell, I was missing a lot more than simple details.

Why is my mind so foggy?

Where the fuck am I?

And why do I know this woman?

"All the more reason to tell her everything so she can be prepared to fight him. She's already weakened him substantially. It won't take much to finish the process."

The female shook her head, disagreeing. "This has to be done properly. Siphon the light, then negotiate. You know everything is about deals, darling."

My gaze narrowed. *Darling* was the term my mother used for me. It sounded sweet, but it was actually meant to be condescending. And it seemed she'd learned it from this woman.

"Why do I know you?" I demanded, somehow finding my voice. It came out strong, pleasing me greatly.

However, it had the opposite impact on the black-haired angel before me.

She gave me a look so deadly I almost took a step back. "I'm your flesh and blood, girl. That's how you know me."

I started to shake my head but stopped when her eyes narrowed.

Wow, if looks could kill, I would be a dead fae.

Something about that thought triggered an onslaught of rules to roll through my mind.

Hell Fae Rule #2: Don't Draw Attention.

Hell Fae Rule #3: Know Your Enemy Before Engaging.

Hell Fae Rule #1: Don't Die.

They weren't in order, but that didn't matter. They all applied.

"Apologize to your grandmother, Camillia," my mother demanded.

"*Ugh*, enough with the familial title," the female grated out.

"I'm sorry, Vivaxia," my mother said. "Apologize to our Virtuous Fae Queen, Camillia. Right now."

My mouth opened to obey, but the words... the words didn't come out.

Because that name—*Vivaxia*—meant something to me.

Something important.

Something *catastrophic*.

I stared at her. Studied her elegantly beautiful face. Her alluring features. Her familiarity. *Her cruel eyes.*

Vivaxia, I repeated to myself. *Vivaxia... Vivaxia...* My eyes widened. "*Vivaxia.*"

The Virtuous Fae who had caused Lucifer to fall.

The Virtuous Fae who had treated Az like a *pet*.

I recognized her through my mate. Or perhaps both Az and the Hell Fae King. Maybe even through Lucifer's book, Vita.

Regardless of the source, I knew exactly who this bitch was, my soul knowing her dark presence on nearness alone.

Oh, hell no.

"I'll *never* fucking apologize to you," I spat, furious as all the pieces finally clicked together. As all my memories hit me at once. As everything I'd just been through slammed into my mind and heart and *soul*.

I wanted to kill this female instead.

Rip her apart.

Shred. Her. To. Fucking. Pieces.

I rushed her, my palms outstretched as I screamed in fury at everything she'd done to Az. At everything she'd done to Lucifer.

Only to hit an invisible wall.

She tsked. "That's not polite, Camillia. I gave you life and purpose, and this is how you thank me?"

"Thank you?" I nearly laughed. "I want to fucking kill you."

She rolled her eyes like I was an annoying gnat. Then she

flicked her wrist and sent me sailing across the too-white road into the side of a building.

Silver ropes appeared, binding me before I could move.

Then the mirage around us faded to reveal the truth.

No more clean lines. No more blue sky. No more green grass.

Instead, all I saw was gray.

Smoke. Pollution. A world tinted by a blacked-out sun.

And before me was a woman with storm clouds for eyes, her turmoil a presence that existed all around us.

My mother cowered nearby, her expression oddly panicked.

But the female in front of me was all regal elegance, her features exuding boredom.

"All right, Camillia. I can see you require a lesson in respecting your elders." A feather appeared in her hand, her manicured fingers stroking the golden edge. "So let's begin, shall we?"

CHAPTER 16

MELEK

Unease wound through me as I stepped through the library's double doors. I paused once inside, allowing the cooler air from the cathedral-like ceiling to drift down.

The lower temperatures were from the figments. They giggled and whispered but didn't speak directly to me.

Perhaps they sensed my mood—or maybe they sensed *Camillia.*

Whatever the reason, they were wisely keeping their distance.

I wasn't in a playful mood. A rare occasion for me. But nothing about today had been normal.

Feathers, the last week had been atrocious. Having access to Camillia's mind just to be barred from her thoughts had to be one of the worst punishments a man could endure.

And I wasn't even sure *why* she felt the need to block me.

Everything I'd done had been to help her, not hurt her. Yet she'd made it very clear that she didn't trust me. Hell, I wasn't even sure she *liked* me.

Which was an annoying little concern.

Everyone liked me.

I was lovable. Kind. Good-looking. Fun. Confident.

Or I used to be, anyway.

Camillia had made me question myself in more ways than one, which probably explained why I was questioning myself even now.

Because I could *feel* her here. Yet deep down, I didn't trust my instincts.

Maybe my insecurities had something to do with watching Lucifer fall for a second time.

Talk about triggering.

But this time, he accepted my hand...

An eon ago, the situation had been much more dire. Much less *trusting.*

But tonight, we were united, his power literally oozing off of him and permeating the entire realm.

It was so different from the first time he'd fallen. This time was more like a power explosion from above, my king having teleported himself almost all the way to the Hell Fae Realm before losing control and tumbling from the cloudless sky.

His fall from the Virtuous Fae Realm had been from a much greater distance. And the damage that incident had caused had been far more catastrophic. Yet it had also symbolized rebirth, his beautiful power stretching far and wide in an effort to rebuild.

Tonight, he hadn't exuded the same broken stature as before, but the vision of him on his knees had been magnificent. Empowering. The rise of the Hell Fae King.

He seemed to be even more powerful than I remembered, as if Camillia had done so much more than return his Source. It was as though she'd healed that ancient divide that had always tormented us.

Or, at least, started the healing process that I hadn't even realized we still needed.

I owed Camillia a debt of gratitude, one I'd repay once I

found her. *Are you even here?* I wondered, wandering the library, searching for my little angel.

Ajax had felt her in the Barren Lands.

Azazel had flitted off back to the Midnight Fae Realm.

Yet I was sure she'd been here. At least until I'd arrived. Because now... now I was almost certain she wasn't here at all.

"Prince Melek?" a female voice chimed.

I startled as I looked down at the seated female I hadn't even noticed was there in the center of the room. Another sat across from her and stared at me with wide eyes.

Their uniforms marked them as Hell Fae Bride candidates, but neither of them was the one I was looking for.

"Candidate Twenty-Two." I acknowledged the female with silver hair bound in a ponytail, one that revealed her pointed ears. She had a regal posture that reminded me of Camillia's spirit, but that was where the similarities ended.

"Feyre of the House of Iron," she corrected me, but I expected it was less of a correction and more of a hopeful introduction to the Hell Fae Prince.

The bride trials had been halted while the Marsh Lands were rebuilding. The mysterious portal opening near the Naga cavern had not been a coincidence. It'd happened right before the Naga trial, so any trials we planned next would likely become a target.

Meaning the trials were on an indefinite hold until we knew who was behind this, a fact that had upset many of the Hell Fae and Nightmare Fae. But our lieutenants understood and agreed with Ty's decision.

We would find the culprit, and soon.

Because I suspected whoever had opened that portal in the Marsh Lands—the one that had led to the deaths of Nightmare Fae and at least six Hell Fae Brides—was also the villain responsible for whatever had just happened with Camillia, too.

It was all connected.

I have to find her.

"And I'm—" the other female began, but I cut her off with a short bow.

"Apologies, ladies, but I am on an urgent errand. Please, continue your studies and prepare for the next trial."

"But when—"

A figment tugged at Feyre's ponytail, sending her words into a sharp curse as I took my opportunity to leave.

Thank you, I thought at the giggling figments, appreciating them even more.

I had no desire to offend any of the Hell Fae Bride candidates, especially ones who had made it this far. But until I found Camillia, I would not have answers for them.

My lingering sense of unease amplified when I reached a corridor lined with various books that I'd perused once before. A strange realization, as I didn't often frequent the deeper levels of this library. I had a library of my own within the palace, making my visit here moot.

But once upon a time, I'd been drawn to this very aisle, and to the beauty seated at a desk toward the end.

"This is where I first saw you," I whispered as I lightly traced the table's edge.

A female with dirty-blonde hair reading Vita—a book only Ty himself should be able to decipher—was an imprint I would not soon forget.

What have you found, little prince? Ty asked in my mind. *I just felt a jolt of intense longing from you. Is Camillia there? Did you learn something?*

Instead of answering him, I transported myself back to the palace. The Hell Fae King's Warden and Commander were already with him, standing on the wide balcony that overlooked his kingdom.

Ajax's jaw clenched, and Azazel's eyes were a turmoil of

purple and black. Both of them were unsettled and now looking at me for answers.

Unfortunately, I had a sinking realization of what this all actually meant.

I looked at my king as I delivered the news. I was the one who had been pulling all the strings, who had been there when each one of us had fallen for Camillia De la Croix.

"I know why we sensed her in different places," I said. "I felt her at the library because that is where I first met her."

Ajax frowned. "I don't understand."

"That's where I first fell for Camillia," I explained, meeting his gaze.

His frown deepened. "But I was drawn to the Barren Lands. Camillia and I have never been there together."

"True," I agreed. "But what happened to you when Camillia was there? When you thought she died?"

His cheeks lost some of their color, his eyes rounding. "I was broken."

"Because you'd fallen for her," Ty said slowly, following my train of thought. "You were all drawn to places that hold emotional value."

I nodded.

Ajax glanced at Azazel. "You felt her in the Midnight Fae Kingdom. That's where...?"

"Where I stopped fighting my Phoenix," the Commander said solemnly.

Typhos frowned and looked back at his palace toward the statue and the steaming crater next to it.

I didn't have to ask him what that meant.

He'd finally accepted her.

Here.

Earlier tonight.

For the very first time.

And it terrified me that I had finally won, that I had finally convinced Ty of Camillia's place at our side when she was—

"It's the mate-bond we are sensing," Ty interjected before I could finish my thought.

"Yes. Our initial link to Camillia De la Croix." I wasn't sure if that'd been set up by nefarious magic or just our souls trying to find our missing mate.

Ty's jaw ticked before he glanced back at his kingdom. "Then where is she?"

I shook my head. "I don't know…"

CHAPTER 17

CAMI

VIVAXIA'S cold eyes brewed with malicious intent. She wove her feather through the air, inscribing gold-colored spells that scorched my skin on contact.

Her jaw ticked when I didn't scream or make a sound. When I didn't *submit*.

My mother stood behind her, a look of confusion on her face. "Why isn't the spell taking?"

"Because your child is stubborn."

I nearly smiled at her obvious irritation. But each stroke through the air reminded me of Ajax waving his wand around in a similar fashion. And the silver binds holding me against the building reminded me of the snake-vines he'd once used to bind me to a chair.

In fact, this whole situation had me recalling that experience in the Midnight Fae Realm.

Az and Ajax interrogating me.

Which led to them eventually believing me.

And now they're mine.

But I couldn't hear or feel them. I wasn't sure why. My memories of them also kept fading at the edges. I hadn't even remembered them at all while strolling with my mother through her twisted version of utopia.

Hearing Vivaxia's name had brought everything back in a rush.

But I could feel the knowledge flickering away, disappearing into coerced compliance.

Only for Vivaxia's feather to draw my attention again, thus making me think of Ajax's wand, and the cycle continued.

It seemed pretty clear that her spell was meant to alter my recollection of the past, or perhaps convince me to forget it entirely.

But I refused.

So maybe I was stubborn. Because fuck this Virtuous Fae bitch.

If I had my hands free, I'd try to punch her again.

Her gaze narrowed like she could read the desire from my features. "I created you, child. You will do what I tell you to do."

"If you think that's true, then you don't know me very well," I bit back.

"*Camillia*," my mother hissed. "I taught you better than this."

"No, you taught me to be independent through a series of trials," I informed her flatly. "You taught me to fear and embrace abandonment at the same time. And you taught me to never trust anyone. Especially not you or Dad."

She bristled.

But I didn't care.

My parents had raised me in an environment of torment. Being strapped to this building didn't frighten me or make me want to submit. It made me want to *fight*.

Which was exactly what I did when Vivaxia tried yet another spell.

Instead of her voice whispering the incantation, I heard

Ajax. I felt him. His magic. His power. Our bond. I just couldn't *hear* him.

Az was there, too, his power humming through my veins, his Phoenixfire a very real presence inside my heart.

Why can't I hear either of you? I wondered, examining the blocks in my mind. They were unfamiliar and sticky, the weblike substance not one I'd put there.

Ignoring Vivaxia and her foreign words, I started focusing on untangling the web. On finding my mates. On getting the fuck out of whatever mess I'd landed in.

All while piecing together my mother's cryptic statements.

I'd thought I was lost in a dream before, not fully understanding each word she'd said until now. Until I'd realized this was *real*, that I wasn't dreaming at all, and that my mother... *isn't human.*

A shiver traversed my spine with that thought, my mind struggling to accept what was right before me.

Two Virtuous Fae.

That meant *I* was part Virtuous Fae. *Is that why I can read Vita?* I wondered. *Why Melek was drawn to me? Did Melek know?*

Thinking about him had me wondering if I could somehow reach him. The blocks I'd built between us were still there, the structure Az had helped me construct holding remarkably well. Apparently, it was something he'd learned through his mating with Lucifer.

I'd consider that more later.

But for now, I focused on those blocks, trying to take them down piece by piece. That sticky substance didn't exist here, just the barrier I'd created with Az's guidance.

A snap of sound yanked my attention to Vivaxia, her wings having burst out of her back in a flurry of agitation.

Only, the white plumes from earlier were a sooty black now.

Kind of like Lucifer's damaged appendages, I realized, thinking of his powerful form from that day in the Marsh Lands—when he'd been trying to close the portal. Only this female still had some feathers, the fiery remains flapping angrily behind her like a swarm of furious fireflies. *My grandmother.*

That fact hadn't really sunk in yet, my mind rebelling against our familial relation. Along with the understanding that she'd *created* me.

To be a siphon, I thought, trembling.

Fae, it meant I really had been a danger to Lucifer. To his *Source.* I wasn't quite sure what exactly that entailed with being a siphon, but it seemed pretty clear to me that I'd been designed to steal Lucifer's light. To shatter his Source.

"*You're a siphon, darling,*" my mother had said. "*Created with my blood and that of one of his Hell Fae creations. You were designed to absorb the light and restore Virtuous Fae kind.*"

I wasn't sure how that worked exactly, and I didn't want to find out.

"Listen to me, girl," Vivaxia snarled. "You will follow my command and *heel.*"

My back bowed as a bolt of pure, unadulterated power hit me right in the chest, lighting a fire within me that had me gasping and seeing white all around me.

White buildings.

Perfect sidewalks.

A glittering fountain.

White wings tipped in gold.

I frowned at that last part, Vivaxia's form having taken on a renewed appearance. A false one.

Melek, I thought dizzily. *Those are Melek's wings.*

Another crack of energy left me wheezing, my mind flickering in and out of reality. *Gray and white. Polluted and pristine. Fiery feathers and golden tips.*

I blinked, then shook my head, trying to clear it.

But a beautiful face, so feminine and angelic and kind filled my view.

No, not kind, a smart part of me whispered. *Those gray eyes are cruel. Wicked. Exuding evil.*

However, the being smiled, like she was pleased with me. And that had my lips curling in kind, liking her affection. Her *acceptance.*

"Much better," she cooed, tucking a feather back into her wings.

White tipped in gold, I repeated to myself. *Melek...*

"Now where were we?" the woman asked, her name escaping me.

I knew her. Recognized her. But my memory of her was blurred.

"I realize you have some of your father in you and that might be making you somewhat sympathetic to the Hellbeasts, but you have to understand the hierarchy, darling. Virtuous Fae made all this possible. We are the gods of this world. The creators. Our way of life is the superior existence to everyone else's."

Her words rolled through me, making me want to bow my head in acceptance.

But the small voice inside me that recognized her feathers disagreed with every word. *It's a façade. A lie. Don't listen to her.*

I followed that strand of thought, my instincts firing.

Melek, my mind whispered.

Who? I wondered. Then blinked. *Yes, Melek.*

Virtuous Fae.

My Virtuous Fae.

I returned to the barrier between us, pulling away the pieces while Vivaxia prattled on about the glory of her—*our*—kind.

"That said, our superiority gives us a certain amount of responsibility, too. We have to protect those who are weaker than us. Unfortunately, though, living for eternity can morph certain morals and perspectives. And, sadly, that's what happened to Typhos Lucifer."

I faked confusion because I suspected she was the reason my mind kept blanking and the world around us shifted between white and gray.

Vivaxia clearly wanted me to believe something.

I wouldn't, but I would feign interest if it meant she'd stop hitting me with her brain-numbing enchantments. Because the world around us was still white, suggesting my mind was close to falling completely under her spell.

I couldn't allow that to happen.

I refused.

Come on, I thought, focusing on the wall in my mind. *Let me through.*

"At some point, he fell victim to his own creations," she said with a dramatic sigh. "You see, his unnatural beasts clouded his judgment and altered his mind. It's like he completely forgot how and why he'd created them all. Very sad, really."

I frowned, that last part not registering correctly in my head. "Created?" Was she talking about the dark souls he'd turned into Nightmare Fae as punishment?

"Well, yes. Did he not mention his penchant for Shifter Fae pets?" She laughed, the tinkling sound irritating my senses. "Typhos was the king of abominations, which is why he fell into a pit with them in the end."

That... didn't match the story I knew.

Well, it was reminiscent of certain parts—that he fell into what was now the Hell Fae Realm—but he wasn't the one who liked Shifter Fae pets. Vivaxia did.

"It's only suitable that he rules his own mess, I suppose.

But I would love for him to rise again, to return to us and restore the light," she continued. "He made a mistake playing with life the way he did. However, I think he's been punished for long enough."

I fought the urge to gape at her.

She was making it sound like Lucifer had created all the Nightmare Fae, but Az had told me many of the Virtuous Fae enjoyed playing with souls and life, thus manufacturing various types of Shifter Fae to keep as pets.

"I see you've not been told about any of this," she said, sounding sad. "Let me guess—he told you he fell as a result of a deal with me?"

When I didn't respond, she heaved another sigh.

"The 'deal' he refers to is one all Virtuous Fae agree to upon birth—to protect and cherish life. It's more of a vow, but the term is moot, as the moral behind it is what matters. And he broke that moral when he chose to carelessly create souls for entertainment purposes."

She paused, her energy humming around me.

The world pulsed in shades of brighter whites and blues and greens, my hand nearly rising to shield my eyes from the blaring sun.

But a flicker of murky skies blinked in and out of view, reminding me that this was a mirage.

That she was crafting a careful lie.

One that painted Lucifer as the villain, not her.

A few months ago, I might have believed her. However, her story didn't match what I'd seen through Vita, what Melek and Az had both told me about Lucifer.

He wouldn't do what she's saying he did, I thought, returning to the barrier in my mind again. I was almost through. *I can't believe her. I won't believe her.*

Even if her words resonated somewhere deep within.

Even if my mother stood behind her with a remorseful expression.

Even if... my heart ached a little at the possibility of Typhos deserving his fall from grace.

"It took eons for us to gather all his experiments up and give them a new home," my grandmother informed me, her tone holding a touch of sorrow. "They were such broken creatures, their souls morphed for wicked amusement."

Her gaze fell, a hint of regret crossing her angelic features.

But that sadness didn't reach her eyes. Which was strange because there were tears glittering around her irises as she looked at me again, real remorse displayed there, yet all I could see was the cruelty lying deep within. Like those gray orbs were imprinted on my mind, skewing my vision of the sight before me.

"We couldn't kill them," she said, swallowing visibly with the words. "We... we just didn't have the heart for it. So we provided them with a new home, then sent Typhos to join them, hoping he would learn from his mistakes."

I studied her, trying to discern truth from fiction. Her story was so similar to Lucifer's history, and yet... utterly different.

What if her version is the truth? I wondered. *What if... what if I've been clouded by my mate-bonds?*

"Instead, his thirst for power only grew," she continued. "He started collecting pets from all the fae realms, offering them a kingdom to reside within so long as they bowed to his will. That's why he forbade females from entering—it was a way to control the masses, to ensure they never mated."

My mother nodded behind her. "It's true, Camillia. Your father told me all about it. Not allowing mates was a way to keep his Hell Fae loyal."

"And it worked," my grandmother said. "For a long time."

"Until some of the Hell Fae and Nightmare Fae started to

question Lucifer's real reasons for keeping them unmated," my mother murmured. "That's when Lucifer devised the Hell Fae Bride Trials."

"It was brilliant, honestly." My grandmother—*No,* I thought, *Vivaxia*—almost sounded proud. As though she respected Lucifer's decision. "As with everything else, he crafted the perfect setup, one that he controlled. And he used it as a way to punish those who went against him."

"Like your father," my mother added. "He wanted to leave the Hell Fae Realm, and the only way to do that was to sign away his daughter's life. You."

I considered that for a moment, recalling the deal I'd read that had determined my fate.

My mother's summarization matched what I'd seen—my father choosing his freedom over mine.

But something about this explanation didn't feel right. It didn't marry up to what she'd said during our tour, either. She'd told me that she'd used my father to create me... then she'd convinced him to sign the deal with Lucifer.

So which story was real?

The world flickered again, my mind seeking the truth. Seeking *reason*.

I'd been doing something before, too. Something inside me. *Beating at a wall...*

My eyes nearly widened, the thought crashing through my stilled state. I'd fallen under some sort of hypnosis, listening and believing Vivaxia's words. Questioning what I knew. Questioning whether or not Az and Melek had told me the truth.

Typhos has been their mate for thousands of years, a part of me whispered. *They would lie to protect him.*

I almost agreed, the train of thought a dangerous one to follow.

But the use of *Typhos* in the sentence gave me pause.

I didn't call him Typhos.

I called him Lucifer.

My jaw tightened. Something—or *someone*—was in my head.

Magic swirled around me, foreign energy humming through my veins.

The wall, I thought, clawing toward it in my mind while Vivaxia continued droning on about Typhos's fall, talking about how devastating it had been and the aftermath of his punishment.

"He broke all our vows, but the Source still believed in him. *We* still believed in him," she said, the depressed quality of her voice almost sucking me back into the discussion. "So our light followed Typhos into the darkness and tried to renew his purpose. But he never atoned for his sins. Instead, he kept our light, and our Source..."

The sky changed once more to display that polluted state, the gray colors unsettling me inside.

"Our Source shattered because of his selfishness," she whispered. "He refused to come back to us, refused to listen to the light, and this is who we are now. Broken shells, waiting to be reborn in our glory once more."

I stared at the polluted sky, the dimmed sun, the fractured wings at her back, and wondered what the true mirage here was—the utopia or the perceived pain.

Perhaps they were both lies.

Visions meant to manipulate.

A sea of dishonesty encased in a single incoming tide.

That tide was Vivaxia.

Her eyes gave her away. No amount of tears or frowns could hide the evil lurking within.

I shoved through the remainder of the barrier I'd crafted with Az and instantly felt Melek's warmth inside me.

Camillia, he breathed. *Fuck, where are you? What happened? Are you okay?*

I'm with Vivaxia, I told him. *She's doing something to my mind. I—*

Heat flooded my veins, momentarily stunning me into silence as my back hit something hard. I blinked, confused, as a world of fire unfolded around me.

My eyes widened, my feet instinctively moving to carry me backward.

And I... I *moved.*

There was no more wall. No more magic binds.

Just flames dancing dangerously in the wind.

And an angel hovering above it all with large *black* wings. Her matching hair wavered in a violent breeze, fury emanating from her cold gaze. "You will help us right this wrong," Vivaxia said, her voice carrying on the howling wind and wrapping around me in unwelcome torrents of energy. "Or you'll end up in his prison. *For good.*"

With a flap of her massive wings, she stirred a gust of air that shoved me backward.

My arms went wide, my hands grasping for something to hold on to. But her gusts were too powerful, her energy a hot wave that crashed over every inch of me and seared my very soul.

I shifted to block my face, trying to protect myself from her angry howls.

Which was how I ended up facing the other way.

And spotted a familiar sight. One I'd seen in my mind, not in person. *A crater in the ground surrounded by black scorch marks.*

The place Lucifer fell, I recognized, the image perfectly matching what his book, Vita, had once shown me.

Jump, Melek told me, our connection suddenly wide open. *Jump, Cami. Jump!*

I... I wasn't sure... I...

Flickers of power shimmered as more flames ignited, the fires encircling the hole... like Vivaxia was trying to block it from my view.

Or maybe all of this was just a mental mindfuck.

But one thing was very clear—I needed to get away from Vivaxia. From my mother. From wherever I was. *In the Virtuous Fae Realm,* I thought, shivering as ice shot through my veins.

Hell Fae Rule #13: Nothing Is What It Seems.

Fuck it, I told myself, taking off toward the hole. Because what did I have to lose?

Vivaxia screeched behind me, the sound reminding me of a predatory bird.

I ignored her.

I blocked everything out.

Leapt over the fire.

And fell into the black hole.

CHAPTER 18

MELEK

My wings beat at my back, my heart threatening to pound its way out of my chest.

I'm coming, Cami, I promised her. *I'll catch you.*

Nothing.

Just static.

Like her brain had gone offline.

Fuck, I thought.

What's happening? Ty demanded. *I can feel your panic.*

Cami's falling! I shouted at him. *Vivaxia had her. She jumped, Ty. She fucking jumped.*

Which was what I'd told her to do because I knew it would bring her here. But that didn't stop my insides from shattering at the thought of her *falling*.

This wouldn't be like Ty falling from the Midnight Fae Realm.

This was something else entirely.

From a realm that hovered above us all, one that shouldn't exist but did. And that distance couldn't be measured in time or space.

Because Cami was falling from the heavens themselves.

Just like Ty.

Broken wings shredded.

Fire enveloping his form.

Blood everywhere.

I swallowed, trying to shove the vivid image from my mind, the pain of that day threatening to derail me.

Az and I are on our way, Ty told me.

My feathers strained, my ethereal magic surrounding my form as I misted myself to the center of the red sky, my gaze frantically scanning the horizon for Camillia.

The two suns blazed hot, their colors vibrant and illuminating every inch of the Hell Fae Kingdom.

Lucifer's palace was in the distance, glittering like a beacon. Camillia might appear there—in the place where Ty had originally fallen. I told him with a thought to station himself above our home, just in case that was where she landed, too.

He didn't reply, merely appeared in position with his fiery wings glowing at his back.

Az's Black Phoenix cawed as he ascended nearby, the powerful being searching, *hunting,* for our mate. His tracking abilities would allow him to potentially find her before I did, his senses heightened even more via their connection.

But if I couldn't feel her, he might not be able to sense her either.

Come on, little angel. Where are you? I thought, my chest aching at our disabled connection. We weren't fully bonded, our souls only loosely tied, and it hurt so much more right now than it should.

I wanted her.

Craved her.

Maybe... maybe even *loved* her.

She'd been my obsession since that day in the library, the

exciting new chapter in my existence. The mate I hadn't even realized I'd needed.

We'll find her, Ty promised me.

I know.

I was just worried she might be broken beyond repair when we did.

Her genetics were still utterly confusing to me, her immortality an unknown. *What if the fall kills her?* I wondered. *What if I sent her to her death?*

Stop, Ty hissed into my mind. *She's going to be fine.*

But I felt his rising concern, his mind gluing all the pieces together.

He'd completed that fall once. He knew what it was like.

And he knew a human could never survive it.

We'll catch her, he vowed. *I've never let you down before, Melek. I'm not going to start—*

He cut off as he shot up into the sky, Cami's tumbling form finally visible and heading right for him. My wings engaged, my ethereal form teleporting me to his side just as he deftly caught our angel in his arms.

Relief struck me.

Followed by instant terror.

"She's not breathing!" I shouted over the wind our wings were creating.

Ty didn't reply, just disappeared with her, his mind telling me he'd teleported to our suite. I followed, my heart shattering in my chest.

She can't be dead. I could still feel her soul. *She'll survive. She has to fucking survive!*

"Melek," Ty said, his voice holding a note of dominance that forced me to look at him. "Listen. Her heart is beating. She's already healing. She's going to be fine."

He laid her on our bed as Az appeared with Ajax right beside him, the pair searching the room with frantic gazes.

"She's alive," Ty told them before they could rush the bed. "Just give her time. That fall... it's brutal. But she's stronger than any of us have realized."

I heard his mind whispering thoughts on why that was, how that could be. *Virtuous Fae heritage*, rolled through his thoughts. *A connection to Melek? Or something else entirely? And what am I sensing...*

He trailed off, his gaze roaming over her mostly nude form. It wasn't a look of masculine admiration so much as curiosity, like he was searching for information about her origin.

With his lips twisting slightly, he grabbed a blanket from the side of our bed and covered her. "She's breathing now," he told me. "The fall just knocked the wind out of her."

"How is that possible?" I asked. "When you fell..."

"I landed in the pits of Hell," he replied without looking at me. "She landed in a pillow of power." His eyes finally met mine. "I caught her with my energy before she landed in my arms."

Az took a step forward, his Phoenix peering out through his blazing gaze. In a blink, he relaxed and then yanked Ajax into a hug. The Midnight Fae male clung to him, showcasing an emotional side I'd never seen from him before, but I more than understood it.

We'd nearly lost her.

I could feel it in my chest, my *soul*.

"Vivaxia had her," I breathed. "But I don't understand how. The Virtuous Fae Realm... it was destroyed." Yet I'd *felt* Camillia's location in my spirit, her mind supplying all the visual details to confirm where she'd ended up.

"Not as destroyed as we thought," Ty muttered, running a palm over his face. He'd taken a step away from the bed, but he was still standing the closest to Cami, his opposite hand opening and closing like he was fighting the urge to touch her. "They're behind all of this. The portals. The attacks. *Cami*."

I swallowed, hating that he was right. But it made too much sense for me to deny it.

She possessed Virtuous Fae power. I'd known that from the beginning. However, I'd thought Vita had chosen her as Ty's potential mate.

Now... now I wasn't sure what to think.

I hadn't been able to access enough of Cami's thoughts to understand what was happening with Vivaxia or how she'd ended up there, but I'd sensed her fear and her inner chaos. She hadn't wanted to be there. That had to mean something, right?

"I don't think she..." I trailed off, my throat working. "She's not cooperating with them, Ty."

He glanced at me, his sapphire gaze thundering with dark oceanic waves. "I know."

I blinked, surprised. "You... you know?" He'd already said that he'd realized she was innocent. But this—falling from the Virtuous Fae Realm after admitting that she was with Vivaxia —was rather damning.

"I'll know for sure when she wakes," he clarified. "But she's a pawn. Another pet. And I'm very familiar with how Vivaxia tames her toys."

"You think she's a puppet," Az translated. "Like I was."

Ty considered him for a moment. "We'll find out when she wakes," he reiterated. "Until then, I have some reading to do." With a snap of his fingers, his book appeared, and he grabbed it from thin air. "You three watch her. Notify me when she's up. I'll be in my den."

He disappeared before any of us could say a word, his presence a passing kiss to my soul. *Why are you running?* I asked him, confused by his abrupt departure.

Because she's not mine to heal, he answered briskly. *And I'm too tempted right now to change that fact.*

My eyebrows rose. *You choose now to be attracted to her? When she's unconscious in our bed?*

We both know I've been attracted to her since the moment you chose her, he returned, not saying anything more.

Part of me wanted to press him, to push his boundaries into admitting more.

However, for once, I was too exhausted to try. Too consumed by the female on the bed. Too startled by her fall to care about planting thoughts or weaving webs.

All I wanted was for her to open her eyes.

And tell me how the hell she'd ended up in the Virtuous Fae Realm.

CHAPTER 19

AZ

Vivaxia had Cami.

That thought, fueled by Melek's statement, set my soul aflame as the words ran on repeat in my head.

My Phoenix wanted to hunt. To destroy. To *ravage*.

But my mind, heart, and soul couldn't leave Cami. Not like this. Not now.

So, instead, I stalked the fiery corridors of Typhos's palace. Our home. Our past. Our present. Our future.

Because Cami would wake up. Hopefully, soon.

She's safe. She's here.

But Vivaxia had her...

There were so many unspeakable things that Virtuous Fae could have done to Cami. I could taste her magic lingering in the air, the perfume eliciting a hoard of bad dreams. Horrid memories. *Fears.*

Growling, I increased my pace.

The Hellhounds smartly kept their distance, no doubt feeling my churning wrath.

I hadn't realized where I was heading until I made a certain turn, my spirit clearly guiding my steps. Typhos and I had some things to discuss. I'd locked him out for over a week, only choosing to let him back in during the ball so I could monitor his intentions with Camillia.

The Hell Fae King and I were at odds.

I didn't like it.

My Phoenix didn't care for it either. Especially right now.

Our alliance, our *history*, was more important than ever.

Thus, it made sense that my instincts had taken me toward his den. I could have just ashed here, but the stroll had helped to clear some of the nightmarish fog from my mind. A little, anyway.

Fucking Vivaxia. I'd loathed her for eternity, wanted her dead for thousands of years.

But this—*taking my mate*—made me want to rip her apart. Hear her scream. Torture her for eons until she begged for death.

First, though, I needed to figure out what the fuck she'd done to Cami. Because that damn floral scent still lurked in my nostrils, Vivaxia's mark all over my female.

Typhos had absolutely felt it, too.

If Vivaxia hurt her...

The Phoenix inside me hissed at the very thought of it, furious that we were still here doing nothing about such blasphemy. All I could do was indulge him with mental fantasies of the ways we would torment the Virtuous Fae once we found her.

I'm going to wring that bitch's neck with my bare hands, then carve out her eyes and leave only her mouth to scream.

That was one of the many deaths Vivaxia had forced upon me; it was only fitting to return the favor.

You taught me what I know about death, I thought at her. *You only have yourself to blame, Vivaxia darling.*

That damn nickname.

Her fucking *voice*.

I shook my head, clearing it from my mind. But her scent still lingered. Still taunted. Still promised there was more to come.

Which was exactly why Typhos and I needed to be on the same page as allies.

But I wasn't sure of his intentions for Cami or Ajax—both of whom I'd left with Melek.

Ajax probably knew where I'd been headed without me telling him, but I whispered a thought to him anyway. Then I asked, *Is Melek behaving?*

He's reading a book on the bed next to her, Ajax replied quietly. *He's oddly... silent.*

Hmm. I'd picked up on Melek being a bit more reserved than usual at the ball, too. His typical devil-may-care attitude and playful riddles had been notably absent from our conversation. *Let me know if anything changes.*

I will, Ajax promised. *And do me a favor—don't talk on my behalf with Lucifer. I can handle myself.*

Yes, you've made that quite clear, Warden, I drawled.

I mean it, Commander.

I'm going to him to talk about Cami, I told him. *I'm sure she would also say she can handle herself, but she's currently unconscious.*

Ajax said nothing for a moment. Then very quietly, he replied, *I can feel her soul. She's alive.*

I know. I'd been checking our connection, too. *She's healing.* But she was also wrapped up in Vivaxia's scent like a damn Virtuous Fae bouquet.

Ajax knew something was off, too. I hadn't needed to tell him that; he could sense it. *Find out what Lucifer thinks,* he finally said. *I'll be here.*

I nodded. Not that he could see me, but he likely felt my agreement. Or perhaps he knew I was now standing outside of Typhos's den.

Rather than mentally announcing myself, I resecured my walls and knocked on the stone door.

"Come in," grated the deep voice of the Hell Fae King through the heavy rock.

Taking the invitation, I stepped inside.

The posh living area was tidy and filled with maps and folders. A feathered pen floating nearby told me that those folders contained a few of his deals, ones he may have just inked. Or perhaps he just hadn't gotten around to filing them.

"Yes, you can release him," Typhos said, but not to me. He was talking to the Unseelie King on the translucent wall monitor.

Erebus was likewise in a luxurious environment, but his office consisted of mirrors. Tons of them. However, each one seemed to reflect the light in a different way, breaking it into rainbowlike patterns that hurt my sensitive eyes.

"We have new information on who has been tampering with the trials," Typhos continued. "It wasn't the fae you have in custody. He and several others were set up."

Erebus licked his lips. "Does that mean the bride trials will continue?"

"Soon," Typhos promised, which surprised me. But maybe it shouldn't have. Even if Cami almost died, even if his own Source was under attack, he would still put his people first.

And what about his own fucking mate-circle? I wondered, my jaw painfully flexing as I listened to the conversation between the Hell Fae King and his lieutenant.

"This pleases me," Erebus said with a smile. "As for the fae, I'm glad I can release him. He's the father of one of the Hell Fae Bride candidates, a position of honor among us that I prefer to acknowledge rather than punish."

"I know," Typhos replied. "Speaking of Hell Fae Bride

candidates, have you located the one who went missing in your territory?"

The light flickered around Erebus in fractured patterns as if he flitted those barely discernible wings of his.

"My soldiers are proving difficult to reach of late. Perhaps the girl is giving them a hard time." He grinned as he tilted his head, the gesture not so much birdlike as mine would be, but playful. One never knew if Erebus was just being himself or hiding something. "You certainly know how to pick them, my king. When I have my hands on her, you will be the first to know."

"Hmm," Typhos hummed, not giving anything away, but I had a feeling there was something in this conversation I was missing.

The Unseelie King flicked his gaze to me as I purposefully ventured into view of the screen.

I was here to give Typhos an update on Cami, which, frankly, was more important than whatever games the Unseelie King was playing.

"I see you have company. I will leave you to your important matters, Your Majesty," Erebus politely announced with a bow of his head. "I look forward to updates on when the bride trials will resume."

Typhos nodded. "As I look forward to your updates, Erebus."

The Unseelie King only grinned as the screen went black.

Finally, Typhos turned to me. "Apologies, but I have been providing all of my lieutenants with an update now that we have more information. I think we can safely assume Vivaxia and the Virtuous Fae are behind the attacks on our realm."

I nodded, agreeing with that assessment. "It seems they're no longer interested in hiding."

"Indeed," he returned, his eyes flickering with dark blue fire.

While I believed and understood Typhos's statement about needing to update his lieutenants, I also knew that wasn't the only reason he'd chosen to retreat to his den. He'd caught Cami in the sky, his body and power cradling hers in the fall, then he'd taken her to his bed.

That'd been instinctual.

Not purposeful.

And I suspected he was trying to digest that realization, perhaps even brooding a bit about the involuntary decision to take her into his inner sanctuary.

He studied me for a moment, then motioned to the leather chair next to a fireplace that lit the spacious office with Hellfire. "Let's talk, Azazel. How's Camillia?"

An interesting question, considering Melek was no doubt providing him with mental updates regarding her condition, just as Ajax had done with me.

So I chose to ignore the question and ask one of my own. "Is there a reason you had me overhear your conversation with Erebus?"

Typhos poured himself a flaming whiskey, always having a bottle from his personal stash in his office. Then he poured me one, too.

I took the glass and sipped from it while I waited for an answer.

He didn't speak right away, instead settling into his leather chair, his muscular body engulfing the entirety of the furniture as his dark hair splayed out behind him. The lock of white hair against his face was an interesting addition, one that made him more approachable somehow.

"There's something going on between Erebus and that runaway bride you lost during the portal madness." He glanced at me, fully aware his words had just struck a nerve. "Do you recall?"

I bristled at the insinuation that my Phoenix and I had *lost* a target. "I did not *lose* her," I said through my teeth. "The Unseelie purposefully diverted me."

And I'd also been distracted by Cami absorbing Typhos's power to heal the vortex in the sky.

But the former reason was the most important—I should have been able to capture that bride in seconds, yet she'd disappeared with the help of the Unseelie surrounding her.

"Can you prove that they interfered?" Typhos asked.

"Can I prove it? No," I admitted. "But it's the only explanation for my inability to track her. Besides, you know the Unseelie. They're even more devious than Melek."

This also wasn't what I'd come here to discuss.

But I supposed I'd angled the conversation this way by asking him why he'd invited me in while talking with Erebus. He'd obviously wanted me to overhear the conversation, yet he still hadn't told me *why*.

Typhos sighed. "Fair. But they're loyal."

I couldn't argue that point, so I didn't comment.

Because yes, they were loyal Nightmare Fae. I wouldn't counter that declaration, as I agreed with it.

"Loyalty is very important to me, as you know," he went on. "But it's something I've been questioning lately."

I arched a brow. "Are you accusing me of something, Typhos?" I wondered aloud. "Perhaps questioning my *loyalty* because I blocked you from my mind and mated the female you view as an enemy?"

His gaze narrowed, his lips sealing around his glass as he took another long, purposeful drink. "No, Azazel. I trust you. But all of this has made me view loyalty in a different light."

I wasn't sure what he meant, so I remained quiet and sipped my drink instead.

He set his glass down. "Hades made me realize that I was being unfair to your brother. I released him while you were away."

"Oh." I hadn't been aware of that. "Hades spoke to you on Maliki's behalf?"

I wasn't quite sure of my brother's relationship with the Mythos Fae, but I'd gathered they had some sort of history. One I hadn't truly cared about before. Now, however, my interest was slightly piqued. Maybe when this nightmare was over, I'd pay my brother a long-overdue visit.

"Hades met with me," Typhos rephrased. "He confirmed what I already knew, that the Virtuous Fae have something to do with the portals and the chaos. Their interference has made me question everyone's loyalty, even those who have proven time and again to have our realm's best interests in their hearts and minds."

"Are we still talking about the Unseelie?" I asked, not quite following his logic.

"Yes and no." He picked up his drink again for another sip. "You asked why I *let* you overhear that conversation. I was showing you that I've seen the error in my judgment."

I leaned forward. "Go on."

His lips twitched, probably because my encouragement had come out more like a demand than a prompt. Our dominant tendencies rarely led to conflict, mostly because my Phoenix bowed to the Hell Fae King.

Or it used to, anyway.

Cami and Ajax had changed that.

Fires, they'd changed *everything*.

"My point is, or rather, the lesson I've learned is that I can't punish the pawns. They were manipulated against their will. Imprisoning them is wrong, even if it was initially for reasons of protection."

I suspected we weren't talking about the Unseelie anymore.

Or maybe we were, but only tangentially.

"Vivaxia has finally made her move after millennia of

leaving us be, and she's using every tactic she can to make me question my own faith."

"Is that such a surprise?" I wondered out loud. "A few thousand years is nothing in our lifespan."

"True," he agreed. "But her methods and desires are not the point I'm trying to make."

"Then what point are you trying to make?" I asked him, not in the mood for riddles. If I were, I'd be with Melek instead of Typhos.

However, it seemed Melek wasn't in the mood, either.

"My point is that I owe you an apology," he said, causing me to nearly drop my glass.

Typhos Lucifer rarely apologized.

In fact, I was pretty sure the last time he'd ever uttered that word in my presence had been while trying to save me from Vivaxia.

"An apology?" I parroted back at him, certain I'd heard him wrong.

He sat up and poured more whiskey into his glass, his gaze slightly unfocused. "Two apologies in less than twenty-four hours. I really must be losing my touch."

A smirk lifted his lips a moment later, suggesting that either he found humor in what he'd said, or Melek had just whispered something to him.

I imagined it was in reply to his admission of *losing his touch*, something I highly doubt was true. The stack of deals nearby was proof of that.

Is one of those meant for Ajax? I wondered. *A penned agreement just waiting to be signed?*

My Midnight Fae mate had asked me not to speak on his behalf, and I'd honor that. But if I found an agreement meant for him, I would absolutely set it on fire.

But this was the Hell Fae King. His entire world revolved around those deals.

They were more than binding agreements—they were his religion.

Each word was doctrine, and if broken, Hellfire met the failed party on the other end of that deal.

Ajax would not be subjected to that fate.

"After everything we've been through, I hope you know what you are to me," Typhos murmured as his gaze returned to mine. "You're my mate, Azazel. And more than that, you're my best friend. I should have consulted you about my intentions with Ajax."

"Yes," I agreed. "You should have."

He nodded. "I'm sorry. It won't happen again."

I arched a brow. "Does that mean the deal is no longer on the table?" This technically wasn't me talking on Ajax's behalf, but me simply being curious as to what Typhos's intentions were now.

He didn't immediately answer, instead swirling his drink. "There is no deal to be made. Ajax's position in Hell Fae society is resolute, his role as Warden having already been reinstated. He's yours; that makes him a Hell Fae. Camillia's status has also been changed to note her as a Hell Fae mate. Both of them are safe here and under my protection."

I waited.

When he didn't continue, I hedged, "In exchange for...?"

"Nothing." He took another sip, then set his drink down again. "If Ajax chooses to mate me, the offer still stands. But it'll be his choice and nothing more."

"You still want to mate him?" I asked, uncertain.

"I want to protect him," Typhos replied. "I don't fancy him the way you do. But I respect him. I care about him. And I want him in my inner circle. However, I won't make him join me."

Studying my Hell Fae King mate, I inquired, "Why the change of heart?" It wasn't a matter of believing him—I did without question. It was a matter of not understanding his choice.

"It's like I said, Azazel. I've been wrongly punishing the pawns and questioning the loyalty of others, even when their actions speak volumes regarding their intentions. This mess with Vivaxia has stirred chaos. And it ends now."

I finished the drink he'd poured for me, then relaxed into the chair across from him. "So what does that mean for us? What does it mean for Camillia?"

"I'm going to train her," he replied, surprising me. "No more punishments. No more threats. No more questioning her intentions. I see her now. I realize the mistakes I've made with her. And I'll atone for them. But before all of that, I'm going to teach her everything I know."

"Why?" I asked. "So you can use her against Vivaxia?"

"No. She's not a toy or a weapon, and I won't treat her like a pawn. I'm not Vivaxia. And you questioning my intentions shows just how tarnished our mate-circle has become. I'm going to fix it. And I'll start by healing whatever spell Vivaxia has put inside Camillia."

I leaned forward, caught up in what he was saying and zeroing in on that last line. "You feel the magic, too."

"Of course I feel it. The stench of it is all over her."

"Like a fucking bouquet of sickly flowers," I muttered.

"Vivaxia's trademark perfume," he drawled. "We're going to dismantle whatever gift she's left inside Camillia, then embolden Camillia with knowledge and skill, so next time, she can properly defend herself. It's what I should have done from the moment I met her. Instead, I tried to imprison her."

"For protection," I translated, recalling his earlier comments about what he'd done with all the pawns. "You feel bad for what you've done to her."

"Feeling bad is irrelevant," he said, his gaze falling to his glass. "I made a mistake. I'm owning that. Apologizing for it.

And now, I'm going to fix it." Tidal waves swirled in his irises as he looked back up at me. "Can you forgive me?"

I stared at him. "Would you forgive someone for trying to corner Melek into a mating agreement?"

His lips twitched. "He asked me something similar."

"And what did you say?"

"That I'd kill the asshole."

I almost smiled. "I suppose that's one answer."

"Are you saying you need to drive that flaming sword of yours through my heart?" he asked, arching a brow. "Would that make us even?"

"Not even close," I admitted. "But I'll consider it as an option for later."

"Later?" he repeated.

"We have more important things to do right now," I told him. "Like help Cami and take down Vivaxia." I pushed away from the chair. "After that, I'll consider stabbing you."

He smiled. "It's a date."

"Don't get too excited, Typhos. You know I'm going to make it hurt."

"You realize that just excites me more, yes?" he said, standing as well.

I shook my head. "You're a sadist, not a masochist."

One of those neatly shaped eyebrows rose. "Been talking to Melek about my preferences?"

"I've been inside your mind long enough to know," I tossed back at him. "But if you hurt Cami, I really will kill you." That part I uttered in all seriousness.

He lifted his hands. "I have no intention of touching your female mate."

I studied him for a long moment, recalling everything we'd discussed. "Hmm. We'll see." Because it seemed pretty clear to me that he was beginning to fall for Cami, just like the rest of us had.

"We won't be seeing anything," he informed me flatly.

I nodded sagely. "Okay." If he kept saying it enough, perhaps he'd believe it.

Az, Ajax said, instantly seizing my attention. *She's starting to stir.*

Melek must have said something similar to Typhos because his entire body went rigid.

We both shared a look, the two of us in sync once more. "Let's go," Typhos said, disappearing in a flurry of fiery embers.

I immediately followed.

Time to open your eyes now, little warrior, I thought as the bedroom materialized around me. *We have a lot to discuss.*

CHAPTER 20

CAMI

Mmm, cinnamon and sin. Such an addictive scent. I wanted to roll in it, swim in it, *live* in it.

I inhaled deeply, my insides coming alive as more delicious aromas taunted my senses. Pine. Peppermint. Bonfire.

All of it together made me think of enjoying a peppermint hot chocolate at a cabin in the woods.

Decadent.

Relaxing.

Safe.

I moaned, the silky sheets surrounding me reminiscent of heavenly bliss. I recognized this bed. Knew it from my dreams.

Which was why it didn't surprise me to find a pair of sapphire eyes staring down at me.

Typhos Lucifer.

My ultimate temptation.

His dark hair framed his gorgeous face, a flash of white a new addition that suited him, his jaw tight as he studied me with his intense gaze.

"You're wearing a shirt," I said, somewhat surprised by his

attire, and even more surprised by the rasp in my voice. Maybe it was supposed to be sultry. Dreams were strange like that.

He arched a dark brow. "Would you prefer me to be shirtless?"

My lips curled. "Well, you typically are..." I glanced over his button-down shirt, the sleeves rolled to the elbows. "But this works, too."

He slowly lowered himself to the bed beside me, his movements different than his usual forwardness. Of course, my dreams almost always started with him naked and hovering over me.

But this was a nice change.

I reached for Lucifer, curious as to what else might be different.

Normally, he tied me down. However, my hands were free now, and I intended to take full advantage.

His eyebrows lifted as I touched his neck, my palm sliding to his nape as I partially rose from the bed. Then I used my strength to pull him the rest of the way toward me.

My name left his lips just before I kissed him, his body strangely rigid beneath my touch. Probably because I'd taken the lead.

Lucifer preferred to be in charge.

Well, too bad. This was my dream. And he hadn't bound me yet. "Shouldn't give me freedom if you don't want me to take over," I said against his mouth, my voice still raspy.

Actually, I felt a bit weak, too. Like I'd just finished an intense workout.

Maybe there'd been a part of this dream I couldn't remember.

Well, I would absolutely remember *this*.

I parted Lucifer's lips with my tongue, demanding that he kiss me back.

But he didn't.

Not quite.

Instead, he palmed my cheek and nudged me back a little. "Camillia."

"Lucifer." I leaned in for another kiss, and this time he *growled*.

I smiled, pleased that I'd pushed his buttons. Because I knew what would come next.

Only, a surprise movement to my left gave me pause. I glanced over to find Melek sitting against the headboard with his long legs crossed at the ankles. "Hello, little angel."

Oh.

I'd never dreamt of Melek and Lucifer together.

Someone else cleared their throat, drawing my focus to Az. He was standing near the foot of the bed with Ajax.

All four men? I thought, my stomach twisting. *All right. I can handle this.*

Cami, Ajax murmured into my mind.

Shh, I hushed via our bond. *Let me concentrate for a minute.*

Az and Ajax had been preparing me for anal play. But that'd been in real life.

In dream world... Yeah. I could handle anything here. Which meant taking three at a time wouldn't be a problem. I'd just have to use my hand for the fourth.

Fae, I can't believe I'm even entertaining this...

But dreams were safe.

Which was why I felt confident enough to lean into Lucifer again. His palm slid to my hair, his touch turning more dominant with each passing second.

He was absolutely going to tie me up soon.

Maybe even force me to take all three men while he watched.

My thighs clenched at the notion, my body more than ready to play.

"Camillia," he said against my mouth.

"Stop talking and kiss me," I demanded.

His grip in my hair tightened, the Hell Fae King not appreciating my command.

And he delivered his punishment with his *tongue.*

Holy. Fae.

We'd kissed in my dreams a dozen times now, but never quite like this.

His cinnamon scent burned through me, the aroma reminding me of a flickering candle. I inhaled deeply, reveling in his taste. His prowess. His masculine presence. His *virility.*

It was all around me, consuming me, owning me, *claiming* me.

Wow, this fae could kiss.

I was so lost to him that I couldn't hear Az and Ajax. They were both speaking into my head, their words incoherent beneath my roaring cloud of need.

This kiss was devastating.

It ruined me for everyone and everything else.

It overwhelmed me. Branded me. Utterly captivated me.

And suddenly it was done.

Lucifer used his grip in my hair to hold me back when I tried to lunge toward him, his blue eyes darkened to midnight pools of need.

So much more intense than my other dreams, probably because his dark shirt highlighted his beautiful eyes.

Cami, Ajax tried again. *Did you hear me?*

I looked his way, my lips curling. "I was a little preoccupied."

He didn't return my smile. "I can see that."

"Are you feeling all right?" Az asked, sounding concerned.

I laughed. "I'm feeling pretty amazing."

Lucifer's lips twitched. "Are you now?"

"Yes," I hissed, stretching my arms over my head. "Now

take off your shirt." Because I wanted to explore his muscular torso—something I never could do in previous dreams because of his penchant for tying me up.

He arched a brow. "Why would I do that?"

"Because you always do."

"Do I?" He cocked his head. "When?"

"During my dreams," I told him with a laugh. "Although, I like having my hands free. So that's a nice change."

"Are you usually tied up, little angel?" Melek asked, drawing my attention to his smoldering gaze.

"You're awake, Cami," Ajax interjected before I could reply to that. "This isn't a dream."

I opened my mouth, then closed it. *What?*

That's what I was trying to tell you—this is real, he stressed via our mental connection. *You're very much awake.*

I looked at him and then at Az.

"You fell from the Virtuous Fae Realm," Az told me, his words like a bucket of ice. "Typhos caught you, but you've been out for hours. We're in Typhos and Melek's suite right now."

"Let's rename it the royal suite," Melek suggested conversationally. "I suspect we'll all be here more in the coming days and weeks."

I blinked from Az to Melek and then back to Ajax and Az.

And eventually to... to Lucifer. "Oh, fae..." I... I'd *kissed* him. His hand was still knotted in my hair, his mouth scant inches from mine. "*Oh.*"

This fae was going to kill me.

Horribly.

Painfully.

His nostrils flared, his lips curling down. "Breathe, Camillia."

I didn't.

Because what was the point? My life was forfeit. Each

passing second brought with it a new memory, starting from our dance to my leaping into that dark hole.

I hadn't felt much beyond that, just emptiness.

Until I'd awoken in this bed and thought it was a dream.

"Sorry," I managed to get out with my last bit of oxygen. It seemed pretty meek and sad in comparison to the apology I owed him. But I didn't have the air to voice much more.

"*Breathe,*" he demanded, his dominant tone hitting me square in the chest and forcing me to inhale. "Good girl, Cami. Again."

His praise had me obeying, my need to please him a unique desire that I didn't want to analyze too deeply. Because I doubted I'd like the reason.

After several more inhales, he complimented me again.

But then he said, "Tell me what happened. How did you end up in the Virtuous Fae Realm? And what did Vivaxia want?"

I gaped at him. How was I supposed to answer that? *If I tell him I'm a siphon, he'll kill me.*

He already knows, Az replied softly. *He's aware that Vivaxia has been using you. He wants to help.*

I nearly laughed.

Because that was impossible.

And just the notion of it being true had me wondering if this was all a dream again.

"I'm not going to kill you, Camillia," Lucifer said after a beat, suggesting Az had told him what I was thinking.

Or maybe Melek had.

Our connection was completely open again, though he hadn't tried to talk to me at all. That seemed odd. *He was constantly talking to me before...*

And you blocked me in response, Melek replied, his trademark amusement missing from his tone. *I would like to avoid being punished like that again, so I'm trying to leave you alone.*

I glanced at him in surprise, his use of the term *punish* one that caught me off guard.

"I apologize," he stated out loud. "I won't use our link again until you're more comfortable."

My brow furrowed. Melek seemed... different. Hurt? Pained? Insecure?

Did something happen to Melek at the ball? I asked Az and Ajax, my mind connecting to theirs with ease. I was finally getting a handle on all these mating links. *Why does he seem so... sad?*

I blinked, that final word reminding me of what Lucifer had told me on the dance floor. My focus instantly went to his unreadable expression, my heart skipping a beat.

He wanted to know what had happened. How I'd ended up in the Virtuous Fae Realm. What Vivaxia had said. And he'd just stated he wasn't going to kill me.

Probably because he couldn't.

But he could imprison me.

Just like Vivaxia had commented.

Just like he'd done before.

Oh, fae, I kissed him... like, really kissed him. And his hand was still in my hair.

He'd let me shift my attention to Melek, but he hadn't released me.

Why? Was he leashing me? Holding me in place? Preparing to throttle me?

"Camillia," he said, drawing my gaze to his mouth. The one I'd just kissed.

Fuck. "I'm sorry," I blurted out. "I thought I was dreaming."

He released my hair, sending a chill down my spine. Then

he grabbed my chin to draw my focus away from his lips and back up to his intense gaze.

"You don't owe me an apology, little one." His soft tones were at odds with the king I knew, the king I *feared*. "But I would like to know what Vivaxia said to you."

I shivered. "You're going to imprison me."

He frowned. "For being a siphon?"

My eyes widened. *He knows I'm a siphon.* Az had already told me this, but hearing Lucifer say it aloud drove the knowledge home.

Lucifer released my chin and sat a little straighter. "I felt you fight the pull, Camillia. You shoved my light back into me when you could have taken it. Maybe it was all for show. But I don't think so. I think Vivaxia is using you to harm me. Convince me otherwise."

The subtle command in those last three words caused my brow to furrow. "Convince you that I want to hurt you?"

"Sure." He stared at me. "Well?"

"I don't want to hurt you," I snapped, fed up with this stupid cycle between us. "And I don't want your Source. But apparently, I was created to absorb your light and restore the Virtuous Fae Realm. Because according to Vivaxia, you shattered their Source when you refused to atone."

I nearly rolled my eyes at that last part. Saying it out loud was almost as insane as hearing it.

But Lucifer's features hardened. "Is that what she told you?"

"Yes. She said you created all the Nightmare Fae and Hell Fae for your own twisted enjoyment, therefore breaking a *vow* —not a *deal*, by the way—to protect life. So you were cast out as punishment, but the light followed you in an effort to help you atone. When you refused, the Virtuous Fae Realm fell apart."

I was surprised I'd retained all that, given how strange my brief experience in the Virtuous Fae Realm had been.

"Oh, and while I'm rambling, Vivaxia is also apparently my grandmother." Might as well get that little fun tidbit out of the way. "And my mother is alive, but my father is dead."

My lips curled down at that last bit.

I didn't exactly like my parents but... but I...

I cleared my throat. "I don't actually know what happened to him, but I think Vivaxia ordered his death?" I phrased it as a question, as my mother had somewhat implied that his passing had been necessary.

I shook my head.

Everything she'd said, that Vivaxia had said... it was... a lot.

"They told me I was created to steal your light and rebuild their realm." I had no idea how it worked or how to stop it. "Vivaxia kept trying to imprint a spell on me, one that altered my reality. I kept forgetting things, then seeing mirages, and... and..."

I wasn't sure what else to add. Or what had made me speak in the first place. But I'd said my piece.

"I don't want your Source," I stated in conclusion. "I don't want to be a siphon. And I think I might hate my mom."

My lips twisted as I stopped talking.

No one spoke, causing my insides to churn.

Their sworn enemy is my fucking grandmother. Of course they didn't have anything to say. They probably hated me now, too. As they should.

Vivaxia had imprisoned Az, kept him caged as an animal.

She'd tricked Lucifer into falling.

And I was pretty sure she had something to do with all the security issues in the Hell Fae Realm, too. Although, we hadn't discussed that part. Still, it seemed to be—

"Do you believe her?" Lucifer asked softly. "Do you think I created all these fae for sinful purposes?"

I blinked up at him. "Do I believe her?" I echoed back at him, my eyebrows lifting.

"Yes. Do you believe her?" he asked again.

"Seriously?" I huffed a humorless laugh. "Why the hell would I believe anything she said? That bitch created me to hurt you. Not to mention all the things she did to Az. And now she expects me to bow to her will? To take your light and restore her realm?" Another laugh escaped me. "Fuck. That."

He smiled, causing me to freeze. Because just like when we'd danced, that expression took my breath away.

But it also scared me.

Because a pleased Lucifer couldn't be a good sign. Not in this situation. Not after everything I'd confided in him.

He'd probably just decided what to do with me.

"You're going to punish me now, aren't you?" I asked, swallowing my unease.

I couldn't exactly blame him for whatever he had planned; I was obviously a threat. And I had no idea what Vivaxia had done to me with all those spells. Maybe they'd been meant to brainwash me, but I suspected she'd done something else as well. She struck me as a master chess player, someone always thinking ten steps ahead.

Just like Typhos Lucifer.

"Oh, Camillia, I suppose I am," he murmured, reaching forward to tuck a strand of hair behind my ear. "But not in the way you fear."

I frowned. "I don't understand." Pretty much everything he did evoked fear inside me.

"I'm going to teach you how to use my Source," he replied. "It won't be easy, and it's probably going to hurt. A punishment, as you suggested, for the gift inside you."

What? I gaped at him. Because I still didn't understand.

"Vivaxia wants to use you as a pawn," he went on, his knuckles brushing my jaw. "So I'm going to counter her."

"How?" I breathed, both curious and terrified to hear his response.

Especially since he was smiling again, the action reaching his dark blue eyes.

"By changing your position on the board," he replied, his words complementing my thoughts about Vivaxia being a chess master.

Because it seemed Lucifer was just as skilled.

And eager to make the next move.

"When we're done training, you'll no longer be a mere pawn, Camillia De la Croix. You'll be a queen. *Our* queen. And together, we're going to destroy Vivaxia and take down the Virtuous Fae Realm once and for all."

CHAPTER 21

MELEK

I PACED MY BEDROOM, the sound of running water taunting my instincts.

Cami's naked and wet. In. My. Shower.

I could easily envision her standing beneath the various showerheads, the droplets caressing her exquisite form as they washed away the residuals left by the Virtuous Fae Realm.

Of course, she still smelled like Vivaxia. Even from here, the aroma of dead roses had my nose curling.

She'd definitely done something to Camillia. The *what* remained to be seen.

Ty, Ajax, and Az were all discussing it now. It was an intriguing evolution in the conversation they'd been having moments ago—whereby Ty had informed Ajax that his Warden status had been fully reinstated, no strings attached.

I couldn't read Ajax's mind, but I suspected he'd been shocked.

However, according to Ty's thoughts, the Warden hadn't displayed an ounce of emotion.

Which naturally had earned Ty's approval.

He liked that Ajax was a strong fae. I did, too.

Now the three of them were discussing next steps regarding Camillia, something I only knew because of my link to Ty.

"We need to talk," Ty had said about thirty minutes ago, his words for Ajax.

"The deal," Ajax had replied.

"Indeed." Ty and Az had shared a look before Ty had suggested, "Let's go for a walk. There are some things I'd like your opinion on."

"What about Cami?" Ajax had asked, our mate having just wandered off to take a shower.

"Melek," Ty had prompted. "Can you look after Camillia?"

His tone had suggested it wasn't a question so much as a request, but his mind had gently stroked mine, aware that I was feeling a bit uneasy around Camillia at the moment.

Still, I'd agreed to stay here. It was where I could be the most useful—if Camillia allowed me to be, anyway.

As a result, the three of them had wandered off for a stroll through the palace courtyard.

Ajax might not realize the purpose, but I did—Ty wanted everyone to see them together. To know that Ajax had been accepted into the inner circle. That he was more than just a Warden; he was Ty's confidant. His friend. A being deserving of respect.

With how much the Hell Fae in our kingdom enjoyed chattering, word would spread quickly.

And Ajax would soon realize the importance of their stroll.

However, Ty was as productive as ever, using the opportunity to not only solidify Ajax's status but also discuss what he felt in Camillia.

"*Maybe we should consult Zakkai,*" Ajax had just

suggested, the words playing with my king's mind as he tasted the opportunity. *"If anyone can unwind a spell, it's him."*

He wasn't wrong, something I'd been about to whisper back to Ty when the water shut off in the other room.

I swallowed, my body going rigid.

When Cami had gone into the shower, all of us had been out here. She had no idea that I was the only one waiting for her, and I wasn't sure how she would react to that.

I eyed the food I'd ordered, the tray having appeared a few minutes ago. Cami had to be hungry. But I wasn't sure if she'd like what I'd requested from the kitchens.

This is ridiculous, I told myself.

Never in my entire existence had I ever felt this insecure about anything or anyone. This lack of confidence was going to be the end of me. This uncertainty about Cami was going to drive me mad. And this—

The door opened, distracting me from my inner turmoil, because an angel had just popped her head out to look around. Droplets of water lingered in her dirty-blonde hair, their alluring sheen trailing a slick path down her neck to her collarbone where she held a towel tightly against her chest.

"Um." Her lips twisted, her eyes scanning the empty room.

"They went for a walk," I explained, my voice a little deeper than I'd intended. I cleared my throat, again hating all this uncertainty. It wasn't me. It wasn't how I worked. It wasn't who I wanted to be or should be with her.

She'd blocked me from her mind because she didn't trust me.

Fine.

Enough brooding.

Except I couldn't seem to stop brooding because it had really fucking hurt to be cut off from her like that. Then she'd very clearly believed I'd enchanted her dress, and had continued to assume that even after I denied my involvement.

Obviously, I'd pushed her too far with the sensual invitations, but that...

That's who I am, I thought.

And if Cami didn't want that—didn't *accept* me—then I... I didn't know how to proceed.

"Melek?" Cami prompted, drawing my gaze to hers. I'd apparently been staring at the ornate rug beneath my feet, which was a strange thing to do with a nearly naked Cami standing in the bathroom doorway.

She'd moved completely into view, her head no longer hanging out to the side, but upright as she stood there in just a towel.

The plush fabric wrapped around her in a fluffy white dress that ended well below her knees.

My lips twitched at the sight. She'd chosen the towel Ty typically used for himself, and he stood well over a foot taller than her five-foot-four frame. Thus, the material resembled a blanket more than a towel.

When she cleared her throat, my amusement waned. She likely assumed I'd been checking her out. Which I probably would have done if I were in any other state of mind.

But I was lost in this cloud of uncertainty that hung over me like a dark fog.

"I ordered some food for you," I told her. "I also wasn't sure what you would want to wear, or if you would be okay with me going through your things in the other room, so I... haven't touched anything yet. If you tell me what you need, I can grab it. Or you can grab it. Or..."

I trailed off, feeling somewhat like an idiot rambling on about nothing.

This isn't me.

Then stop overthinking everything and be who you are, Ty

growled into my mind, obviously hearing my flustered thoughts. *If she rejects you, then she isn't good enough for you.*

I don't think that's how it works, I told him. *Typically one rejects another for not meeting their standards.*

That won't be the case with her, he replied. *If she can't see how amazing you are, that's on her, not you.*

The classic "It's not you, it's me" saying, hmm? Any other day, I might have laughed. However, I wasn't feeling all that humorous at the moment.

"Melek," Cami repeated, this time from a few feet away.

I'd dropped my gaze again on impulse. Looking at her *hurt*. And I really didn't want to give her any other reason to question my loyalty to her.

Yes, I'd played games. I'd woven everyone together in this circle, knowing it was how we would all thrive. If she hated me for that, so be it. I couldn't apologize. Because I knew it was right.

She might be Vivaxia's granddaughter—a reveal I questioned, as I didn't trust a single word out of that bitch's mouth. And she might be a siphon meant to bring down our realm. But I saw something deep in her soul that I couldn't ignore.

It'd been there from the very first moment in the library.

A knowledge I couldn't quite define.

I just... knew.

She was mine. *Ours.* The key to uniting the Hell Fae Realm once and for all.

Camillia De la Croix was a goddess in disguise, a queen destined to rule. I just had to help her see it. I'd had to help Ty see it, too.

Now he did.

I felt his acceptance deep inside, his intrigue finally piqued. We'd reached the endgame.

The final move.

The moment that would hopefully unite us all.

But if Cami couldn't forgive me for the role I'd had to play in all this, then I would be left on the outside. Partially mated for eternity. Because I couldn't force her to take the final step. I wouldn't bind her to me unless she wanted it.

And right now, I was pretty sure she wanted nothing to do with it or me.

Which was why I'd dutifully stayed out of her mind.

I also didn't want to risk feeling her rebuilding that wall; it might break me.

Although, I might already be broken, I thought, my mouth curling downward. *I definitely don't feel like myself at all.*

Warmth caressed my skin as Cami pressed her palm to my cheek, her nearness surprising me. I'd stopped looking at her... *again.*

"I'm sorry I accused you of bespelling the dress," she said, her voice soft. "I should have believed you when you said you didn't do it."

My shoulders lifted and fell. "I—"

Her touch moved to my lips. "I'm also sorry for blocking you from my mind. I didn't want you to hear our counter deal with Lucifer. I didn't trust you not to share it with him since everything you do is for him."

"That's—"

"That's what I've believed," she interjected, the heat of her body bleeding into me as she moved even closer. "But I'm starting to understand a little better now."

I frowned. *You are?* I wanted to ask. However, her hand was still over my lips, so I didn't try.

I am, she replied, surprising me with not only the response but also her use of our mental bond.

She didn't block me again, I realized.

No, I didn't. Her answer shocked me even more.

Because I hadn't telegraphed that via our link.

I'd said that to myself.

Her fingers moved, both of her palms coming up to cradle my face. "I'm so sorry, Melek. I'm still learning how these connections work, and, um, I've been sort of hearing all your thoughts since I stepped out here."

My brow furrowed. "Even my conversation with Ty?"

She shook her head. "Not exactly. I could sense you were talking to him, but couldn't hear the words. However, I felt your emotions. And, well, I picked up enough to understand what you might have been talking about."

I stared at her.

We'd bonded on the second level, thus marrying our minds, but I hadn't realized how open I'd been to her. In my effort not to touch her thoughts at all, I'd actively tried not to link to her. However, I hadn't created a barrier or protected my mind from her. I'd just... fought the temptation to mentally connect.

"I hadn't meant to share all of that with you," I admitted. "I..." I blew out a breath, my head falling back. "Fuck, Cami. I'm not feeling like myself." I wasn't sure what else to say. Which also wasn't like me at all.

"I know," she whispered. "But I have an idea on how to help."

My gaze fell to her mouth before slowly returning to her pretty eyes. She was so gorgeous it hurt. All I wanted was to wrap her up in my arms and claim her. To be with her. To let her see and experience how I felt about her.

She'd said I did everything for Ty.

That was partly true. I'd seen her as a potential mate for him, but I'd claimed her for myself. Claimed her to protect her. Claimed her because I *wanted* her.

She might argue that I barely knew her. But my soul had immediately recognized her soul. And I'd lived too long to ignore that sort of connection.

So I'd coaxed her into a mate-bond, knowing it could never be broken. Knowing that she would forever be tied to my spirit.

It would hurt if she rejected me. Fuck, it already had when she'd blocked me out.

However, I could live with that pain if it meant she would always be protected through my immortality.

Cami's eyes held mine, her gaze searching. "I finally see you, Melek. The real you beneath the riddles. The man who follows his heart, no matter the risk. You do everything for Lucifer. He's the center of your universe. His wants and needs come first."

My lips parted, my eyebrows coming down. Because that wasn't quite right. "Cami—"

"Shh," she hushed me, her fingertip pressing to my mouth once more. "I also see where I fit now, too. How that same care and consideration applies to me. You risked his wrath when you claimed me. He's still the center of your universe, but at some point, you added me to that circle as well."

I swallowed. "I think I put you there the moment we met." It had been instinctual. I'd recognized her as my soul's mate. My missing half. Perhaps as a result of something Vivaxia had done. Or maybe it was just fate.

Regardless of the reason or the purpose, we were here now.

She existed in my orbit.

And her needs now came first, too.

Balancing her and Ty hadn't been easy, but we were finally on the same page. Finally at a point of collaboration. Finally ready to embrace whatever came next.

If Cami would have me, anyway.

"That, right there," she said, her fingers gliding back into my hair. "*That* is what I can fix."

I stared down at her, my hands hanging at my sides as I

tried to discern what she meant. "What do you want to fix, Camillia?"

"You," she replied as she went up onto her toes. "I want my bold Melek back. The one who keeps teasing me with wicked thoughts." She pulled my face down, her lips a hairsbreadth from mine. "The one who promised to tie me up in his ropes."

Her mouth brushed mine, causing me to go rigid against her.

I was afraid that if I moved, that if I even breathed, I'd devour her.

Because Cami had never kissed me first. It'd always been me sneaking in an embrace or tricking her into letting me taste her.

But this was all her.

Her fingers in my hair.

Her breasts pressing against my chest.

Her mouth ghosting across mine.

"The one who sets my soul on fire every time he touches me," she went on, her voice a mere whisper. "The one who is impossible to resist."

Another meeting of mouths, brief... Too brief.

"The one I've wanted for far too long but kept denying. The one who makes me feel things I shouldn't." Her eyes held mine, our lips touching with each word. "The Melek who marks me with his golden essence because he knows deep down that I secretly like it."

I shuddered, her words seeming to mend something inside me. Not completely, but partially. Enough to coax me into moving my hands to her hips. "It's ethereal magic," I corrected her. "It's yours, too."

"Brought out by you," she replied, her arms encircling my neck. "Az and Ajax are addicted to the flavor of it."

I swallowed, my tongue craving a taste. "I imagine it's quite decadent."

She shrugged. "Why don't you make me come and find out?"

I stared down at her, both aroused and terrified. "Don't tease me, Cami." She could shatter me right now, destroy the vestiges of my resolve, and kill me with her rejection. If she—

"I'm not teasing, Melek." Her lips boldly claimed mine before I could respond, before I could even think.

Then she released me as quickly as she'd kissed me, causing my heart to leap into my throat.

But she didn't step away.

She simply tugged at the towel.

Let it fall to the floor.

Then cocked her head to the side. "Come play with me, Melek. Tie me up. Fuck me. Claim me. Do whatever you need. I'm ready."

CHAPTER 22

CAMI

My HEART THUDDED RAPIDLY in my chest.

I tried to exude confidence, to tempt Melek into taking me.

However, inside, I was vibrating with nerves.

Not because I didn't want this, but because I'd just realized how much I *needed* this.

Fae, hearing his mind... feeling his emotions... It had undone something inside me. Something fragile yet utterly impactful.

In the shower, I'd started thinking about him, recalling his reserved behavior while Lucifer had been discussing his thoughts on my training. It'd been a brief conversation, one sparked by his comments about turning me into a queen— which was an entirely different notion that made my heart race.

But Melek had been quiet throughout most of the discussion.

I'd picked up on the sadness Lucifer had mentioned during our dance, and I'd started considering it more while standing in the shower.

In doing so, I'd connected to Melek's thoughts, had heard him second-guessing every move, trying to determine the perfect meal for me. Debating clothing options, then disregarding all of them because he didn't want to push me away more than he already had.

Those concerns had reached a crescendo when I'd stepped out of the bathroom, Melek's insecurity a bruise I longed to heal.

Because this wasn't him.

I'd hurt him. Badly, it seemed. I hadn't meant to. I'd meant what I told him about not trusting him while discussing the deal, but it all felt trivial now.

Lucifer had reinstated Ajax as Warden without strings— something I'd learned through Melek's thoughts and had confirmed by asking the Midnight Fae himself.

Do you trust him? I'd whispered to Ajax minutes ago. Because I... I was beginning to believe Lucifer had all our best interests at heart.

Oh, he'd done horrible things, things I might never forgive him for. But the more I understood him, the more drawn to him I became.

Just like with Melek.

Only my draw to Melek was that much more impactful due to my connection to his mind. Because I finally saw him. The real him.

Not the insecure fae worried about losing me.

But the man beneath—the one who *cared*. The one who wanted a chance to be with me. To cherish me. To show me what it meant to be *his*.

I wanted to learn more. To see what he meant when he promised to worship me. To experience his ropes. To indulge in this connection between us and see where it went.

I didn't hide that desire from Ajax and Az. They knew.

And while they both exuded possessive auras, deep down I felt their acceptance.

Melek was already part of me. Already bonded to me on a level that could never be undone.

Yet he thought I meant to reject him, to block him indefinitely from my mind, and force him to live with a one-sided link.

He'd been willing to accept that.

Protecting her is all that matters, some part of him had whispered, telling me his true feelings. Confiding his intentions. Letting me finally unravel the riddle that was the Hell Fae Prince.

Yet he simply stared at me now, like he couldn't decide how to proceed.

And for an instant, I wondered if he would reject my offer.

It was a mere second in time that gave me an immediate glimpse into how my potential rejection had affected him.

I didn't like the way it made me feel, the insecurity it inspired inside me, the sensation of confusion that swirled around my soul.

Melek and I were already tied together.

Our only path was forward.

I'd thought he'd bonded me for some nefarious reason, or simply as a means to protect Lucifer. But Melek's reasoning went so much deeper. It was rooted in his own version of righteousness. His own version of *loyalty*.

And saturated in his unrestrained *need*.

Melek was a fae who fought for what he wanted but never let anyone see that fight. Instead, he used games to sway his opponent to his side.

I'd played.

Some might say I'd lost.

But as he took a step toward me, his multicolored eyes glittering with sinful intent, I knew that I'd actually *won*.

He clasped my nape, his palm a brand against my skin as he yanked me into his hard body. The silk of his suit felt decadent against my heated flesh, his kiss a benediction I felt all the way to my soul.

Finally, some part of him breathed, the thought one that rivaled my own.

I'd fought this attraction since the first time we'd met. The male exuded sex, his erotic appeal one I'd struggled to deny. But I no longer had to fight this.

He was mine.

I was his.

And I wanted him to show me what that meant.

His hands slid to my hips, his touch hot and possessive as he started walking me blindly around his room. When the back of my knees met his mattress, I smiled with relief.

But then he took a step back to evaluate me with careful consideration. "I can't tie you up yet, Cami."

I blinked at him. "Oh." I swallowed. "Right. Yeah. Of course not. I..." I started looking for the towel I'd lost, my skin suddenly on fire.

However, he caught me by the hip before I could move, his opposite hand going to my chin.

"I can't tie you up until you trust me," he clarified, his beautiful gaze holding mine captive.

My lashes fluttered again, confusion lancing my heart. "I do trust you."

"Not completely," he replied, wounding me more. "I'm not saying that to hurt you, love. I'm saying it so you know I'll always put your safety over my own desires. I'll always protect you, and I'll never hurt you."

"I know," I told him. "I told you—I see you now. I *know* you."

"Which means we're on the right path," he whispered, his forehead touching mine. "I want to stay on that path, Cami. I want to feel you beneath my silk, make you writhe. But first, I have to show you what it means to be mine. To properly earn your faith. Then, one day, when you're ready, we'll play."

He kissed me again, this time with intention. Sensuality. The sweetest hint of seduction. By the time he finished, I was panting and praying that he planned to do more.

Because I wanted his mouth on other places.

His hands roaming my bare skin.

To feel the strength of his thrusts between my thighs.

"I want to finish the bond," I told him. "I want to be yours." Yet I had no idea what that required.

However, a part of me hoped sex was involved.

His lips curled like he could hear me. And he probably had. I wasn't masking my emotions or my thoughts from him or any of my mates.

I was just being me.

Trusting my fae to respect my mind and honor my desires.

Az and Ajax had already proved more than capable of doing both.

And Melek... Well, it was like he'd said—we were wandering down the right path.

Renewed respect and understanding blossomed in my mind as I started to comprehend his comments on trust and how we weren't fully there yet.

He was right.

But I wanted to be there.

And the first step toward that fate was to acknowledge our bond. To complete it. To officially become *mates*.

"I would ask if you're sure, but I can hear the resolution in your mind," Melek breathed, his gaze seeming to memorize my features.

His thoughts told me he couldn't believe this was happening. Mere moments ago, he'd assumed I intended to reject him entirely.

Now, I was asking him to claim me for eternity.

"Tell me what to do," I said.

"Oh, the ways I could interpret that statement." He kissed me once more, his tongue weaving dark promises against mine. He didn't pull away again until I was panting, my brain solely focused on him. His nearness. His decadent scent. *Like sin,* I thought. *Pure, unadulterated sin.*

His eyes smiled, the multicolored irises gleaming with wicked intentions.

Wicked intentions I longed to experience.

Because I was done fighting this attraction. Done denying how I felt.

Maybe everything that had happened had jarred my brain, forced me into a mode of compliance. Or maybe it'd made me want to *live.*

I chose to believe it was the latter.

I'd been fighting for freedom my entire life, desiring my independence and a normal existence. Something that didn't involve random camping trips or being left in the middle of a forest fire. But I was never meant to be normal.

I was me.

Part Virtuous Fae, part Hell Fae.

A siphon, apparently.

Well, fuck that part. I wouldn't do what Vivaxia claimed I was born to do. I'd rebel instead. I'd make my own choices.

Like mating Melek.

That was all me. My decision. My fate.

"How do we finish our bond?" I asked him. He knew that was what I'd meant when I'd asked him to tell me what to do. But he'd distracted me with his mouth. Now I wouldn't let him *interpret* my words in any other way.

No games.

No riddles.

Just us.

Just *this*.

He moved backward, his hands on the lapels of his jacket as he guided the fabric away from his shoulders and down his arms. "If we're doing this, it's only fair that I'm naked, too." He folded the expensive-looking coat on a nearby chair, then loosened his tie to pull it over his head.

I swallowed as he took off his cuff links, then started on the buttons of his dark dress shirt. All black. A contrast to the gold-and-white feathers that I'd seen last week.

The feathers I'd remembered while lost in the mirage of the Virtuous Fae Realm.

Melek had been a big part of why Vivaxia's mind manipulations hadn't worked. My memories of him had kept pushing forward, helping me to see through the charade and remember who I was and who my mates were.

Az had also been integral to grounding me, his story about Vivaxia so powerful and profound that I'd been able to realize the woman's true nature. Recall her history. To know her claims about Lucifer were lies.

Then there had been Ajax, our link an anchor that had held me captive in reality.

But it'd been Melek's feathers I'd recalled first. Then the statue of Lucifer that Melek had shown me.

He was meant to be mine, my heart and soul knowing him in a time of intrinsic need.

I hadn't meant to hurt him or lead him to feel rejected.

However, I fully meant to heal him now. To bring back the playful Melek, the one who exuded confidence in all ways.

Some of that confidence showed through as he lost his shirt, his sculpted form a pleasure to observe. He knew he was beautiful. But I confirmed it anyway by saying it aloud.

I specifically enjoyed his tattoos, the symbols ethereal and otherworldly in nature. They were practically glowing gold right now as well, suggesting they were tied to his Virtuous

Fae heritage, and not necessarily art he'd imprinted on his body.

I would have to ask him more about those markings later.

Because right now, all I could focus on was his belt—and his hands unfastening said belt.

"Not as beautiful as you, little angel," he murmured, replying to my comment regarding his beauty. His gaze ran over me with unrestrained interest as he undid the button of his pants and drew down the zipper.

I wasn't surprised at all that he was bare beneath. It just seemed appropriate that Melek would forgo undergarments. Though, he would look really nice in a pair of silky black boxers.

"Next time," he murmured, kicking off his shoes and bending to finish disrobing.

I assumed the "next time" referred to the silky black boxers I was currently fantasizing about.

But as he straightened to reveal himself in all his naked glory, I wondered if boxers would be uncomfortable. Because wow, Melek was... impressive. In every way.

Information I did not need to hear about Melek, Ajax grumbled into my mind.

Sorry, I said back to him, once again struggling to control the mental links within my head. Seeing Melek like this had broken my brain.

You're making me jealous, little warrior, Az murmured. *Do I need to ash over there and remind you what I can do?*

I shivered, my insides turning to liquid fire at the very intimate knowledge of what Az was capable of doing to me. *As much as I love your cock, I need to let Melek have his moment right now.* It was purposely worded in a way I knew Az would like.

His responding growl proved me right, his approval

warming our bond. *I'm going to make you show me how much you love my cock later while I fuck your mouth.*

I swallowed. *I'll scream it for you,* I promised.

Good girl, he replied. *Now go show Melek what Ajax and I have taught you.*

Ajax released a sound of noncommittal agreement, his possession wrapping around me in a warm mental kiss before he released me to Melek's touch.

"Tell them I'm going to make you glow," Melek said against my mouth, his hands on my hips. "And maybe I'll let them help me lick you clean afterward."

He ensnared me in a kiss before I could react to the vivid mental picture his words had just painted in my mind, his embrace all-consuming and overpowering.

It felt like the last few months of knowing one another had been a prolonged game of foreplay, like we'd been dancing around the inevitable for eternity.

His tongue parted my lips, his hands lifting me onto the bed.

And suddenly I was sprawled out beneath him, his wings stretching out over us in a cloud of white and gold.

I stared up at him in wonder, his glorious form both regal and godly. Gorgeous and sinful. A fallen angel sent here to corrupt my soul.

But my soul was already partly his.

Soon to be fully his.

"Mate me," I whispered.

He smiled. "You have no idea how much I needed to hear you say that." He pressed his forehead to mine. "I've craved you since that first day in the library, Camillia De la Croix. It was so hard being a gentleman when all I really wanted to do was strip you bare and take you against the shelves."

My insides burned at the thought. Would I have let him? Maybe. Probably. Because I'd been just as taken with him that day. Scared, too. But the attraction had definitely existed between us from our very first meeting.

Melek rolled to the side and propped himself up on an elbow, his wings disappearing in a flourish. "The final level of mating requires a blood exchange from the same hands we cut before. And the ancient incantation must be voiced in unison as well."

I stared at him, waiting for him to continue. "Anything else?"

He shook his head. "It's a fairly simple process in our physical forms. It's our souls that have to do all the work."

I considered that for a moment. "Why does that sound like another one of your riddles?"

"Because it's a mystery even to me," he replied. "We'll mate in corporeal form, but for the bond to truly thrive, our souls have to mate, too. Neither of us can control that outcome. Either our spirits will accept our intertwined fates, or the bond will shatter for good."

My eyebrows lifted. "You're saying our souls could reject each other?"

He nodded. "That's how Virtuous Fae bonds work—it's about our ethereal energy matching another's ethereal energy. In theory, not all souls desire the mate-bond."

"So we might not be mates?" I asked, suddenly panicking. Because that seemed like a pretty fucking big deal.

Yet all Melek did was grin. "We're mates, Cami. I'm sure of it."

"I'm glad you're so sure," I muttered.

A dagger appeared in his hand, the same bejeweled one that had magically manifested itself when we'd engaged in the second mating level.

"Faith, little angel, is the key to everything." Another knife materialized beside the first, and he held them out to me. "Pick one and we'll begin."

CHAPTER 23

AJAX

THIS IS SO FUCKING SURREAL, I thought, glancing around the Hell Fae Realm. It wasn't being here that aroused that sensation so much as being here beside Lucifer.

He was walking and talking to me like an equal, something he'd done a bit before, but never quite like this.

And definitely not since the incident with Cami in that fucking chain-link dress.

What the hell are we even doing? I wondered, glancing around the fiery courtyard that surrounded the Hell Fae Kingdom Palace.

Lucifer is making a statement, Az replied, clearly having overheard my thoughts.

What kind of statement? I asked, wary. Because most of Lucifer's "statements" involved punishments, and I really wasn't in the mood for one of his infamous lessons.

The kind that's meant as an apology, Az told me.

I nearly snorted. *Right.* Typhos Lucifer did not apologize. That would require him to admit fault.

Oh, he might have told me that I no longer had to mate him—though the offer, he'd said, was still there should I desire it. But that didn't mean I believed him or the explanation that had accompanied his declaration.

"I realize now that demanding a mating under those circumstances was wrong. A fae should want to mate me, not do it out of obligation," he'd said a bit ago. "But make no mistake, Ajax, I still want you in my circle. However, I realize I need to demonstrate that desire rather than force it."

Kuro ruffled his feathers on my shoulder, drawing me back to the present. He'd arrived shortly after Lucifer's proclamation, no doubt responding to my internal stress.

Because it was all too good to be true.

And just because he'd changed his terms didn't mean he wasn't planning to punish me in some way. I'd defied him. Chosen Cami over him. *Left* him.

He wouldn't let that go unanswered.

He couldn't.

Az sighed into my mind. However, he said nothing more. His ties to Lucifer clouded his judgment. Or that was my opinion, anyway.

Az disagreed, muttering something about how he'd put me first, but didn't otherwise press the issue. Instead, his mind shifted to thoughts of Cami.

And Melek.

My hands curled into fists.

I might not be in the room with them, but I knew what they were doing.

Was I jealous? Yes.

But it went so much deeper than jealousy. I didn't fucking trust Melek. However, whatever he'd said and done had made Cami feel differently.

I could hear her mind processing Melek's intentions, could feel her arousal as she looked at him, could sense her interest in *more*.

It had my teeth grinding together. Az's, too.

Though, if it bothered Lucifer, he didn't show it. He simply sauntered along the courtyard, head held high, and nodded at Hell Fae as they passed.

"Is there anything you'd like that I haven't covered?" Lucifer asked, drawing me out of my thoughts and back to the deal he'd told me no longer applied. Instead, he was listing one-sided terms for me to accept.

Except, he hadn't called them "terms" or referred to this as a "deal." Just a way to comfortably restore my status, with no strings attached.

I'd believe that when it came to fruition.

Still, I pondered his question as we exited the courtyard and turned onto the main street that ran through the center of his kingdom.

The skyline glowed with Hellfire, the sight making me feel at home despite its differences from the Midnight Fae Realm. Fortunately, Kuro didn't seem to mind. He simply relaxed on my shoulder like he was settling in for the long term.

I sort of hoped he was.

I'd missed the little guy. And I was forever thankful to Shade for keeping an eye on him when I'd disappeared.

Typhos thinks you're goading him with your silence, Az warned me.

I'm not.

I know, he replied. *Just sharing his mood.*

As a warning? I guessed.

No, as a way of demonstrating good faith, he told me. *Typhos doesn't like being goaded, yet he's exuding the utmost patience right now while your mind wanders. It's a sign that he cares about your well-being, Ajax. He's not trying to force you to answer him. He's waiting for you to come to him. I imagine that's why he's left the mating open-ended, too. He wants you, but he won't force you.*

I nearly snorted at that. Typhos Lucifer gave orders. I

obeyed them. That was how our relationship had always worked.

But rather than release the sardonic sound, I focused on Lucifer's question again. *What else do I want?*

"Honestly, I just don't want Cami to be hurt," I told him by way of a reply. He'd offered me my old job back and then some. "And I want to be able to see her whenever I want, even when she's in your bedroom."

A new suite. Amenities. Additional staff. Even a new weapons collection.

That was what he'd offered me thus far, in addition to my title.

But those bribe-like offers meant nothing to me.

Cami and Az were all I cared about. I wanted access to both of them, even if they were in Lucifer's personal territory. They were my mates. *Mine.*

"I'll never keep you from Camillia or Azazel," Lucifer told me. "I respect mate-bonds."

The *as should you* was definitely attached to that statement, probably because he'd picked up on my frustrations around Melek and Cami mating. Or maybe he'd caught the uncertainty through Az's thoughts.

Regardless, I nodded. Because on that term, we could absolutely agree.

I might not like Melek mating Cami, but I trusted her to make her own choices. I'd also vowed to never force her hand again—after that incident in Lucifer's nightclub.

A nightclub that was slowly coming into view now.

Fuck.

I hadn't realized where we were going until now, my mind too consumed by Lucifer's comments and Cami's arousal.

We were no doubt headed here for whatever act of humiliation Lucifer had in store for me.

Fine, I thought. *Fucking fine.*

He's not planning anything nefarious, Az promised me.

I nearly shot back a snide remark about not trusting him either—especially after what he'd done to me the last time we were here. However, I bit my tongue.

I'd leashed Az with that spell. He'd leashed me with his mind. Our crimes might have varied, but the results were similar.

And bringing all that up now would put us at odds with one another.

We couldn't live in the past any longer. We needed to move together into the future. As mates.

His palm ghosted along my lower back, like he'd heard my inner turmoil and agreed. Flames, he probably had. Because he leaned in to kiss my neck just as we stepped up to the nightclub entrance.

If Lucifer noticed the fleeting expression of appreciation, he didn't show it. Instead, he held open the door and waved for us to enter.

The moment I stepped inside, I vividly remembered exactly why I didn't trust Lucifer at my back.

Hellfire burned in winding red and blue pyres that lined the walls, surrounding the stage where Cami had been on display. A stage I'd been forced to stand guard beside, while paralyzed, thanks to Az's suffocating power.

So what's your next move, Hell Fae King? I wondered, glancing back at him. *Going to force me to parade around naked on that stage? Show off how aroused I am by what your prince is doing to Cami right now?*

Lucifer ignored me, though I suspected he no doubt felt my irritation. We didn't have to be bonded for him to sense my ire. I wasn't masking my facial features at all. Because I no longer cared to hide.

He'd pissed me off.

Now he wanted to play nice by giving me everything I desired—and more—without anything in return?

Yeah. Like I believed that.

"Your Majesty," a Hell Fae greeted, the male wearing leather pants and a long red tie over a bare chest. Then he glanced at Az and bowed again, only to pause when he saw me. The note of surprise in his eyes wasn't unexpected. I rarely spent time like this with the Hell Fae King.

And the last time I was here, he'd made a fool of me in front of his kingdom.

"Benedict," Lucifer said, causing the Hell Fae to snap his attention away from me to focus on the king before him. "A bottle of Hellfire whiskey with three glasses, please."

The male flinched, then bowed low enough for his dark hair to fall over his face. "Y-yes, right away," he said and scurried off.

Lucifer turned and moved through the crowd, his mere presence causing everyone to step out of his way as he approached his usual booth.

Sometimes, he chose the throne on the stage. But apparently today wasn't one of those days.

That night with Cami hadn't been one of those nights, either. A special cage had been brought out for her instead.

I idly wondered if another would appear for me soon.

Kuro nibbled my ear, likely sensing my growing agitation.

An agitation that reached a boiling point as Lucifer said, "I brought you here for a reason."

No shit, I thought.

Az nudged me into the booth as Lucifer took over the bench across from us, the Hell Fae King's large form appearing even more pronounced than usual.

"Whatever punishment you have in mind, I'll accept so long as Cami is unharmed," I told him, my voice unwavering.

Two females—illusions crafted by the nightclub's magic—

appeared with our drinks before Lucifer could reply. The glasses were garnished with red flames, the fires making Kuro bristle on my shoulder.

When one of the illusions set the glass down, he nipped at her translucent form.

I smirked. "You never did like figments. I suppose it makes sense that you wouldn't like this magic, either."

Kuro huffed.

"I think he's just mirroring your mood," Lucifer said, humor in his voice. "That's what familiars often do, yes?"

I grunted, not at all surprised that he understood Midnight Fae bonds with their familiars. But I opted not to give much away anyway. Because I didn't trust him. Not one bit.

"And what mood do you think that is?" I asked him, my tone holding an edge to it.

The Hell Fae King hadn't responded to my punishment statement, which only confirmed that was his exact intent for bringing me here. So of course I was in a testy mood.

And so was my owl.

"You're angry," Lucifer said. "And rightly so."

I arched a brow. "Oh?"

He gave me a look before knocking back his drink. One of the figment-like waitresses appeared again with a refill, but he ignored her as she set it down before him.

"Look, I said I brought you here for a reason, and yes, it's punishment-related." He leaned forward, his blue eyes flickering with fiery intensity. "But it's not *your* punishment that I seek."

I frowned at him. "Then whose?" In the next moment, my heart stopped and I instantly connected to Cami's mind, needing to know that she was safe.

But all I caught were consuming thoughts of Melek and ropes and bonds.

"I'm punishing myself," Lucifer said, his words shocking the hell out of me. "I brought you here so I could face my wrongdoings and apologize for them. I took your punishment —and Camillia's—too far. I understand that. I own it. And I apologize for it."

"Because you give a shit now?" I blurted out, not following this turn of events at all.

Az made a sound and shot me a look that said he was about to tackle me.

But I ignored him.

Because this was between me and Lucifer.

"Actually, yes, I very much *give a shit* now," Lucifer said. "Melek's my prince. And he's about to mate Camillia for eternity."

"He initiated that bond almost two months ago," I pointed out. "And you certainly didn't care then."

"Oh, I cared." He knocked back his drink again, then waved off the incoming refill. "But I also thought she was a threat. Now I realize I was wrong. She's a pawn in a game that started well before her creation. A pawn that was literally crafted to hurt me. And, well, I have a penchant for saving the fae Vivaxia sends my way."

He looked pointedly at Az.

Then glanced around his nightclub.

"My realm is filled with Vivaxia's former playthings. Now Camillia is one of them, and both of my mates appear to be quite taken with her. So, yes, I officially give a shit."

I stared at him, still uneasy. "And how do you feel about her?"

He smiled. "To be determined, Ajax. To be determined."

I arched a brow. "That doesn't make me feel all that confident in your intentions, Lucifer."

"No, I imagine it doesn't. But all I can promise now is that I want to save her, empower her, and turn her into a queen.

Whether or not she becomes *my* queen, well, that remains to be seen, yes?"

I was about to question that further when a screen flickered in the air before him, drawing his attention away from mine. He frowned. "Hades is calling. I need to take this."

I blinked, surprised he'd told me who was calling. And also surprised to hear that particular Mythos Fae—the God of the Netherworld—was ringing Lucifer.

Any idea what that's about? I wondered at Az.

He shook his head. *Things have been going on while we've been gone. I haven't received the full rundown yet.*

Oh. My jaw clenched as I finally took a drink. Unlike with Lucifer, the figments didn't immediately return to fill my glass.

Not surprising.

I wasn't even a real Hell Fae. Not to them.

"What's your take on his comments regarding Cami?" I asked Az out loud.

"I believe him when he says he won't hurt her."

"And do you think he intends to mate her?" I pressed.

Az considered me. "Would it bother you?"

"Yes," I replied immediately.

"Why?" he asked.

"Because he's not worthy of her."

Az's eyebrows flew upward. "Not worthy?"

"He's keeping her alive for you and Melek, not because he wants her alive," I said, my teeth grinding together.

Az looked ready to speak, but I wasn't done.

"Lucifer's motives revolve around his kingdom and his mates. Until he can see Cami for who she is and wants her for her, then no, he's not fucking worthy." I picked up my drink again, intending to finish it, and found it already empty. "*Fuck.* I need another drink."

A Hell Fae male turned nearby, no doubt having heard my

comment and taken it the wrong way. I'd sounded ungrateful. That hadn't been my intent.

But as he stormed toward us, I realized he'd absolutely read my hostility wrong. And now we were about to have a problem.

Kuro launched from my shoulder before I could stop him, his beak going straight for the Hell Fae's eye.

I called him back to me before he could truly strike, but the Hell Fae shrieked in alarm anyway and tried to swat at my owl.

"*Kuro*," I commanded when he righted himself in a position to strike again.

Fortunately, my familiar obeyed me and puffed out of existence just to reappear on my shoulder again with an indignant squawk.

"Little asshat beast!" the Hell Fae roared.

"He—"

"Take that *thing* back to the Midnight Fae Realm!" he shouted, cutting me off before I could utter more than a word. "And why the fuck are you even here, *ex*-Warden? You're not a real Hell Fae. You're *nothing* to us. And you sure as fuck don't deserve a seat at His Majesty's booth."

My jaw ticked, his words ones I'd definitely heard before. Well, maybe not the *booth* part, but I'd definitely dealt with other Hell Fae telling me I didn't belong here and saying I shouldn't have the title of Warden.

Usually, I demonstrated my power through a sparring lesson.

Today, I just stared him down.

Because I had nothing to say back to him. While my position as Warden had been officially reinstated, there hadn't been any sort of official announcement yet. At least, not one that I'd heard, anyway.

And I probably shouldn't be in this booth, either.

"He's right," another Hell Fae chimed in from a nearby seat. "You don't belong here, *Midnight Fae*."

"I disagree," a voice boomed from the other end of the room as Lucifer appeared, a screen in front of him.

I frowned, assuming he was arguing with Hades.

Instead, he said, "I'm going to have to call you back," to the Mythos Fae before disconnecting.

Did he just hang up on Hades? I asked Az, somewhat shocked by that move. I highly doubted the godlike entity was used to being disconnected in that manner.

It seems so, Az said, sounding more amused than irritated.

"Perhaps Ajax's presence at my side today hasn't been noted by everyone in this room," Lucifer said, his voice carrying throughout his nightclub. "But let me be clear. Ajax is my Warden. He's also officially a Hell Fae now, as he's mated to my Commander."

Several Hell Fae exchanged looks, then glanced back at us with wide-eyed expressions.

"And for those of you who really need a lesson in respect, let me remind you that Azazel is one of my mates." The words echoed on the screen, suggesting he was broadcasting these words to the entire Hell Fae Kingdom. "Which means Ajax is now linked directly to me."

He locked eyes with the Hell Fae who had snapped at me over Kuro.

Then looked at the other fae who had echoed his opinion of me not belonging here.

"I strongly encourage you to remember these mate-bonds and their importance to me as your Hell Fae King. Because the next time you choose to insult *my* Warden, I won't be kind in return."

Both Hell Fae looked pale, the pair of them mumbling apologies before quickly heading toward the nightclub exit.

I gaped at them, then at Lucifer.

He'd just... *claimed me*.

Not in an unbinding mating, but in his own way as king. And he'd ensured the entire kingdom knew I belonged to him.

Which meant Cami belonged to him, too.

Or she would, anyway, as soon as she finished mating Melek.

"Now have I made my intentions clear?" Lucifer asked as he returned to our table. "Or do you still have questions?"

I stared at him.

Did I still have questions? Yes. Thousands.

But I couldn't organize them all in a coherent train of thought, so I just... shook my head.

He smiled. "Good. Then let's move forward, Warden. I'll earn your forgiveness in time, prove my worth to you as a potential mate—not just to you, but possibly to Camillia, too—and maybe one day, we'll complete this circle. Until then, I could use some insight into this Vivaxia situation."

Shit. He must have overheard my comments about him not being worthy enough for Camillia.

Or perhaps he'd read them through Az's thoughts.

Regardless, Lucifer didn't appear to be angry so much as invigorated. He'd also stated that the onus fell on him to prove his worth—an interesting way of phrasing it.

"What kind of insight?" Az asked, focusing on the last part of what Lucifer had said. "Do you have an idea of what Vivaxia might have done to Cami?"

My jaw clenched, the reminder of what Az could sense inside Cami suddenly the most important topic in my mind. We all knew that Virtuous Fae had done something to her. The question was *what*?

That'd been one of the only reasons I'd been okay with leaving her in Melek's care. If anyone could solve this riddle, it was another Virtuous Fae.

But naturally, he was choosing to play with our mate instead.

Maybe finishing their bond would help protect her.

Or maybe it would make things worse.

"Perhaps I should talk with Zenaida," I said, voicing the thought out loud before I fully considered it. Yet it seemed like a good place to start. If anyone could provide us with information on the future, it was her.

Of course, it would be uttered in the form of a riddle.

But I'd grown up with Shade. I understood riddles well, thanks to his many teachings.

Melek also might be able to help, I realized, his mating Cami suddenly having a bit more of an appeal. Because the riddle master himself would finally be on our side.

Lucifer studied me for a moment and nodded. "Zen might offer some interesting insight. We should also consider asking Zakkai to come by for a visit."

My brow lifted. "Zakkai?"

"Yes. He's the Midnight Fae Source Architect. He might be able to help."

I knew what and who Zakkai was; I was just surprised Lucifer wanted to invite him down for a visit. "I can talk to him, too."

Lucifer gave another dip of his chin. "Meanwhile, I have some texts to review."

"What would you like me to do?" Az asked him.

"Can you accompany Ajax?" Lucifer phrased it as a request, not a command. "I'd prefer to be able to maintain communication, should something happen. And I don't have that sort of link to Ajax... yet."

My eyes almost narrowed as I repeated that final word in my thoughts. *Yet.*

"I can do that," Az said, his arm stretching out behind me on the booth. "But I'll want regular updates, too."

"Of course," Lucifer replied. "I'll be starting with Vita, then working from there."

Az reached for his untouched drink and downed the contents. "Then let's get started."

Take us to Zenaida first, he added in my head. *We can pick up some cookies for Cami. I suspect she's going to be famished by the time Melek finishes with her...*

CHAPTER 24

MELEK

CAMI STARED at the blade she'd selected, her brow furrowed. Doubts played through her mind, concerned that doing this might dismantle our bond.

A few weeks ago, she might have been okay with that.

However, something had changed between us, something profound.

I wasn't sure when it had happened, but she finally understood our potential as mates.

The attraction had always existed between us. I assumed it was because our souls recognized one another. Cami hadn't reached that level of certainty, though. She was still trying to wrap her head around the risk of failure.

"If our bond doesn't take, then we were never meant to be together," I told her. "As disappointing as that would be, there's nothing we can do to change it."

I caught her chin and guided her gaze away from the knife and up to my eyes.

"I didn't tell you this to worry you. I was trying to explain why the ritual seems easy. It's because our souls will be doing most of the work, which should result in another energy exchange." I smiled. "You enjoyed that before, which means you're going to love it this time."

"If it works," she whispered.

"Ah, little angel, I'm both pained and pleased by your worry." I leaned down to kiss her softly. "Pained because I don't enjoy your predicament, but pleased because you're concerned about losing me."

I palmed her cheek, noting the fear lurking in her pretty sea-gray eyes.

"I wouldn't do this if I thought it would be the end, Camillia. I only want forever with you. So I need you to take a leap of faith, love. Please. For our souls."

Sitting up, I took my blade and drew it across my palm—the same one that had just been on her face.

Then I waited for her to join me.

Cami pursed her lips but otherwise didn't move.

"Where's my confident, gorgeous angel?" I asked, my voice low. "The one who faced a Manticore with nothing but a book. The one who saw through the trial mirages. The one who stood up to me at every turn. The one who lets Az and Ajax share her, knowing full well they could destroy her in an instant."

She glared at me. "They wouldn't destroy me."

"Because you're miraculous and perfect and a goddess to be worshipped. But I want to know where my Cami went, the glorious fae with a smart mouth and a penchant for danger."

"Now you're just using words against me," she muttered, sitting up. I was very pleased that she hadn't tried to hide her body from me, especially now as her bare breasts swayed a little.

She was so fucking sexy like this—exposed, vulnerable, and *in my bed*.

"I said I wanted my Melek back, and now you're saying

you want your Cami back," she went on. "Not very clever, Hell Fae Prince."

I cut my palm again, aware that the wound had already closed. "It made you move, didn't it?"

Those pretty eyes of hers narrowed even more. "If we do this and it breaks our bond, I'm going to be pissed."

I arched a brow. "Oh?"

"Wait." Her expression changed from heated annoyance to confusion. "Lucifer wants to mate Ajax. Does that mean...?"

"He suspects his soul is compatible with our Warden's?" I finished for her. "Yes."

"But what if he's wrong? Will that negate the deal?"

"There is no more deal," I told her. "Ty already reinstated Ajax's role as Warden, and he's in the process of confirming his place as a Hell Fae." Along with a few other details—like ensuring everyone knew Ajax was part of his inner circle now.

She blinked. "When did that happen?"

"While you were showering," I replied. "Well, technically, he made the decision after catching you in the sky. Or maybe even before that. But—"

"He caught me in the sky?"

I hummed in confirmation. "And then he put you in our bed."

Her eyes widened. Then she shook her head. "We'll come back to that." She cleared her throat. "If he knew this third phase might not work, then he had a loophole set into his own agreement. What would have happened if Ajax and Lucifer couldn't mate?"

I considered that for a moment, then shrugged. "Knowing Ty, he would have written in a clause that stated Ajax had to claim him as a Midnight Fae mate. But it's a moot point now —there's no deal."

"So he wouldn't have reneged on the offer?" she pressed.

"Are you worried he had that as a backdoor escape to show

unfaithfulness on Ajax's part?" I wondered aloud, my brow furrowing. "Because Ty may write deals in his favor, but he's not Vivaxia." *She* would have written such a loophole into her own agreement, and often did.

"No, I..." She frowned again. "So Ajax would have had to claim him with his Midnight Fae power—because he could still do that."

"Yes, but I doubt it would be necessary. Their souls are as compatible as ours." Well, perhaps not as compatible, but definitely complementary.

"So if this fails..." she went on, ignoring me, her expression clearing as her eyes radiated stark resolve. "If this fails, then I'm going to figure out how Hell Fae claim mates, and force you to be mine."

The conviction in her tone and her words made my dick throb.

Because yes fucking please.

"I think I like where this is headed," I admitted. "Will you tie me down and have your way with me, too?"

She growled, the sound reminding me of the night we'd first met. She'd growled at me then, too, infuriated by me not helping her.

Little did she know how much I was assisting her that night.

And always.

I would never have let anything happen to her. But I did want her to realize how much she could accomplish on her own. I'd recognized her strength and spirit, her power a beacon to my senses.

That night—and all the days since—had showcased her talents in a myriad of ways.

I'd done what I could to protect her. And now, I would provide her with the ultimate form of protection—by marrying my soul to hers. *Indefinitely.*

If the impossible happened and our spirits didn't mate, it would hurt. A lot. It'd be the equivalent of feeling her death.

I kept that part to myself, though, as only I would experience that pain. Not her.

Besides, I was certain our souls would accept each other. There was no alternative. Camillia De la Croix was meant to be mine.

And one day soon, she would become my Hell Fae Queen.

Her jaw ticked as she glowered at me.

Then she took her dagger and sliced her palm.

I cut mine for a third time, ensuring the wound was still open, and grabbed her hand before she could pull away.

"Now we say the words together," I reminded her. "Ready?" She nodded, so I counted down from three, and after I reached *one*, we both said, "*Nadeehar Laki Nafsi.*"

Warmth flooded through me as ethereal energy flowed around us.

Cami gasped, her hand clutching mine. "*Melek.*"

I yanked her into my lap, my wings flaring from my back to wrap us in a cocoon of feathers. But the magic was too powerful, the essence bleeding into every inch of our beings as our souls connected for eternity.

I told you we were soul mates, I breathed into her mind.

She clung to me, her legs straddling my hips as gold flares flickered around us. *This is amazing.*

This is just the beginning, I replied, my lips seeking hers as warmth blossomed inside my chest. Searing warmth. *Exciting* warmth.

Because our bond was complete. Our souls fully joined. Our powers mingling.

My wings stretched again, my feathers ruffling as our energy created a long golden ribbon of silky vitality. It wound around our joined hands, sealing our bond in a symbol of unity.

Cami sighed, her skin glittering with the evidence of our connection. "I feel so alive." Her voice held a wistful note to it. "Like I'm *flying*."

"Mmm, I'll happily take you to the stars, little angel." I tugged on our bound hands, my opposite palm going to her hip. But before I could kiss her, she glanced down.

"Another rope." She stared at the item in question. "Is this why you always talk about ribbons? Because of the bond magic creating them?"

I grinned. "The bond didn't create them, love. My power did. It's a symbol of our mating—a gold strand that can never be broken despite how soft and delicate it may appear."

She studied the pretty fabric. "It's unending."

"Indeed." The ribbon might appear neatly bound now, but there were no ends to the fabric. When unraveled, it would go on and on for as long or as little as we desired. "It represents us."

Cami pulled on the bond, the silk easily falling into her hand as she slowly unwound it from our joined palms. "I want to understand you better, Melek. I want to trust you."

I admired her profile, my mind helping me to understand what she was really saying. "You want me to tie you up."

She gazed up at me through her thick lashes. "I want to learn."

Hmm. If I recalled correctly, she'd asked Az for a similar lesson—something I'd overheard in her head last week. Except that lesson had been about his need to release his excess power.

This was about my preference for rope play.

My desire to bind her.

To dress her in silk and tease her until she begged me to fuck her.

Or begged for Ty...

Alas, we weren't ready yet for what I truly desired. But I could slowly introduce her to my games.

"All right," I said, my energy swirling around our bound hands to finish unbinding the silk. Then I wove it through my fingertips as I indulged in the soft texture. "Sit in the center of the bed."

It would require her to slip off of my lap—an act that didn't appeal to my dick. But the delayed gratification would be worth it.

Cami moved to where I directed her.

"Go up on your knees, then sit back on your heels and place your palms on your thighs."

She did as I commanded.

And fuck if that wasn't a stunning sight.

"Now close your eyes," I told her.

A flush stole over her cheeks, her tongue licking her lips, then her lashes fluttered as her eyelids shut.

I waited a beat, purposely drawing out the moment.

"Rope play is about teasing your senses," I said softly. "It's about anticipation and blocking out the rest of the world." I shifted to kneel behind her. "But trust is the heart of the experience."

I leaned down to kiss her shoulder.

"I'm not going to bind your arms or your hands, Camillia." I drew my teeth along her skin and up her neck to her ear. "Not today, anyway. But some day, I'll enslave you with my ribbons."

Then leave her for Ty to unwrap while I watched.

That was a fantasy I couldn't wait to play out.

But tonight was about me and Camillia. About me worshipping her. Cherishing her. *Loving* her. And showing her who we would be together.

No games. No puzzles. No teasing truths or riddle-like statements.

Simply Melek and Cami.

I kissed her thundering pulse as I gently touched her

arm with the silky fabric. She jumped, just like I knew she would. It was part expectation, part fear of what was to come.

Which was precisely why a gradual introduction was needed.

"Shh," I hushed her. "Relax and let me take care of you." I drew the material up and down in slow caresses, giving her time to adjust. "Rope play is an art form, one that requires patience. But the end result is quite beautiful."

"So you... you have a lot of experience doing this? To Lucifer?"

I chuckled, the rope closer to her shoulder now. "Ty has indulged me once or twice, but he's not a being who allows others to bind him."

"So he ties you up?" she guessed as I lowered my touch to her collarbone.

"He has before, yes," I told her. "It's important for a master to experience the rope for himself, to understand the intricacies and sensations. It makes rope play even more sensual and safe, because it allows the dominant of the pair to properly respect the submissive's limits."

She shivered. "You're the dominant?"

"Between us? I think so, yes. But I can switch." I kissed her pulse again. "And for you, I would be anything and anyone."

My preference would be to lead. However, I'd kneel if Cami desired it. I'd do anything she asked.

I sent my touch downward toward her chest, drawing a gasp from her as the silk nearly reached her nipples. "So how do you know how to do this?" she asked, her neck arching as she swallowed. "If Lucifer doesn't let you tie him up... and he's only tied you up a few times...?"

I pressed another kiss to her neck, my gaze on the ribbon between her breasts. "Ty usually watches me tie up others," I explained.

She stilled. "He doesn't mind you playing with someone else?"

I chuckled. "Ty and I have always been very open with each other. He chooses monogamy. I... I choose loyalty. But just because I've used my ropes on others doesn't mean I fucked them. I usually wrap them up as a gift for someone else. Then watch the scene play out while Ty indulges me."

It wasn't a traditional relationship. But then again, nothing in my world could ever be considered traditional anyway.

Cami said nothing for a long moment, her breathing heightening as my touch reached her belly button. "Will you... still play with others?"

My hand paused, my mind finally understanding the point of her questions.

She hadn't been interested in my experience from a trust perspective—I'd assumed she just wanted to ensure that I knew what I was doing. No, she'd been asking from a relationship perspective.

"You want to know how I feel about monogamy," I translated out loud. "What it means now that we've mated."

"I..." She didn't finish her statement, just snapped her jaws closed as an adorable flush stole across her features.

My lips curled. "Mmm, my little angel is feeling possessive."

"You're my mate."

"I'm also Ty's mate."

"That's different," she muttered.

"How so?" I wondered aloud, resuming my path with the ribbon against her flesh.

"He's Lucifer," she said, like that explained everything.

"So you're okay with me fucking him and him fucking me?"

That flush continued down to her breasts. "Y-yes."

"You want to watch?" I guessed.

"I..." She trailed off again, then cleared her throat. "That's not what I mean. I... He's already yours, and I understand that. But the others...?"

"Hmm," I hummed, moving to her side so I could properly take hold of her chin and bring her eyes to mine. "First, there are no *others*, Camillia." I allowed the rope to unravel a bit, part of it pooling over her thighs. "Second, I need you to hold your arms out."

Her gaze narrowed. "Melek."

"Arms, Camillia," I repeated.

With a cute little growl, she complied, but her eyes told me she wasn't pleased. "You've tied up other people. That means, by definition, there are *others*."

"I've played in a club setting where other fae have asked me to tie up their mates," I clarified, my focus going to her abdomen as I wrapped the rope around her once.

Then I met her gaze again, wanting to finish this conversation so we could properly begin.

"I enjoyed playing with their mates because it provided a sense of calmness for me. There's a certain level of give-and-take that comes with tying up another person. It's all about trust and patience. The responsibility for pleasure falls on the dominant, and the submissive is actually the one in charge. It's a power dynamic that I find freeing."

Her expression told me that while she heard what I was saying, she was still wrapped up in thoughts of me with other women.

And men, I realized, hearing it in her mind.

She knew I obviously indulged in both. Ty made sense to her. Everyone else... did not.

"Do you want to know why Ty has always respected my need to play?" I asked her.

Her teeth gritted at my choice of words, her mind

changing *play* to *cheat*. Normally, I would have some qualms about that phrasing and quickly correct her. But I knew this was the fresh mating bond talking more than Camillia.

She was experiencing a new wave of possessiveness and desperately trying to fight it.

Rather than wait for her to reply, I attempted to put her out of her misery by answering my own question. "He let me play because he knew I needed the outlet. He's known for a very long time that I would eventually take another mate because he's aware that he couldn't give me certain things. And he wants me to be happy."

I palmed her cheek, my eyes going to her lips before slowly tracking back up to her stormy gaze.

"Camillia, you give me the things he can't. You give me everything I desire." The words were like a benediction, one I hoped she understood and felt as a vow.

Because I meant it.

She was my world now.

"I've been looking for a mate like you for thousands of years, and now that I have you, there will be no *others* for me, Camillia. It will only be you and our mate-circle. *Us.* That's what I need. What I want. What I *crave.*"

I leaned in to press my lips to her ear, her resulting tremble one I felt to my very soul.

"I'm going to give you more than loyalty, Camillia De la Croix. You have my heart. My utmost devotion. My *faith.*"

Releasing her face, I grabbed the ribbon on either side of her abdomen, the rope tightening beneath my grip.

"And now I'm going to show you what that means. So I need you to close your eyes again and focus on what you feel. Because you're my life now, and I fully intend to tie you up for eternity."

CHAPTER 25

CAMI

I CLOSED MY EYES, my mind and heart a mess from Melek's words.

Loyalty.

Devotion.

Faith.

My possessive instincts had flared when he'd mentioned Lucifer being okay with him playing with others. Because I'd realized that I... I wasn't okay with that.

Melek playing with Lucifer was fine.

Melek indulging others... was not.

The distinction was confounding, and a bit hypocritical given my relationships with Ajax and Az. None of us had discussed monogamy. It'd just been an instinctual expectation, but Melek tested the boundaries of my instincts. He always did things I didn't anticipate.

Like now with the ribbon.

He was wrapping it around my upper abdomen, his fingers smoothing the flat silk against my skin as he carefully maneuvered upward to my breasts.

The sensuous touch had goose bumps pebbling across my

chest, my nipples beading in expectation. It almost distracted me from my thoughts. From Melek's words playing through my mind.

They'd resembled promises I longed to believe in, statements I hoped were true.

The tiny hint of hesitation inside me—the voice that questioned Melek's motives—confirmed what he'd said about trust. The fact that he knew we were still growing in that area, and respected that growth, spoke volumes about our impending relationship.

He paid attention to details. Paid attention to *me*. And honored my feelings.

It surprised me. I'd assumed Melek simply enjoyed chaos and riddles, that he liked playing games with me. And he did; that much was true.

But his games possessed layers, all of them built with good intentions.

An intriguing realization to have as he created *layers* of ropes around me now, each one seeming to be purposeful.

I held my breath as the silk skimmed my areolas. The next one would cover my stiff peaks, providing a sense of—

My brow furrowed when the ribbon... did not... go over my nipples. It... it went above them instead.

I waited, wondering if Melek would go back down to cover the skin he missed, but he continued upward until the ribbon went right beneath my armpit.

Maybe he'll start downward again now?

No, I realized in the next breath. *He's... he's tying a bow at my back.*

I could feel the strands tightening, the ends of the bow feeling complete. But it was an illusion. I could sense the endless quality of the ribbon, how it would grow and grow and grow with a single command.

Melek played on that now, taking one edge like a leash and pulling it around to my front.

"You can lower your arms now," he told me softly. "But don't open your eyes yet."

The *leash* he'd created slid around to my front, the edge of it teasing my upper leg as he released it between my thighs.

I bit my lip when the bed shifted, his weight disappearing behind me.

My ears strained to hear him, curious as to where he'd gone. But he was silent.

Everything was still.

I swallowed, my nerves ratcheting up with each passing second.

Melek? I whispered via our bond.

He didn't reply.

I almost peeked, slightly nervous about what he might be doing. But his demand not to open my eyes held me captive.

This was about trust. And I trusted him not to hurt me.

He was just heightening the moment and drawing out the anticipation.

I focused on my breathing, as well as the strands on my skin. They were so soft yet firm. He'd left my arms free, but I still felt constrained.

"You look so fucking beautiful, Cami," Melek said, his voice seeming to surround my senses and captivate me. "Spread your thighs a little more for me."

I shuffled, eager to comply.

"Mmm, yes, just like that."

I waited for him to do something, to say more, but he fell quiet again.

A shiver rolled through me, followed by a tightening in my lower belly.

I was exposed. On display. A *gift* wrapped for his pleasure.

Something about that made me feel cherished. I felt so alive. So safe. So *ready*.

Because I wanted more. I wanted him. His mouth. His tongue. His touch. His cock.

I could already feel him between my splayed thighs, imagine him thrusting in and out of me, feel his *claim*.

"You're getting so wet for me," Melek murmured. "Fae, I can't wait to taste you. In fact..." The ribbon moved against my thigh, confusing my senses, as I hadn't felt him come back onto the bed. Maybe he was leaning over the mattress?

I so badly wanted to look at him.

But I refrained.

He wanted my eyes closed for a reason.

I jolted as the silk touched my core, the unexpected movement drawing a gasp from my mouth.

"You have no idea what I want to do to you, Camillia," he murmured. "I want to wrap up your pussy, apply ribbons in just the right place, so that your clit is stimulated with every thrust." He ran the material over my clit, applying the barest hint of pressure. "I'll slide the rope between your legs..."

He demonstrated, eliciting a moan from me.

"Up along your ass," he went on, reaching behind me to pull the rope upward against my backside. "Then I'll secure it to your middle." He brushed the bow. "And do it again and again until you're fully bound." The strand went taut against my middle, causing my lips to part in pleasure. "Then I'll make you fly, little angel."

The ribbon moved against my core as he tugged it back the way it'd come, dragging the silk against my damp flesh.

"I'll suspend you in the air, too," he whispered, his lips suddenly at my ear. "And fuck you while you're hanging over our bed."

I panted at the image his words painted inside my mind. "Yes..."

He kissed my neck, his touch moving to my sides as he tugged on the rope in a way that squeezed my nipples.

"When we do this next time, I'll bind your arms so that every move"—he tugged again—"will tease your pretty tits." Another pull, this one sharper. "You'll drive yourself crazy, then beg for my mouth. My touch. Your *release*."

He proceeded to demonstrate, his clever fingers working the silk around me and creating an inferno inside me.

Every move barely touched my aroused peaks. It was just enough to tease, but not enough to please.

When the ribbon returned to my core, he replicated the sensation there, dragging the silk against my clit without applying enough pressure.

"Melek," I whispered.

His mouth touched my throat, his heat suddenly engulfing me from behind. I wasn't sure how or when he'd settled on the bed, my mind too caught up in the sensations he was eliciting with his *silk*.

When he pressed on my back between my shoulder blades, I bent forward. "Keep your hands at your sides," he told me. "Pretend they're bound."

It was hard to do, my instinct to break my fall one that had my fingers flexing in response.

But I trusted him to catch me.

And, oh, I was so glad I did because he used the rope to guide me downward, the taut strands applying even more pressure to my aching breasts.

He moved my head at the last moment, tilting my face to the side before I face-planted into the mattress. Then he used the rope he'd threaded through my legs to pull my ass up, the pressure from the lift fully on my clit.

I groaned, the sensation nearly undoing me.

But then his hands were everywhere, mapping my form,

memorizing every inch, and in an instant, the ribbons vanished, leaving me utterly free and incredibly turned on.

"When we do this again, it'll be for much longer," he promised. "But we've been dancing around our attraction for months. And I can't go another moment without being inside you, Cami."

He spread my thighs, his cock already at my entrance.

I barely had a moment to react before he was filling me, his thrust powerful and intrusive and utterly flawless.

My hands went to the bed, my fingers digging into the comforter as Melek fucked me from behind, his movements wholly *him*. Because he exuded sensuality. I could feel his urgency, hear his boiling need, yet he somehow managed to emit his usual sensuous perfection.

I moaned, the sensation of fullness an alluring antidote to all the teasing. My insides clenched, my stomach twisting with renewed passion.

And suddenly I was on my back with Melek above me, his wings stretched out as he entered me again.

"You're so beautiful," I told him, only belatedly realizing I'd opened my eyes. But he'd freed me from the ropes, shattering the illusion of being under his command. My arms had already moved. Looking at him had just felt... natural.

"Not as beautiful as you, Cami," he said, capturing my mouth as he palmed my breast.

I screamed, startled by how sensitive my nipple was beneath his hand.

He responded by rubbing the stiff point, then lowering his lips to kiss my breast as his pace slowed below.

I writhed beneath him, lost to his tongue, his mouth, his everything.

I hadn't realized just how much the rope had teased me. Now it felt like I was bathing in relief, reveling in pleasure, losing myself to *him*.

I let myself fall. Gave in to his touch, his kiss, his everything.

By the time he kissed me again, I was no longer Cami. I was simply Melek's angel. His female. His fae. His *mate*.

And he worshipped me, just like he'd promised.

With his hands. His mouth. His tongue. His cock.

Every part of him complemented every part of me, our bodies engaging in a sensuous dance that was all Melek.

Because he could well and truly lead. I was a slave to his motions, utterly devoted to his every whim.

He smiled against my mouth. "Are you falling in love with me, Camillia De la Croix?"

"I don't know," I admitted.

"Mmm," he hummed, nipping at my bottom lip. "I'll accept that. But you should know, I think I've loved you from the moment we met."

I shook my head. "That was lust."

"That was our souls knowing each other," he corrected me with a thrust I felt through every inch of my body. "My heart beat for you then, and it sings for you now."

He captured my mouth before I could reply, not that I knew what to say.

Melek, the fae of riddles, was speaking truths. Confiding his feelings. And expressing his adoration in a way only he could.

We'd finally reached the last play in this game between us.

And it turned out that we were both winners here.

Both of us chasing the same end goal.

Screaming for each other in unison.

Chanting the other person's name.

"Melek!"

"Cami!"

I clung to him, my heart racing in my chest as an explosion built inside me. An explosion born of months of uncertainty.

Months of yearning. Months of confusion. Months of teasing. Months of *need*.

"Fly for me," Melek demanded, his mouth against mine. "Fly for me and shout my name."

I squeezed my thighs against his, my arms wrapped firmly around his neck.

Then I flew, just like he'd ordered me to.

The sensation of falling overwhelmed me, the airlessness a feeling that nearly caused me to panic.

But I let go. I let *everything* go.

And trusted Melek to catch me.

Because he was my Virtuous Fae mate. My soul's confidant. My future.

His wings surrounded me, his devotion a warmth I sensed in every inch of my being.

He was there, holding me through his own fall. The two of us soaring without a care in the world. Simply to land on a bed of feathers, both of us winded, replete, and finally fully mated...

CHAPTER 26

TYPHOS

Explosive.

The word utterly defined Camillia De la Croix as she detonated in my bed. I wasn't there, but I could feel it. Smell it. *Taste* it.

All through Melek.

And not because he was pushing the sensations through our bond. It just existed between us, the temptation a sin I was almost considering falling for. The pain of crashing into the Hell Fae Realm again would be worth the experience of seeing Camillia detonate.

I ran a hand over my face, then palmed my nape as Melek's renewed arousal warmed my blood.

He hadn't said a word to me, hadn't invited me to play, hadn't described Camillia's naked form or provided any sort of provocation.

Yet it existed nonetheless.

Swallowing my urges, I focused on Vita. On the words painted out before me. On the utter uselessness that had been the last hour while I'd searched and hunted for answers that didn't seem to exist.

Something has to be in here, I thought, growling to myself.

"What aren't you showing me?" I asked as I turned Vita's pages, hunting for a lost thought from my mind.

Because I recognized that power inside Camillia. Deep down, somewhere, I knew what it meant.

Therefore, the details had to be in the book. Yet the truth eluded me.

Why can't I remember?

Do I not want to remember?

Was it something Vivaxia had done to someone else I cared about? Something she'd done to me?

My lips curled downward at the thought of Camillia's grandmother, the very woman who had destroyed my life.

Thousands of years later, and I was still tired of the ancient games she and I had once played.

I had vowed never to engage with her again.

And yet, here I am, setting the board with my strategic pieces.

With a new queen.

But I was missing something. A burning sensation deep within my soul churned with uncertainty, warning me with a sense of urgency that didn't make sense.

Camillia was safe.

She was with Melek.

So why do I feel this deep-seated concern for her well-being?

Because Vivaxia had given her back far too easily.

She'd done something to the girl.

But what? I wondered as I studied the magical book that held memories I could no longer access via my own mind.

One's memories grew fractured throughout time. Vita had been my way of protecting my sanity, of storing important knowledge and maintaining ancient recollections.

There was so much history here. So many lost thoughts.

Yet, instead of answers, I found white spires depicted on

Vita's pages, the scene garnished with pristine streets and plentiful flowers. Winged beings drifted in the distance underneath a brilliant golden glow that seemed to come from everywhere.

Vita rarely showed me the Virtuous Fae Realm, given that I preferred not to think about that time, but it was a part of my history that couldn't be erased.

"Where Camillia went was a forgotten nightmare of that place," I informed Vita as I turned the page.

The past was gone. Whatever remained was a ghost that my enemies should have left behind.

The next image was a familiar woman's face, and that gave me pause. Her features were slightly blurred on the pages as if water had stained the ink. I ran my fingers over the depiction, confused by the stirring of loneliness and longing the image brought me.

Dark hair.

Vibrant white wings with black-tipped feathers.

Ah, my mother.

The sight of her struck me with sudden certainty as the bitter memory took hold.

My parents should never have had me.

My conception had cost them their lives.

Why was that, again?

Turning the page once more, I found a young boy with midnight hair and ocean-blue eyes. Even then, the wingspan was an impressive one, as was the smile of a youthful innocent who never imagined he'd become the Hell Fae King.

Me.

A woman—presumably my mother—held the boy, but I couldn't see her anymore. The ink around her splotched and blurred, as did the masculine shadow behind them.

Ah. That's right.

I remembered now why I preferred to keep this particular memory within Vita instead of in my head.

Before I'd reached adulthood, I had slowly drained their gifts, taking their Virtuous magic into myself to build my power that had now become my Source. I'd had no idea what I had been doing, of course, until it was too late.

I had been just a child.

But once I'd realized what I'd been doing, I'd altered myself. I'd made it where I could never again drain another being's power like that and make it my own.

But it hadn't been enough. My parents had died because I was...

My eyes widened when I realized the correlation.

"I was a *siphon*, just like Camillia," I murmured to myself as I turned the pages again.

I'd forgotten about that, because after the death of my parents, my powers had been altered. Not by Vivaxia, but by *me*. I'd been a siphon only very briefly because I had permanently broken that part of myself, changed it into something different that wouldn't be as dangerous.

No one knew how my parents had died. I wasn't from a royal line—or any family of notice, even, when it came to the Virtuous Fae—so my family had been forgotten. I'd also moved to the central city, seeking to escape a past I'd longed to forget.

But I remembered the parents I'd lost, even if it had only been in Vita's pages.

And now my power leaned on an eternal source of energy.

My raw emotion.

I had created an entire realm from my grief. There was power in emotion, especially such deep-seated pain that manifested into raw energy when in the hands of an immortal.

Turning the page again, my heartbeat quickened. I walled

myself against Melek and Azazel so they wouldn't sense my discomfort.

Because they couldn't know how Vivaxia had managed to create Camillia.

Not until I confirmed it.

The next page wasn't an image but a script that was a memory of a discussion I'd once had with Melek long ago.

I didn't want to remember.

But if I was going to face the future, I first needed to recall the past.

Many, many years ago...

I stared at Melek's beautiful face.

Gorgeous.

Breathtaking.

And yet, I barely recognized the male I intended to mate. His multicolored irises exuded a hatred that I'd never witnessed before. A hatred that had my heart beating rapidly in my chest. That day had been the only time he'd ever looked at me like he hated me.

When I brushed his mind, all I felt was disgust.

But the words he'd just spoken... the bold statement he'd just uttered...

I swallowed.

"You... you slept with her?" I asked, not even sure how I repeated his claim without screaming.

Or killing someone.

He said he fucked her. Why would he do that?

And yet, I had just found him naked in her bed.

Exclusivity wasn't always a requirement between us, but

sex with Vivaxia was a betrayal. She was devious and powerful and had the ability to rip apart life from the inside out.

I wasn't mated to Melek, not fully. Although, we had been planning it, once it was safe to do so.

Melek knew my history. He also knew I would never risk overpowering him or consuming him like my energy craved to do.

Now, it wouldn't be possible to attempt if what he was telling me was true. If he was compatible with Vivaxia, there was no way a final mate-bond between us would work on an ethereal level.

Because I would never be able to risk being connected to her. Not even for him.

Melek scoffed as he flicked away hair that had fallen in front of his face. His wings behind him flared with challenge, when they were usually soft and supple, curling around me with an intimate embrace.

Vivaxia wasn't even home, as far as I was aware, but I had come early after reading an urgent note from Azazel saying that he was being sold.

I couldn't let that happen.

And when I had found her mansion empty except for the scent of ambrosia, I never expected to find my lover in my rival's bed.

I should have been tipped off by the utter lack of servants or guests. Vivaxia was flamboyant with her status and was rarely alone, unless she was playing a game.

Melek stood, letting the sheets fall from his naked body.

"You're one to judge," he said. "I saw the deal, Ty. I know what you're planning to do with Vivaxia. How you lied to me about wanting to mate me, and only me."

"Melek—" I began, not having a clue what the fuck he was talking about.

He snarled as he cut me off. "No. You sent me on a fool's errand to search for some flaming text." He grappled for a book on the nightstand and held up the tome in question. The one my mother had favored. The one I desired to repurpose as a text-like catacomb for the important notes from my mind.

Anger flared in my chest when Melek held the book up by the cover, not the spine or as a whole, just haphazardly dangling the item between us from his fingertips.

"I was hunting for *this* all while you were here engaging in another infamous deal, one meant to tie your soul to hers. Well, now my energy is tied to hers instead."

My heart skipped a beat. *The mating bond. He's initiated the mating bond.*

I couldn't sense it. But I... I had never known Melek to lie.

I shook my head, not wanting to believe any of this was happening. How life could take a turn so damn quickly.

Melek was from one of the noble families, and we had fallen in love despite all my efforts to not let anyone in. I'd promised to mate him.

Yet he'd... he'd seen a *deal* that had suggested otherwise.

And he'd believed it? After everything we'd been through?

Fuck. We'd been studying my magic for years, learning how it worked and how I could wield it.

That had led us to crafting deals *together*.

I ran everything by him. Every caveat. Every clause. Every agreement.

Yet he'd lost all faith in me over a piece of paper that suggested otherwise. A document that stated I wanted to mate Vivaxia. "Let me guess," I said through my teeth. "Vivaxia showed you this deal?"

"Of course she did," Melek bit back. "She thought I should know the truth, which is more than I can say for you."

I grunted. "Melek—"

"No," Melek hissed with a vehemence to his tone I had never heard before. "I'm done, Typhos. Let this be the last memory you have of me."

He threw the book on the floor and stormed out, leaving me without a backward glance.

I'd stood there for hours, unsure of how to proceed or how to fix this.

His lack of faith in me had broken me. His energy mingling with Vivaxia's had shattered me. And his easy dismissal had infuriated me.

When Vivaxia waltzed into her bedroom some time later, I was still there. And I'd been so incredibly vulnerable.

Vulnerable enough to sign the deal that soon led to my fall.

A deal that had changed us all.

I CLOSED VITA'S COVER WITH A THUD AND STARED at it as the truth seeped into me. It left me feeling trapped, like the walls were closing in around me.

That had been the only time Melek had ever lied to me. He'd allowed me to think he'd slept with Vivaxia because that deal had been the only way for me to achieve my dreams.

Had I not signed it, had I not fallen, had I not been *broken*, the Hell Fae Realm would never have existed.

Melek's cruelty—his *lie*—had cost him dearly. It'd nearly broken him, too.

But in the end, it'd been the right thing to do.

Because the alternative would have hurt so much more. Living in the Virtuous Fae Realm with no means to protect the innocent would have driven me mad. With the limitations of my power, I would never have saved Azazel.

I would have grown spiteful and angry.

I would have pushed Melek away and become destructive.

My prince had known that. That was why he'd played along with Vivaxia's plan. He had even proposed the façade of having slept with her. She'd been delighted, given that she had only asked him to help convince me to sign the deal, not break my heart.

But Melek was the only one who knew how my power worked. He knew it wasn't just in the language of my deals but also in the emotion storming in my heart.

That was why he had deceived me.

And he vowed to never do it again. He had completed our mate-bond shortly after, and of course we were compatible. I should never have doubted him.

But had I seen the truth; we wouldn't be where we were today. And that... that I would never change, even if I had the chance to go back and do it all over again.

I forgive you, my prince.

I didn't let him hear those words. I had already spoken them to him long ago, but now I better understood why he had done it.

The only way we could be at peace was to start over. The Hell Fae Realm was my dream, one he shared.

It had been created in an explosion of grief.

If reversed in the same manner, if everything I had done with good intentions was instead perverted and undone, it could be destroyed.

That method did not come in the form of a spell, or brute force.

It was in the perfect shape of a female not only designed for me but destined for my inner circle.

Camillia De la Croix was meant to be a corruption from the inside.

Vivaxia had finally figured it out, somehow, that I had once been a siphon, too. I didn't know how she had learned it, and I didn't really care. But if she knew my history, then she knew so much more than simply how to create a siphon and how to reverse everything I've built.

She's been watching me, I realized as my jaw flexed.

That was why she had taken so long to act. She had been observing.

Learning.

And now she's figured out how to destroy me and everything I care about.

She might have lost our battle long ago, but now she knew how to win the war. She had made sure to prepare for this.

And she'd sent a pretty little Hell Fae Bride as a Trojan horse.

But it went deeper than that. Vivaxia's games weren't one or two plays.

She's after more.

She didn't just want my power. She wanted to break my heart.

Again.

My nostrils twitched as the heat of ash tinged my nose. I'd locked Melek and Azazel out of my mind, but it seemed I hadn't done a good enough job of it with my Commander.

Or perhaps it was my blocking him that coaxed him to visit.

Because I'd promised to keep our communications open, which I had. They'd just been a bit... throttled.

"Why does your mind feel like stone?" Azazel asked as he lingered behind me. "What have you discovered, Typhos?"

I didn't turn around to face him. Everything felt too raw

after Vita had forced the ancient memories back into my mind, memories I had intended on burying indefinitely.

Alas, now I needed to recall everything.

Every. Dark. Piece.

"I know what Vivaxia did to Camillia," I said as I brushed my fingers over Vita's leather cover. "And if we don't act fast, it could be the end of us all."

The Story Continues with Hell Fae King...

EPILOGUE
A NOTE FROM MELEK

Hello Loves,

Have you ever wondered what would have happened if I'd been a little more forward in the beginning? If I hadn't issued my riddles or played with words, and just... took what I wanted?

Because I was wondering how this story would have begun had I just fucked Cami from day one.

And after conferring with my loving figments (also known as the muses of my world), they agreed to let me play.

For a sneak peek at what could have been, flip the page.

Until next time, my loves.

Remember to hydrate.

Choose silk over wool.

And please, for the love of the fae, follow your dreams. You might end up with a sexy Hell Fae King, too. Or maybe an impish prince who just likes to play.

Bye for now...

Love,
Melek

MELEK

BONUS SCENE
MELEK'S FANTASY

Dedication: To those who want to be wrapped up in Melek's ropes, this one is for you...

MELEK

I RAN my fingers along the worn spines, only vaguely aware of the ancient texts lurking on the library shelves. Power bristled in the air, telling me I'd stepped into a sacred row, one littered with Ty's most prized books.

But there was one in particular that called to me.

Vita.

Her pages were spread, her energy creating a beacon that drew me forward on curiosity alone.

No one should be able to read the secret words scribbled on her old parchment. Yet a beautiful female sat at a lone table, utterly engrossed in the book sprawled out before her.

Candidate #66 her shirt said. *Hmm.*

I quietly opened a device from my pocket, searching for her details.

Camillia De la Croix.

Half human, half Hell Fae.

I scanned the rest of the details, finding them unhelpful. They were too generic. And very likely *wrong*.

Because this female was *not* half human. Not if she could read Vita.

I crept forward, my gaze admiring her long, dirty-blonde hair. She had it pulled back into a ponytail, the edges of it reaching her upper back.

From here, I could tell she was athletic, yet curved in all the right places, too.

Perfect for my hands.

Perfect for my tongue.

Perfect for my ropes.

What has you so intrigued, little prince? Ty whispered into my mind, his interest a palpable presence that thrived between us.

A Hell Fae Bride, I told him.

Surprise filtered through my mate-bond with Ty. *Oh? Which one?*

Candidate Sixty-Six, I said, leaning against the shelves. *I haven't seen her face yet, but I'm certain she's beautiful.* I could have looked on my device, but I didn't want to ruin the moment. That first pull of attraction was my favorite part of finding a new bedmate.

Determining seductive methods was my second-favorite part.

I see, Ty replied, his tone giving nothing away. *Are you wanting company for your playdate?*

I smiled. *I always want your company, my love.*

Hmm, he hummed. *Tell me when I should join, and I'll be there.*

My blood heated at the prospect of what he was really saying—*tell me when the female is ready, and I'll fuck her for you.*

Give me thirty minutes, I murmured, pushing away from the shelves and stalking toward my prey.

She was too engrossed in her reading material to notice my approach, her head bent over in a way that made me want to palm her slender nape.

There was just something about her. Something powerful. Something *otherworldly*.

As I rounded the table, I studied the angles of her face, the pretty slope of her jaw, and her full, fuckable lips. She was mouthing the words to herself, confirming her ability to read Ty's book.

Fascinating.

I would have to ask her more about that later.

Maybe learn who and what she was, and decipher her true purpose here.

But first, I wanted to fuck her.

To wrap her up in my silver ribbons and watch as the Hell Fae King desecrated her gorgeous body. I'd lick away her tears, shower her in pleasure, and then fuck her again.

Fae, I was hard. *So fucking hard*.

Who is this angel sent from the heavens? I marveled. *Is she a sinful treat left out for me to devour? A temptation to test just how far I've fallen?*

If it was the latter, I'd fail.

I was in the pits of Hell, just where I belonged.

And I fully intended to drag this beautiful creature down with me.

I observed her mouth once more, noting the way it curved downward at whatever she'd just read. "That's not possible," she whispered to herself.

"I would tend to agree," I replied as I sidestepped to stand right behind her.

"Uh…" She glanced over her shoulder, her pretty sea-gray eyes going round at the sight of my nearness. Or perhaps that was simply a reaction to my appearance. Most fae found me attractive. Beautiful, even. And the reddening of her cheeks told me she absolutely felt that way about me, too.

I waited, giving her a moment to enjoy the view, all the while reveling in that first sight of attraction that I so loved.

She was positively stunning. Breathtakingly so. And it created the most alluring sense of excitement, knowing she was admiring me just as much as I was admiring her.

That tight shirt on her did wonders for her breasts. I was sure that when she stood, her pants would also accentuate her ass.

Mmm, yes, this female was designed for my ropes. Curved in all the right places. Strong. *Interested*.

I could see it in the flare of her pupils, the way her tongue snuck out to dampen her plump bottom lip.

"Hello," I finally said, glancing over her again.

"I, uh..." She trailed off.

"You were busy reading," I finished for her. "Yes. I've been watching." *And admiring,* I thought.

"It's engrossing material," she told me.

"I have no doubt that's true," I agreed, canting my head to the side. "You were so consumed by the engrossing material that you missed curfew."

She blinked, then glanced at a nearby clock. "Oh, shit."

Oh, shit indeed, I thought. "Our king takes his rules rather seriously," I warned her. "I think it's his penchant for punishments; he likes having reasons... to play."

Her long lashes fluttered again. "And you're here to...?" She trailed off again.

"Help administer punishment, I'm afraid," I told her with a sigh. It wasn't exactly a lie; she had broken the rules, and Ty really did take that sort of thing seriously. But we would both ensure she enjoyed it. *Thoroughly*.

The female surprised me by straightening her spine, her

shoulders falling back as she faced me head-on. "Fine. Punish me."

"Oh, I won't be the one punishing you, Camillia De la Croix," I said, my lips curling into a sensual grin, one I knew brought most fae to their knees. "As I said, I'm just here to *help*. So, if you'll follow me..."

I took a step back, my left arm sliding out to the side in a gesture that indicated I'd like her to stand and leave the aisle.

Her lips twisted, then she shook her head and pushed away from the table. "Sure. Why not?" The confident air swirling around her was quite becoming. It gave her the appearance of a Hell Fae Queen, not a Hell Fae Bride.

She strolled by me, allowing me to check out her backside—and yes, those pants firmly showed off her ass. *Beautiful.*

Your excitement is distracting me, little prince, Ty murmured into my mind.

I think you're really going to enjoy this bride, my king, I told him, admiring the stubborn set of her jaw.

Oh?

The female paused at the end of the aisle and looked back at me expectantly, her bold stare doing pleasant things to my insides. *Yes, you're* definitely *going to like her.*

"I'm Melek, by the way," I told her as I started toward her.

She arched a dirty-blonde brow. "No title?"

I studied her. "Why would I have a title?" I did, of course. But she shouldn't know that.

Unless her Hell Fae father had educated her on Hell Fae politics.

But she hadn't looked at me with recognition before, just interest. And that expression hadn't changed even now.

"Well, the Warden insisted on being called Warden. So I just assumed..." She trailed off.

"I'm not like our Warden," I murmured. "I'm far more

comfortable with just being called by my given name—Melek."

Her pretty sea-gray eyes ran over me. "Melek."

"Prince Melek," a figment whispered loudly from above.

"Pretty Prince Melek," another added. "So dreamy."

I smiled. "Now, now," I told the invisible beings. "Don't spoil my fun."

But it was too late.

A chorus of voices sounded, all of them commenting on me and my identity.

"King Lucifer's mate."

"So handsome."

"A catch, indeed."

"Lucky girl to grab his interest."

"A virtuous pleasure, yes?"

"Virtuously paired."

"Will they share her?"

"I hope so."

Sighs followed that pronouncement, all while Camillia glanced around with a mixture of wonder and confusion on her face.

"Prince...?" she repeated.

"Only if you want to get technical," I said. "Which I don't."

"You're a prince?" she sputtered, looking me over again. "I guess that explains the suit."

I glanced down. "My outfit has nothing to do with my title and everything to do with taste. I wear suits well, and they bolster my confidence."

Her brow furrowed a bit like she didn't believe me.

"Okay, you're right. My confidence is always bolstered. But women adore me in suits, so I wear them when I'm hunting for a playmate."

"A playmate?" she echoed.

"A fuck," I clarified, not bothering to hide my intentions. We could engage in a game, flirt a bit, and draw this out. It might be fun, too. But part of enjoying the first moment of mutual attraction was acting on the animalistic instinct to fuck.

And that was entirely what I wanted to do with Camillia De la Croix.

The question was: Would she agree? Or would she flee?

The board has been set.
The players have been chosen.

Vivaxia tried to make Camillia a pawn in our eternal game—
when she's wrong about her.

She's not meant to be a pawn. She's our queen.

The Hell Fae Realm is in dire need of one, especially when
rogue Virtuous Fae magic strikes.
Who is an enemy? Who is being controlled?

The last thing I want to do is punish the innocent, but that's
all part of Vivaxia's game. She wants to hurt me, and deeply.
That means dismantling everything I've built, finding ways to
make all of the kingdoms turn on me.

Had she planned for every outcome, she might have won. But

I know something a creature like Vivaxia will never know, no matter how much she observes, schemes, or plans.

My realm is not built on fear. My subjects are loyal because of what I represent. I am everything the Virtuous Fae were not.

I don't control them. I let them exist exactly as they are—I let them fulfill their destiny how they see fit.

Destiny isn't designed by those with power.
It is forged with love and grief, and most of all...
With *Hellfire*.

Authors' Note: *Hell Fae King* is a dark paranormal romance with four tormented mates and no choosing required. If you like your antiheroes dominant and sexy, you've come to the right realm—the Hell Fae Realm, where the romance is hot and no forgiveness is required. This is the final book in the Hell Fae Series.

Amazon

Their Lethal Pet
A Monsters Night Standalone

Run. Hide. *Fight*.

It's Monsters Night, the annual event where the portals to other realms and realities open, and monsters flood the streets to search for their potential mates.

And I'm one of the candidates.

Why?

Because I broke all the rules. I fought back against the elitist system hellbent on enslaving humankind. And f-ck if I'm going to let one of these monsters take me. Let alone *three* of them

Orcus.
Flame.
Reaper.

They saved me from a compromising situation, all because they think I'm a rare Omega. A Goddess. *Their chosen mate.*

You can run and hide, little one.
But we're the monsters of the night.
And you are our chosen bride.
So be a good girl and let us worship you.

Author's Note: *Their Lethal Pet* is a standalone dark paranormal romance featuring three Nightmare Fae and their chosen female mate.

Their Blood Queen
A Monsters Night Standalone

Three sexy vampires haunt my dreams, and they love to make me scream.
For all the right reasons.

The nightmares started on Monsters Night. I figured my overactive libido was just tripping out because of all the monsters on the news. Some portal opened up, and they were terrorizing humans in particular.

But seriously, who hasn't thought about that monster under the bed in a sensual light? There's just something about danger, about fangs, about long tongues...

So, I let the dreams happen. I *invite them in*.

But one night, when I open my eyes and they're literally feasting on me... I realize it's no dream.

This is real.

"Get off me!" I scream, not because it doesn't feel *good* what the one with an unnaturally long tongue is doing, but because this was supposed to be a dream.

"Not a chance, sigil."

Why do they always call me that?

I move to push the one between my legs away, but I realize I can't. My muscles don't comply.

Red eyes glow at my right. Eyes that belong to a face crafted by a master sculptor, but his fangs dripping with my blood suggest he's anything but a benevolent being. *"You're far too delicious to release now. Plus, you invited us into your mind. You told us to play."*

Yes, but that had been when this was all a fanciful dream full of forbidden desires.

I opened my mouth to say as much, but the creature on my right groaned at the sight. "Yes, open that mouth wide, our sigil. We're starved for more of your screams."

Their Blood Queen *is a standalone paranormal romance with three monstrous vampires that feed on blood and dreams from their chosen mate. There is NO OWD and always HEA.*

Their Pixie Mate
A Nightmare Fae Standalone

Run, little pixie.
But stay away from my soldiers—they're far worse than me.
And don't believe what you see, because this is my land, little pixie.
I'm the Unseelie King, and you stepped into my fairy circle.
You accepted my gift.
That makes you our queen.

All I did was step into a damn circle that had a cupcake in the center.

I like cupcakes. Does that make me a criminal?
With icing still stuck to my face, he appeared. The gorgeous, incredibly lethal Unseelie King.
But I know the Unseelie. I know the stories.
They're tricksters. They act on a whim and will just as quickly kill you as help you.
They love their pranks and especially misfortune.

Now I'm running for my life because I've attracted the worst Unseelie of them all.

Not just their king, but his elite soldiers, too.

And now they all want a taste.

And I don't think it's the cupcake they're interested in.

It's me.

LEXI C FOSS

USA Today Bestselling Author Lexi C. Foss loves to play in
dark worlds, especially the ones that bite. She lives in North
Carolina with her husband and their furry children. When
not writing, she's busy crossing items off her travel bucket list,
or chasing eclipses around the globe. She's quirky, consumes
way too much coffee, and loves to swim.

Where To Find Lexi:
www.LexiCFoss.com

J.R. Thorn

Reverse Harem Paranormal Romance - Never Choose.

J.R. Thorn is a Reverse Harem Paranormal Romance Author who loves coffee, stormy weather, and heated discussions with her inner muse. She can often be found scribing her steamy stories in her writing cave far away from the prying eyes of her toddler, husband, two vocal cats, and canine pack!

Learn More at: www.AuthorJRThorn.com